THE MAYOR OF NOOB TOWN

THE MAYOR OF NOOB TOWN

Ryan Rimmel

HARPER
Voyager

Harper*Voyager*
An imprint of HarperCollins*Publishers* Ltd
1 London Bridge Street
London SE1 9GF

www.harpercollins.co.uk

HarperCollins*Publishers*
Macken House,
39/40 Mayor Street Upper,
Dublin 1, D01 C9W8
Ireland

Previously published as *The Mayor of Noobtown: Noobtown Book 1*
(*A LitRPG Adventure*) in 2019

First published by HarperCollins*Publishers* Ltd 2026
1

A catalogue record for this book is available from the British Library.

ISBN: 978-0-00-883635-1

Set in Garamond Premier Pro

Printed and bound in the UK using 100% Renewable Electricity by CPI Group (UK) Ltd

IN THE BEGINNING

I REMEMBER THE BRIGHT LIGHTS, THE SEMI SUDDENLY lurching from its lane and driving straight towards me. I tried to swerve, but it had been rush hour; all I managed to do was slam into the car to my right, the one that didn't move far enough. Then pain. Then nothing.

I floated in an abyss for some time afterward. It was an empty existence and I remained there for an eternity or a second. I was neither hungry nor tired. My mind was rational, yet I could not focus sufficiently to do anything.

Finally, I heard voices.

"What are you going to roll up?" came one that seemed to fill everything. It was a higher pitched, nasally voice. It was the kind of voice that just makes you dislike someone instantly.

"I'm thinking a Warrior," came the response. It echoed even more powerfully. It was also far huskier and far more annoyed.

Suddenly, there was a flash and I began staring around the cavernous room I was now in. It was enormous, mostly empty, and made absolutely no sense. I was dead and yet this wasn't limbo anymore. I could feel the rough stone beneath my bare feet.

I'm going to be honest: I stood there for several minutes, playing back memories through my mind. Despite the sudden change, I wasn't worried, though. I wasn't anything. There was an absolute emotional void.

I recognized that lack of feeling was wrong. I was in a new room after being somewhere else and I had no idea how I got there. I tried to freak out, but for whatever reason I couldn't get a head of steam built up. Instead, I looked around to find the source of a new noise. I recognized it as the rattle of dice, a frequent sound from my years of D&D. Alas, even that didn't break me out of my reverie as I tried to peer into the empty cavern.

"Ohh, that's a high one, on the supplementary expansion table," came the first obnoxious voice's whine.

"Ashes! Are we using that table?" asked the husky one. "I only have the main chart. I'll need to look up what it does."

"You said I could use anything, so I did," replied the nasal voice, tartly.

I saw a light out of the corner of my vision. Swinging my head around, it remained firmly in place in the corner. While it wasn't distracting, it was annoying, and I tried to focus upon it. Suddenly, words appeared in front of my vision.

You have gained the trait Unbound.

You are not bound to level restrictions when selecting any perks, skills, or talents. Traits are the highest type of power that a person can possess and will override any restrictions placed upon them from non-Traits. Unbound is a unique Talent—no one else in the world possesses this Talent. Good Luck!

I put my hand through the words several times. It was something like an AR display, but a quick check revealed that I wasn't wearing any AR devices. Or my glasses. Yet glancing around the room, I realized that I could see everything perfectly, which was generally not the case. In my youth, I'd worn abnormally large coke bottle lenses; with modern technology, they had become more manageable, but still absolutely required if I wanted to see anything. Until now, that is.

"Hello?" I called out, suddenly recognizing that I *could* call out.

"I've never heard one talk before," came a new rumbling response.

"Ignore it. I'm going to find out what Unbound means," came the husky voice again.

"It might be able to tell us what it means from its character sheet," noted the first, his voice becoming quieter as it trailed off.

Quieter ... then quiet.

Oh shit, that can't be good. So, I looked back to the prompt I'd seen. Concentrating on it, a more detailed image appeared.

- Name: Grebthar the Destroyer. Would you like to confirm your name? (Yes/No)
- Race: Human. You have rolled the racial ability: Unbound.
- Class: None. Please select a class.
- Note: Wipe Memory was not performed. Would you like to perform a memory wipe? (Yes/No)

I focused on Name and a menu appeared, giving me a start. There was a large text box that was prefilled with "Grebthar the Destroyer." I mentally clicked the backspace button on the keyboard and the name vanished. I replaced it with "Jim," because I recalled my name was Jim and also because Grebthar was a stupid name. There was a prompt asking to confirm, and I selected "Yes." My name is Jim. Not James even, Jim. Only my mother ever called me James.

Pushing that aside, next I focused on Race. It was Human and when I tried to change it, the prompt indicated that it was already locked in. And apparently I'd rolled the Human racial ability, Unbound. Well, at least I was still a human named Jim.

The voices had mentioned Unbound, so I focused on that. Instantly I was prompted with "You are not bound to level restrictions when selecting any perks, skills, or talents." That meant exactly nothing to me. I'd absorbed, not read really, the more detailed description earlier and that still didn't mean very much. Perks and talents could mean a great number of things, so I continued checking the sheet.

Class was interesting. When I tried to focus on it, a number of statues out in the cavern started glowing in my vision. It was enough like a video game that I instantly recognized what was happening. I started walking down a set of stairs made of the same cool stone. I swear I stepped on a few sharper bits of rock, though nothing seemed to bother my feet. So I carried on at a brisk pace.

Part of my mind considered that I should really be more upset about my current predicament. However, it was hard to work up any sort of serious mental steam about anything; I felt very blasé about my circumstances. I was aware that this was all incredibly strange and that I *should* be feeling something. Emotional engagement towards anything simply seemed out of reach. As I walked, I brought up my character sheet again. If anything could engage my mind and awaken my hitherto missing emotions, having a prompt would do it. And as I examined the sheet, I realized that there was more than one page. I knew instinctively the second page was for stats.

- Name: Jim

- Stats: Unassigned, no class has been selected yet.

I didn't have any stats! I couldn't worry my pretty little head over this. Indeed, I couldn't worry my pretty little head over anything. The entire sense of apathy I had been feeling all came down to this. Would I even be able to chuckle at my own witticisms? Could I even make witticisms? I instinctively knew I had to select a class, so I continued down to where the statues were.

They were standard fantasy fare. There was Warrior, Woodsman, Wizard, and Thief. Several more statues actually, but those were the first ones I saw. All looked pretty iconic for being made of grey stone. There were lots of them, probably twelve or so, but the terrible lighting made them difficult to count initially.

I touched the Warrior statue and became aware that they were proficient in Light and Medium Armor, all Weapons, and Shields. Pulling my hand back, I stared at the statue for a moment. I hadn't seen words or been told that would happen. I just somehow knew. That was intriguing. It was an instant transmission of knowledge and, after removing my hand, I retained the information, however less firmly. It was akin to seeing something written on a page or recalling that information after the fact.

The room was actually getting stuffy. Another thing I "knew" was that the only way to leave was to select one of the statues, thereby selecting a class. In fact, as I looked around, I saw three large doorways leaving from the cavern. One seemed to go towards a church somewhere, the second towards a beach, and the third towards some mountains. The urge to select a class and go was itching at me. However, I needed to collect as much intelligence as possible about this peculiar place before making a choice.

I buckled down. I was concerned that the voices were going to select my life for me if I didn't do it for myself. I had no clear idea if I was racing some unseen clock, but I felt as if time was of the essence.

I waited a moment and touched the rogue statue. I instantly became aware of Sneaking, Dodging, Light armor, and skills with various knives and smaller crossbows. Touching the Cleric and Wizard also brought along knowledge of Holy magic and Arcane magic. I observed that there was a different feel between the two and that the cleric required a commitment of some sort that I couldn't quite place.

Touching the statues didn't give me the ability to do their specific skills; however, I did understand the skills that both Rogues and Wizards possessed. I also had an awareness that whatever class I chose, I would be gifted with their abilities instantaneously. It would be like going to college without any of the work. You'd go from nothing to a graduate in the blink of an eye.

Intrigued, I considered my options. I listened for the voices while I walked around a bit, touching the other various statues. There was the Woodsman statue, all of the outdoorsman archetypes from fantasy, and the Druid statue, representing primal spirits. As I completed my circle, I came to another door in the floor. It didn't open, though.

The three gateways leading out of the room resembled translucent, glowing blue vortexes in space. However, I couldn't get anywhere near them. I actually tried walking into one as hard as I could, but it was like an invisible force field was blocking me. On one level, that was cool; it was like the universe protecting me from leaving without choosing a class. On another level, it underscored that I needed to make a choice to leave.

It was only then that I discovered the spiral pattern covered in arcane symbols on the floor. When my foot initially stepped on it, it was colder and more solid. I could feel that it was not stone like the rest of the floor. Glancing around, I saw a small pedestal with a red orb upon it.

"I'm sure this will be fine," I said as I started walking over to it, but my voice trailed off into nothingness. My cavern was much more like a platform in a large void than a room surrounded by walls. In fact, glancing behind the gateways, I realized I was surrounded by empty space.

Could I fall off this platform?

The orb was pulsing a deep red color, almost as dark as the room itself. The area around it was dusty, as if no one had disturbed it in quite some time. However, there seemed to be a hand-shaped impression on the orb itself. Haltingly, I placed my hand upon it. Lights flickered in the orb and an ominous voice filled the cavern.

"Only the worthy may proceed. Are you worthy?"

"I guess," I said confidently.

"You have completed zero other lives in this realm and have no achievements to speak of," replied the voice of the orb. "Only the worthy may proceed."

"Oh," I muttered. "Well, that was fun. Maybe I could try Warrior." As I tried to pull my hand away, however, I found it stuck fast, as if melded to the sphere. Incessant tugging for a few moments confirmed that I was not leaving that way.

"You will need to achieve level 0 in 3 additional classes to open the door," stated the voice with grave formality. The orb's glow began to fade but my hand would not release no matter how hard I pulled.

"So, I've achieved all the requirements?" I asked.

And with that, the world seemed to vibrate for an instant. The orb sputtered and flared as if it were trying to respond but failing. It felt a bit like computer lag, as if the game had locked up for just a moment. However, as quickly as the stutter began, it ended. Everything resumed normally.

"All requirements have been achieved. The door shall be opened!"

With that, the doorway in the floor opened into a spiral staircase leading down to another layer of the cavern. My hand popped free with an audible snapping sound that seemed out of place, and I started walking even before the stairwell was fully formed.

In for a penny, I thought, before flipping open my character sheet. I glanced at the memory wipe option and dialed it to "No" before locking it in and walking down the stairs.

It opened into a second cavern, which was smaller and only had two gateways leading out of it. They both opened into large cities I noticed, but this time there were only nine statues as opposed to the twelve I'd seen earlier. Looking back up, I could see the floor above me simply hovering much like a flying saucer. Again, I was faced with the surreal knowledge of the strangeness of this accompanied by a general apathy.

The nearest statue to the stairwell was a large man wearing wizarding robes and hat and carrying a large rod. Placing my hand on it, I became aware it was a "Mystic Theurge." They could use both Arcane and Holy magics as well as some unique hybrid spells that blended both. Furthermore, they had the potential to be just as powerful as a Wizard or a Cleric in their respective magics.

That was interesting. The advanced classes seemed to adopt powers from several previous classes. From my own experience, that could be a blessing or not, depending on how the system worked. You could end up being really powerful or a jack of all trades and master of none.

Circling around the statues, I saw several more: there was a Spellsword, which blended Arcane magic and Melee, and an Arcane Thief, which was the same, but with the skills of a Rogue. I also saw statues for some sort of Woodsman/Druid hybrid and a Warrior with a sword and dagger. As neither of them really interested me, I figured I'd give them a once over after I reviewed the other statues.

Around the outer edge, there were three statues that stood separately and instantly drew my attention. One was a Sky Pirate, whose powers were both Pirate- and Airship-based and started with their own personal airship. I felt sorely tempted to select that and move on because, hey, who doesn't want an airship in a fantasy setting? Also, there was a Mage Hunter statue who could nullify magic and a Great General whose powers seemed to focus on battlefield tactics.

So, there were not only hybrids, but also classes that were built around unique mechanics. The more I walked around, however, the more I began to feel like myself. And the more I felt like myself, the more I realized I had just died . . . and that I urgently needed to get out of this room.

I had a family. They needed me. Well . . . maybe. If I died, they got a hell of an insurance settlement. And I did remember dying. That would check every box in my death and dismemberment policy. There would be enough money for them to take care of themselves. I didn't know if I could get back to them anyway.

Because I had died.

Then again, this might have been some sort of lucid dream. I could just be in a coma after the accident. I will admit my memories were kind of fuzzy after the impact. Perhaps, I hadn't died instantly and an ambulance was really close. Logically, though, I was in a car and that semi must have been going at least sixty and there had been a vehicle behind me. What could the odds of survival possibly have been?

I continued walking around the statues until I saw a second pulsing orb glowing red. The light from the orb did not generate shadows, and as soon as I recognized that, I was even more sure that something was wrong. *Well, if this is a lucid dream, I suppose I should make the most of it.*

I grabbed the second orb, even though this one contained no impression on it. Regardless, I figured that if the first one had worked by me putting my hand on it, the second would as well. The light went from a dull throbbing red to a powerful flashing light that seemed to bake me from the inside out.

"Only the worthy may proceed. Are you worthy?"

"You'll find that I am," I said resolutely.

"You have completed zero other lives in this realm and have no achievements to speak of," replied the voice. "Only the worthy may proceed."

"What will I need to do to complete the requirements?" I asked.

"You will need to achieve level 0 in 6 additional classes and complete a world quest. Once all requirements are confirmed, you may proceed. However, if you have not yet completed a world quest, you must achieve level 0 in 12 additional classes," stated the voice with grave formality.

"So, I made it?" I asked.

With that, the world seemed to vibrate for an instant. Instead of lag, this time it felt like the world locked up for just an instant. I could sense and think, but my ability to move was gone. I could sense and think, but my ability to move was gone. I could sense and think, but my ability to move . . .

It suddenly snapped back, and the world came rushing back to normality.

"All requirements have been achieved. The door shall be opened!"

A doorway again opened in the floor leading down to a deeper level in the void. Describing it as a cavern no longer felt apt, as I discovered more of its depths. I found I was actually curious to see how deep the rabbit hole went.

Then I heard the booming voice again.

"WHERE IS HE?"

My trek down the stairs was performed at a suddenly-breakneck pace. Literally.

I fell.

However, apparently when one has no stats, one can take no damage. This staircase was longer, and despite the lack of a handrail, I managed to stay on them for the entire path down. Bouncing down the stairs on my face was probably quite a bit faster than running, I rationalized. Standing up revealed I was correct in my assessment of damage; I was none the worse for wear.

Suddenly I felt like someone was staring right at my back.

"Did he leave already?" came the husky voice.

"I'm looking at his sheet now," replied the nasal voice. "No, he's still there. *Jim?* What kind of name is Jim?"

"He named himself," called out the husky voice, now far more annoyed than before.

"Ash and fire, I had the memory wipe option off!" replied the nasal voice.

Then there was a pause, which I used to look around my current room. There was a way to put the stairs up, so I pushed that. The staircase slowly slipped back into the roof of the room.

"YOU DID WHAT?" screamed the husky voice.

"Well, I just re-rolled three other characters. None of them needed memory wipes so I just . . . turned it off."

"You are an idiot," said the husky voice. "We have to find him. How can he hide? There is just the one room."

"The staircase leading to the middle is down," squeaked the nasal voice.

It was then that I realized that, while I repositioned the last staircase I used, I left the first set of stairs completely exposed. It was like a big blazing arrow pointing directly to me.

"ASH AND FIRE!"

So I scooted. There was no other word for it. I needed to get out of there quickly and, well, this wasn't the time for careful consideration. There were three statues here and one gateway. The first one was a Sage. It had ultimate control over magic. The second was an Archangel, who had fundamentally impressive control over the universe, as well as what amounted to super powers. The third was a Chosen One, who, by divine providence, was set to lead the world into the next age.

All three sounded great. But you see, there was this green orb.

Also, the stairwell from above was opening again. I mean I could have selected any of the statues and headed out the single doorway but . . .

Green orb.

"I'm qualified! Let me down," I said in a rush, as I grasped the emerald orb.

"This is true. The path to ultimate power lies beneath."

I dove down the stairwell just as the room I had been in began to glow an ominous red. This light, as if from the orangish red fires of hell, cast flickering shadows from some impending terror. A terror that was annoyed with me. I was going to jump down the stairs, pick the first statue I could, and run out the door while hoping whatever doom was on my tail could not follow.

This floor was different from the others. Previously, the rooms had been made of stone and set in a void. This room was crystal and looked down over a world from very high above. It was amazingly beautiful. I had all of a quarter of a second to take in my surroundings while I was running like a man being chased by an angry demon down the stairs.

There were exactly two problems with that strategy.

The first problem was time or, more specifically, a serious lack of it.

When I rushed into the final level, the statue was right by the stairwell. I touched it, the Godling, and started to feel a rush of power as the class abilities began to flow through me. It was a feeling that was quickly stopped when my character sheet appeared.

You receive 5 stat bumps from picking a god-tier character. Please select which stats you want to apply your stat bumps to.

I didn't know what that meant. I understood it in the basic sense of assigning points, but I didn't know *how* to assign points. As it turned out, I didn't have time to even select the class; the statue exploded as a spike of green fire passed through it, utterly obliterating the stone. The prompt, the bumps, the class all vanished. In its place, the biggest, fattest, angriest demon I ever expected to see in my life stood before me. At that point, I decided running was the best option.

Which led to the second problem: there was no door out.

See, I didn't have stats, so I wasn't very quick. The demon *did*, and whatever they were, his Speed and Agility were both WAY higher than my nothing. He had me in his beefy clawed hand in less than a second and was holding me high in the air like I weighed nothing.

I might have. I don't know. I certainly would have been pissing myself if that was an option, however it wasn't. So instead, I was just suspended by his claw overtop the crystal floor, quietly realizing that while I couldn't feel much of anything else, I could still feel some degree of terror.

"You *moron*!" screamed the big, fat, ugly, terrifying, husky demon.

"Me?" I wheezed, because I am apparently a moron. The demon glared at me an instant and then slammed me into the crystal floor of the final room with the force of a semi-truck. Scratch that, I'd had some experience with semi-trucks and this was worse.

"I'm sorry," replied the much thinner, nasal voice, weenie of a demon. I mean seriously, even as I was embedded in the floor, this demon screamed dork.

We know our own.

"ANY CLASS, ANY POWER," growled the husky one, "but you forgot to do a mind wipe, so we have to delete him."

"Maybe we could let him decide," replied my dorky savior.

"I'm with him," I groaned.

The husky demon, who had anger issues, lifted me back into the air and slammed me back into the crystal floor again, harder than last time. Thirty percent harder, I realized, because that was something I just knew now. I was definitely about to die again.

"No! He knows too much; you'll never be able to control him," stated the angry demon angrily.

"I'll do whatever you tell me to," I groaned, so he slammed me into the ground three more times in rapid succession. The crystal floor under me was developing an interesting cracked pattern as my body was being driven into it repeatedly. Now that my head was on backwards, I could see the indents my body was making.

Oh, that's why Rumiko did it.

"What if we directly bound ourselves to him?" asked the dork.

The angry demon paused, his hand still firmly attached to my throat, which was in turn firmly implanted into the crystal floor with the rest of my body. He was polite enough to grab my head and snap it back in line with the rest of my body. So . . . there was that.

"Perhaps," he said after a moment, the anger in his voice cooling. "But with his abilities, I'm not sure if we could actually control him. After all, if either of us were to actually go down to the mortal plane, we'd have to do so in our least forms."

"We could get injured or even die," the nasal voice agreed. "However, if we overwrote him, we could just edit a few key portions of his mind and then set him loose. It would be almost as good! We could do it here, in the great chamber, before I pick his class. I'd also be able to change his name."

"That is a stupid name," stated the husky demon.

As much as I *didn't* want to die, getting my mind rewritten wasn't anything I actually wanted either. I tried to squirm, but the demonic claw might as well have been a steel vice wrapped around my windpipe. They continued discussing what they could still change on my sheet after they took me to the great chamber and I'd had about enough of it. I could stand dying, but not getting my mind rewritten by these assholes.

"Hey, Fatty," I stated to the angry demon, who had unfortunately calmed down.

"I forgot you could talk instead of making mewling noises with your mouth. However, you are incorrect if you think your petty human insults have any bearing at all on one such as myself. I will enjoy modifying your mind."

"You have terrible breath," I croaked.

"Thank you!" he chuckled.

"Your mother stinks of elderberries and your uncle's cum."

"You fail to disparage my uncle-dad," he stated.

"Your horns are crooked."

"MY HORNS ARE FINE!"

The crooked-horned demon was sensitive about that, it turned out, and so he slammed me into the crater again. I figured this one would kill me; it was at least five trucks worth of force. It failed, however, to end my life. Instead, the floor shattered and the three of us were sucked out into whatever passed for space in this place.

CHAPTER 1

AN UNINTERESTING GRASSY FIELD

I CAME TO IN THE MIDDLE OF A GRASSY FIELD, NAKED AND sore as hell. I was aware of two things: I had to go to the bathroom and my neck hurt.

That came as a shock, so I stood up, looking around the area. It was a grassy field, with beautiful flowers in all directions. Various herbs and plants were scattered throughout the area, breaking up the line of the simple field. It was very picturesque except for the crater where I had landed. That was still smoking slightly.

I was seeing yellow, so I found a nearby tree and relieved myself right there. It was satisfying, but now instead of seeing yellow, I had a small yellow blip in the side of my vision. It was that prompt again. I was surprised, to say the least, but before I could react to it, I heard a gargling scream.

"What are you doing?" came the squeaky response.

I looked down half expecting to see a mouse, but instead was greeted by the image of a small, rotund little demon with crooked horns. I aimed at his face. It had been a while. It splattered all over him, but the demon had changed significantly. When I'd last seen him, the demon had been massive, at least thirty feet tall, and enormously powerfully built.

This demon was about a foot tall and just about as far around. His head was larger in proportion to his body than even a baby's, but his arms and legs were comically small. He couldn't have even put his hands on top of his head and his attempted dodgings demonstrated that walking was going to be a serious challenge for him. His skin was still red, but it was a darker red now and his glowing eyes had been replaced by more cat-like ones. He had dropped down on the threatening meter from "it's going to kill me" to "I don't know what this is but I'm going to stomp it until it's not a threat anymore."

"I will kill you for this," gargled the demon. "I'm a powerful demon giant!" I presume that's what he was saying, at any rate. Afterwards, he began first wiping the urine off his face and then using a leaf to attempt, unsuccessfully, to sop up the rest.

"And I am Jim."

The demon's eyes suddenly went wide in horror, which is an expression I'll always treasure. It, well obviously he, jumped up and tried to fly with his wings. But now they were not well-suited for him and he barely managed to hover briefly.

"Well, I don't care what you want to call yourself; we need to find a demon door and return to the citadel."

"So, I can be reprogrammed," I replied. "Not gonna happen."

Suddenly, my head flared in pain: deep agonizing pain that drove me right to my knees. In my vision, a red prompt flickered to the side, creating a sudden awareness that I'd been bound to a demon.

"I don't see that you have much of a choice, human," the demon chuckled. "As long as I am bound to you, I can use this power to 'advise' you into doing whatever I want."

As I stood up to calmly discuss this with him, the demon turned on the juice full force, driving me back to the ground. It was like the worst migraine you've ever imagined, but with cymbals crashing at the same time. I started dry heaving.

He relented after an eternity.

"You can do that whenever you want?" I croaked.

"Yes, as long as I can see you." He grinned. "Now, you will call me Master and I will call you—"

"My name is Jim," I stated, standing back up, now brandishing a largish tree branch. The demon examined the stick for a moment before laughing.

"You are going to defy me with a *stick*?" he laughed. "You would need a mighty tree the size of my body to even stand a chance."

I had played baseball in college and I'd like to think he realized at the last moment that the tree branch was every bit as large as he was and I was swinging with as much force behind it as possible. It was actually less than I expected, as the stick was not very well balanced and I was having trouble getting it just right, but the demon was too busy laughing at me to dodge.

It impacted with a meaty thud and the demon went flying, slamming into a nearby tree. Instead of bouncing off, however, he stuck there with a mighty thunk. I walked over to look, hoping he was dead, but no such luck. His horns had pierced the bark and he was almost skull deep into the tough wood.

The demon came to a moment later and the pain flared in my head, dropping me to the ground. "You will pay for this!" was the last thing I heard before I passed out . . . again.

I don't know how many hours I was asleep, but it was more than a few. I was aware of a few new icons in my field of vision, even though my eyes were closed and I wanted to die, so that was nice. Opening my eyes, I examined the demon, still firmly stuck in the tree.

I sat up and groaned. The echoes of pain were still there, but it was mostly gone. I decided to review my icons while I tried to figure out what to do with the demon. There was the demon's icon, which looked like blood on a black circle which I figured was a very bad thing. Another icon was that of a golden star coin. A third looked like a bronze triangle. Also, and I had to be paying attention for this one, there was a small exclamation mark.

Since those were unknowns, I started off by looking at my character sheet.

- Name: Jim
- Class: Undefined
- Awaiting Level UP Warrior!
- Strength: Average
- Dexterity: Average
- Endurance: Average
- Willpower: Average
- Spirit: Average
- Charisma: Average

Skills:

- None
- Demon Lore (1 SP): Unskilled

Awaiting Rank Up!

- Simple Weapons (10 SP)

I'd earned a few XP and SP when I'd hit the demon with the stick. That was nice. I wondered what the little bastard was worth. I clicked on the exclamation point next. It turned out to be a notification for my combat log, which dutifully reported my victories in battle. The thought of all of my accomplishments being noted for posterity was not a good one.

As if I wasn't self-conscious about farting already.

- You have defeated an ELDER DEMON through immobilization by causing 5 points of damage.
- You have gained 999,999,999,999,999 XP and gained one class level in Warrior, additional experience points over level maximum are wasted.
- You have gained 999,999,999,999,999 SP and gained Amateur rank in Simple Weapons, additional skill points over maximum are wasted.

WHAT? He was worth . . . a *trillion* XP? Fuck. But experience through over level was wasted. That was good to know, I suppose. Also fuck. Also, I was in a world where there were experience points. Finally . . . FUCK. That honestly bothered me more than the icons I could always see out of the corner of my vision. And a trillion XP gone.

FUCK.

Inhale, exhale. Maybe it's easy to earn a trillion XP . . .

It's not going to be easy.

Simple weapons 1 was the bronze triangle. It popped up and showed me I was now at Amateur skill level with simple weapons. I could see a whole string of abilities behind it that I couldn't select. Storing that question for later, I went to the next icon.

The golden star coin flashed before me and I was prompted with:

- Level UP, Warrior 1
- You have selected the Warrior Class. Please choose two stat buffs for yourself at first level!
- You have gained the skills Light and Medium Armor, as well as all Simple Weapons.
- You already have skill with Simple Weapons. Please choose another skill or one will be chosen for you.
- Your Hit Point total is increased by 10. Your Stamina is increased by 10.

I considered for a moment and instantly knew I had 30 hit points and 30 stamina as well as 20 mana. I don't recall ever being able to quantify my exact health before, so this was new. I resolved to consider this at a later date, as well. My to-do list was becoming rather extensive.

- You are bound to a Demon.
- You and the demon are Tightly Bound.
- You have not accepted him as your Master.
- He has not accepted you as his Master.
- He has not granted you any boons.
- He can apply punishments to you as he sees fit.
- Your demon's rank is 999. Elder Demon.
- Update: Your demon has been defeated in combat and has had his power level reduced until he returns to the Citadel. His current power is Rank 1.

- Your bond level is Tight, which
  allows the more powerful of
  the two to exert direct force
  over the weaker member of
  the pair if neither is Master.

Well, ain't that karma.

"What is a Rank 1 Demon?" I said cautiously, walking up behind the newly minted rank 1 Demon.

"It is the weakest kind of demon, barely a threat to anyone, an annoying, mewing cur," he grumbled, trying to push himself free of the tree and failing. He had hit the tree horns first, I knew that, but in his current form his arms were too short to actually reach above his head. Also, his neck was mostly solid, so he didn't have the movement a human would have.

Basically, with his tiny arms and legs, he was never going to pull himself free of the tree.

"Could a Rank 1 Demon cause pain to me?" I asked.

The demon paused for a long moment. "Yes, if you were bound. However, it would be only a very limited form of pain, like a mild itch," he finally replied.

"Which means that since you are a Rank 1 Demon, I can basically ignore you," I said.

The demon paused, finally accessing his own menus or whatever he did. He then began struggling for a long thirty seconds before finally stopping, defeated. "What do you want?"

"So many things, you little turd," I replied gravely. "First off, what can I call you? Because it sure as hell is not going to be master."

"I cannot give you my true name. You may call me Sir," he responded.

"So Shart it is," I said. "Shart, what did you do to me?"

"What's a 'shart'?" he asked, struggling harder to remove himself from the tree, still quite unsuccessfully.

"*You* are a Shart, and you bound yourself to me. Explain that, and I might think about considering removing you from the tree," I replied, sitting down and getting comfortable.

Shart continued squirming for a good two more minutes before finally sighing audibly. "I bound you like a familiar so that you would DO MY BIDDING AND RELEASE ME!"

"So, what does that entail?" I asked politely, as I found a particularly comfortable spot of moss.

"It binds our souls together so that I, as the more powerful of the two of us, can force you to do my bidding."

"And now that you are Rank 1?" I asked.

The demon, to his credit, had actually managed to sound arrogant up to this point. However, at the solid reminder of his new status, he cracked.

"This whole thing is a terrible mistake. I'm not even supposed to be here today." Shart wept for a few long minutes before he finally, *finally* gave up on trying to break his head free from the tree. He hung motionless for a few more seconds as if coming to terms with his fate. "So now that I'm Rank 1, I'm not going to be able to command you to do anything, am I?"

"Very doubtful," I responded, "but I may release you from the tree fort of solitude, if you are polite and answer a few of my questions."

Shart hung quietly for a long moment before nodding. Well, probably nodded, since his neck wasn't really developed enough for that. He mainly kind of bobbed. Supporting your whole body by your neck looked painful.

"So, where are we?" I asked. "I'm guessing this isn't the same world I started on."

"You are mostly correct," stated Shart. "We are in one of the Eternal Realms. You are on Ordinal, one of the first realms to be exact."

"How many Eternal Realms are there?" I asked. I had the feeling this could get long-winded and the last thing I wanted was a detailed description of the history of the universe.

"Many," responded Shart. "But most are newer, more refined than this older realm. My associate and I were hoping to renovate it somewhat until the . . . accident."

"Where you got blasted down here and lost all your powers?" I asked.

"Yes," replied Shart slowly. "Anyway, Ordinal has some unique properties and many powerful souls that could have been harvested. However, there were difficulties that led to us ultimately having to import fresh souls from other realms . . ."

"Wait, Earth is another Realm?" I asked.

"I'm going to say yes, but only because your puny mind would not be able to comprehend the magnitude of it all," replied Shart smartly.

"Fine, didn't really care anyway. Any way to get me back to Earth?"

"No," stated Shart. "Your earthly body was shattered and we caught your soul exiting it. If we were to restore you on Earth, you would come out as a babe. Your past memories would be wiped. Those are the default settings on that planet."

I nodded. I had already figured getting back to my previous existence was a long shot. His explanation was pretty straight forward and it meshed with what I knew of Earth. Mainly, that people didn't come back from the dead. Especially considering my conception was not immaculate.

So, I wasn't just dead. I was *dead* dead and there was no going back. I would have slumped down, if I wasn't already sitting. Instead, I just sat quietly for a long minute. I had a wife, and a family. The marriage wasn't always great, but we'd been happy. The kids weren't always great—no kids are—but they were good. As a family, we loved each other. We just clicked, with all our various quirks and all. If I hadn't had such a great insurance policy, I'd see no silver lining. But there would be enough for the kids to go to college and my wife to survive. I sat for what seemed like ages, remembering them. At last, I stored away my memories in a mental box to be looked at again later. For now, I had other issues.

When I finally spoke again, I asked, "Okay, why can I see myself in this amount of detail?"

"Explain," ordered the demon.

"I have, for lack of a better term, a character sheet that shows me all of my abilities, stats, and skills. There was a tab for powers and the like."

"Oh, I forgot they don't have those on Earth," replied the demon, thinking. "You've played video games before, right? It's pretty much the same thing. Just think about it and you can access that information."

"I didn't expect it to be that easy," I said. "If Earth is part of the Eternal Realms, why didn't it have that option?" Character sheets would be really handy, I thought.

"First off, Earth *wishes* it was part of the Eternal Realms. In this case, we didn't really have the <processor power> to activate it and Earth was a bit of a test case for a class-less non-magical realm anyway."

"So, having character sheets is normal and Earth is weird?" I asked.

"Yes. On Earth you don't even have health bars; I don't know how you survive," replied Shart.

"So, I got a Level UP in Warrior," I stated. "What does that mean?"

"You had access to Godling and you picked *Warrior*?" Shart gasped. "That's stupid! You had access to all of the classes, and you picked *Warrior*? That's a primary class, man. They suck."

"Well, I didn't choose warrior. I just got a level in warrior after I . . . defeated you."

"You got lucky," said the demon. "That tree trunk was very large. But you need to be level 60 before you get through the Demon Door to be reborn. With a basic-bitch warrior that's going to take years. I'm going to be stuck here forever."

You have been offered a Quest: Take <Shart> to
the Demon Door; this will allow the Elder Demon
to reclaim his powers. Reward: Unknown.

"And I just got a quest prompt," I said, "to return you to Demon Door."

"I need you to take that," said the demon.

"That's probably not going to happen," I said, pushing the quest away without accepting or declining it.

"If you don't accept the quest," stated Shart, "I'll be stuck here forever."

"I could leave you in the tree, then," I offered.

"Please, no! All I can see is that rock and I already hate it," replied the demon, his struggles beginning for a few moments before finally stopping. "Fuck you, rock."

"I don't see any real benefit to bringing you along, though."

"Well, you are bound to me, so if I get too far from you it's going to be uncomfortable for both of us. Don't worry, I can turn invisible and immaterial so I can hide very well. Only someone with true sight can find me, and you won't be running into anyone like that for a while," continued the demon as he pleaded with me.

"That's not really my concern. I don't really see that as being necessary at all."

"You are a basic-bitch warrior. I could also give you a boon, so you might live a bit longer," he said.

"Explain."

"I'm at Rank 1 now, the weakest power of demon, so I can only grant you my least impressive boons. If I find a source of raw magic, though, it will get more powerful. However, right now, I can grant you demonic regeneration. This will cause you to heal ten times faster than normal. You will be able to quest more and level faster and get me home quicker."

"And when are you planning on betraying me?"

"When we get to the door. I'll try to get in first, and if successful, no matter how powerful you are, I'll be much stronger then," replied the demon earnestly.

"Why would you tell me that?" I asked, a clear note of incredulity in my voice.

"I'm blue," he said, and I instantly knew it was a lie; he was red. I could see he was red. But beyond that, through the bond we now shared, I knew he was lying. I knew it as surely as I knew my name was Jim.

"You can't lie to me," I stated as fact.

"Would make life so much easier," muttered Shart. "After we get to the Demon Door, I can send you back to your family."

Again, I knew he was lying.

CHAPTER 2

STILL IN THE FIELD

I HAD TO FIND A REPLACEMENT FOR THE ALMIGHTY STICK of Demon Smiting, which had flown from my hands after I smashed Shart with it. Fortunately, there were several stands of trees nearby, although they were just far enough away to start to feel the tug of the demonic bond. Ultimately it was easy to find a tree branch of the same approximate size and composition. It was both long and hard, just the way my wife liked it, and I returned.

"This is going to hurt," I informed him as I adjusted myself down into a batter's stance.

"Well, I think that if you were to use the root over there as leverage—" started Shart. He was right; that probably would have worked. However, I used an alternative method of striking him about the head until he finally, on the sixth swing, broke free.

He landed with a groan. "Why did you do that?"

"I said it was going to hurt; I didn't say it had to," I said.

The demon groaned and got up, attempting and failing to fly. He landed with a plop and I glanced down at him, adjusting my new staff in case it suddenly needed to become another Almighty Stick.

"I don't have enough power to fly," stated Shart . . . who immediately vanished. But I could still see him, somehow. His skin had become transparent, but the outline was clearly visible to me. I just stared directly at him while he settled himself and scraped wood off of his horns by brushing them against a rock.

"Which way should we go?" I asked.

"Oh, I think that way." He pointed in a vague direction. Lacking any sort of better route, I started walking for only a short while before I became aware that the demon was getting farther away from me. I was aware of this because of the throbbing pain that was only getting worse.

I turned around and noticed that he was not the fastest little mover in the world. He might have been okay if his little wings had been functional, but on the ground, he waddled like a one-year-old and couldn't make any time at all. Being immaterial was even worse, because he had to be material enough to not slide through the ground. This meant that all the wind and grass he was bumping into was bouncing him around.

The little baby demon didn't know how to walk.

"Can I ride on your shoulder?" he asked, after he spent entirely too long trying to catch up.

I agreed, because I eventually wanted to get someplace. Shart scaled me like a miniature King Kong, and we were on our way again. While we were walking, I brought up my character sheet. I had to get to level 60, and I needed to see what that meant. I also had those two stat bumps to think about and Endurance was sounding pretty good right now. Walking through uncut virgin forest was tiring.

- Name: Jim
- Hit Points: 30
- Stamina: 30
- Mana: 20
- Class: Warrior 1
- Strength: Average
- Dexterity: Average
- Endurance: Average
- Willpower: Average
- Spirit: Average
- Charisma: Average

You have 2 stat bumps available.

Skills:
- None
- Demon Lore (5 SP): Unskilled
- Light Armor (100 SP): Amateur
- Medium Armor (150 SP): Amateur
- Shields (100 SP): Amateur

- Martial Weapons (10 SP):   • Simple Weapons (10 SP):
  Amateur   Amateur

Awaiting Rank Up!

You have one bonus skill selection at rank Amateur.

Well, the stat bumps were easy enough. I dumped one into Endurance, to ease the tiredness from walking, and one into Strength. Experience in my old D&D days taught me that Strength was a Warrior's primary attribute. Nothing seemed to happen until I mentally clicked a prompt to confirm. At that point my entire body shuddered.

I'd worked out when I was younger. I'd actually had some physical labor jobs where I'd gotten pretty muscular at a few points in my life. This was entirely different. My body went from doughy average dad bod to toned college kid in the blink of an eye. My endurance was harder to see, but I could immediately tell it had gotten much greater as well. My body had a leaner quality about it. The walk had been tiring, if not exhausting so far, but suddenly I felt like I'd been doing light labor instead of this grueling hike. My perspective shifted as well; I think I got taller.

That was cool. I could also sense that my hit points went up. Physical stats increased hit points and Endurance at varying ratios. My point of Endurance increased my HP and Stamina while my Strength just increased my hit points. In short, I had gotten much tougher just by deciding I needed to be tougher.

Next, I glanced at my skills tab. This caused an enormous, detail-rich skill tree to appear. Light Armor had a variety of sub skills, but apparently I needed to have the base skill up to a certain level to use them. I could see a skill called Hardened Light Armor, but it required at least Initiate Light Armor to use, and level 0. That was the Unbound rearing up again. It appeared that Unbound just defeated level requirements, not skill rank requirements. Of course, it probably meant I could get access to them at a much lower level than someone else.

All of the skills were laid out on a huge skill board in front of me when I zoomed out. There were literally thousands of skills, and most of them were entirely undefined. The skill tiles were there, but I couldn't tell if it was some super advanced skill or the most basic of skills. I had the feeling that randomly guessing was far more likely to earn me a skill like Sewing rather than something more powerful. But a handful of the tiles, particularly tiles close to other skills that I did know, were more visible. I could see some of the skills past Light Armor, or Simple Weapon, but I didn't qualify for them.

Looking at the entire board, I decided to go with the simple approach and looked at skills I had that were not of a rank of Amateur. Given that my traveling companion was a demon, I decided it was probably in my best interests to get more well acquainted with him, so I selected Demon Lore.

Demon Lore: Amateur. You know a Succubus from an Incarna, you know all basic stats about demons equal or less than your rank. Level up this ability to learn more about additional demons.

Glancing at Shart, he had a Hit Point, Stamina, and Mana counter over his bald, cantaloupe shaped head. This informed me that even at Rank 1, he had over 400 hit points. However, his Mana and Stamina were both very low. Whether or not they could increase, I didn't know. What I did know was that right now he would take forever to kill, assuming I even could. He glared at me when I thought about that, so I moved on to the next skill set and started reviewing all of them.

Simple Weapons granted me general proficiency in all simple weapons. There were some specializations there for clubs, axes, and other reasonably straightforward weapons. I saw a skill for pitchforks and chuckled. One thing I noticed was that the sub skills seemed to add together the benefits of the core skill and the sub skill.

My Staff skill was already at 2 SP of 50 just from walking around with it. I could also look at my staff and know that it did 2–5 points of damage on a successful strike, which was handy. I wondered how much damage my initial stick had done, but then I recalled the combat log and determined that I had caused a critical hit for exactly 5 points of damage. I couldn't see the higher skill ranks, but I hypothesized that the costs would get higher at higher levels. It seemed like every new rank was a pretty big, obvious deal. If there was something that was a minor benefit, it was a sub skill. However, each SP improved the skill, so someone with Simple Weapons Amateur 10 SP was at a significant disadvantage against someone with the same skill and 100 SP.

I wondered what other skills looked like and then remembered my Demon Lore Amateur skill. It didn't have any sub skills, but it did have a cost, 2001/1,000,000 SP. I stopped.

"It takes one million skill points to get to the next rank of Demon Lore?" I asked.

"To Novice," replied the demon. "Yes, it's a higher-level skill. You shouldn't even have it, but you are Unbound, so you don't have a level requirement. I'm a Rank 1 Demon. If you use it on a Rank 40 Demon, you'll find you get many thousands of points. At my full strength, I would have nearly leveled the skill if you glanced at me . . . and survived."

So, each skill had different skill point requirements. I could learn any skill that was only level restricted, but I had to be exposed to the skill first. Furthermore, I gained skill points from just doing mundane things. There was probably a skill for just about everything. That meant that just randomly selecting skill boosts had a very high chance of not being anything useful.

I glanced at the Warrior tab in my character sheet, which just felt odd to say, and all I saw was the token for Warrior. If I focused on it, it felt like the statue in the cavern, letting me know what powers it had granted me. I could vaguely see three oddly shaped tiles after it, so when I got to level 2, I would have another choice.

"Aren't I supposed to have some equipment?" I asked.

Shart focused for a moment. "No, you started with some rough linen underclothes, but you are supposed to get your gear from your initial quests."

"I'm flapping in the breeze here," I noted.

"Probably burnt up on reentry then," replied Shart.

"And where are those quests?" I grumbled.

"Well, here's the thing," said the demon. "I don't think we landed in the beginner village, because there we'd have found some other adventurers right away. I can't sense anyone nearby, but there is a village over there. Hopefully we'll either find someone to give you a quest where you can get some basic equipment . . . or we'll just find some basic equipment on the way. You're fighting with a stick; almost anything would be an improvement."

"Great," I said. "To be fair: the last time I fought with a stick, I kicked a demon's ass."

Shart glared, and I could sense my downfall being plotted through the bond.

CHAPTER 3

ROAD TO THE VILLAGE

- Name: Jim
- Hit Points: 45
- Stamina: 40
- Mana: 20
- Class: Warrior 1
- Strength: (+1) Above Average

- Dexterity: Average
- Endurance: (+1) Above Average
- Willpower: Average
- Spirit: Average
- Charisma: Average

Combat Skills:

- Unarmored Defense (2 SP): Unskilled
- Light Armor (100 SP): Amateur
- Medium Armor (150 SP): Amateur
- Shields (100 SP): Amateur

- Martial Weapons (10 SP): Amateur
- Simple Weapons (12 SP): Amateur
- Staff (2 SP): Rank 0

Non-Combat Skills:

- Hiking (5 SP): Unskilled
- Stealth (1 SP): Unskilled

- Demon Lore (2001 SP): Amateur

I CONTINUED WALKING TOWARDS THE VILLAGE FOR WHAT seemed like forever, though was assured by my demonic companion that the village couldn't be that much farther. Shart proved both invaluable and useless in this. He knew right where he was and where he wanted us to go, but he tended to think like someone who could fly. Because he could not do so, we kept finding dead ends in the most ridiculous places. As I also could not fly, our journey rapidly devolved into a rather wandering trip.

"You are the worst Bitch in a Box ever," I said with some confidence, for we came to the first real rise, which was terrible. It was thirty feet of loose stone and dirt that seemed to defy any effort at climbing it. I had initially thought we were going to just skirt past it but soon realized that Shart had intended for us (*okay, me*) to climb it. Thus began my hour-long ordeal where I learned the difference between hatred and loathing.

Under the blistering sun I toiled. It was slow going, and Shart's under-his-breath critiques of my climbing abilities and physique were not what I would call helpful. After a dusty, fifteen-foot slip down into weeds, Shart grumbled a "Fuck this shit," and gathered himself for a leap. He grunted, like a tiny pig straining to take a shit three times his size, and rose in the air. He honestly reminded me of an ill mosquito as he swayed a bit uncontrollably, and I would be lying if I said I didn't fantasize about knocking him from the sky with a special demon killing fly swatter. Eventually, he found a landing spot far from me.

"Uh oh," Shart called from his new perch high above me, after my fifth attempt to get up a particularly tall rise in the virgin forest. Due to the trees, I hadn't even noticed we were literally walking into a cliff until after we got there. Then Shart, in his infinite wisdom, told me this was the only way up. He had taken a slow, methodical flight to the top of the rise and had told me I could do it. Seeing as I'm an idiot, I agreed and tried to climb my way to safety.

There were two problems I had discovered: One, my demonic lie detector failed or Shart actually thought he was telling the truth. Which meant he honestly thought that I could climb this thirty-foot-tall cliff without any equipment at all. However, I could *not* climb a thirty-foot-tall cliff. Such a climb would be impossible, even if the surface was rough and scattered with roots.

Secondly, Shart was an asshole.

However, Shart had the map and this was the best way to go. He was genuine in his assurance of this. Knowing he was being honest, I decided that I'd better figure out a way to navigate upwards. So far, I'd gotten over 12 SP for crafting due to some particularly ineptly made ropes and grappling hooks.

But "uh oh" was new. Sure, Shart had been enjoying himself, calling down to me from the top, heckling me like you would a bad comedian. He'd even caught the last "rope" and tied it on for me. When it subsequently snapped as I was climbing, causing me to fall and suffer 8 HP of damage for the first time—which I'll write off as highly unpleasant—it wasn't even his fault. I just couldn't make ropes out of vines to save my life. But that hadn't earned "uh oh."

Who could tell what "uh oh" meant?

I turned around.

Starting player forests were often occupied by low-level creatures designed to help starting characters level-up. They typically minded their own business until the player attacked them; only then would they fight for their lives. Wolves were often one of those creatures.

They didn't typically come out in pairs, however, and neither of these looked particularly willing to mind their own business. I could tell this due to my astute senses. The fact that they were both growling and walking towards me with all their teeth bared was another good clue. In my previous life, I wouldn't have given myself odds on even one wolf. In this place, with my enhanced body, I'd certainly give myself a chance versus one.

I seriously doubted they would take turns, though.

Glancing around, I realized there was a spot that I could duck back into that would allow only one of the wolves to attack me at a time. I *might* be able to manage that. However, at my glance, the second wolf ran there, cutting off my avenue of escape.

I examined the first wolf for a moment, but I couldn't see a health bar or his stats; there was no way to know how powerful he was. I lunged forward with my staff, swinging at it. The wolf danced backwards as his mate rushed in from behind me, trying to snap at my ankle. I pulled it away at the last second and swung the staff wildly at her, smacking her on the side.

I tried to move towards a wall. Theoretically, with my back up against a wall, it would be easier to defend myself. In practice, the wall was pretty long and they were attacking from both sides; it wasn't really a perfect system. It might give me an opening though, so I began to move while I swung my staff wildly at both of them.

The Alpha wolf lunged and I swung at his head. There was a meaty smack, and the wolf jerked away. My momentary triumph fled an instant later when his mate grabbed my ankle and began to tear at it. I screamed, pain was pain and that hurt. I swung my staff at it awkwardly and hit the side of its head. Other than an all too brief slightly stunned look, the blow didn't seem to bother her much.

This distraction allowed the larger wolf to recover and he prepared to lunge at me. I was terribly out of position and had just managed to strike the female wolf in the head enough times so that she was considering releasing my savaged leg. I was down 15 hit points from her gnawing on me, so far. That meant I was down 23 total, leaving me with only 17. With the bigger wolf about to attack again, I had to imagine the possibility of it doing more than 17 points of damage to my head.

Suddenly, I heard a whoosh of air, like a long, pent-up fart, and the little demon flew directly in front of the wolf. At some point, Shart must have surmised my desperation and flown down from the rise. The massive alpha wolf snapped its powerful jaw and the demon caught the blow like a special brand of rotting meat shield. Shart was approximately the size of a basketball, so the wolf proceeded to shake him quite vigorously, causing black drops of demonic blood to fly everywhere. Shart had 400 hit points; "had" being the operative word, because the wolf was doing 20 or so damage every few seconds.

It still meant I had a moment of time. The female wolf, not realizing that her mate was distracted, decided to adjust her bite position. This allowed me to yank my leg away. Suddenly, free of worrying about the larger wolf, I managed to smash her with my staff, twice.

The first was to her shoulder which staggered her; the second hit was square on top of her skull. A meaty crunching sound ended the wolf.

The larger wolf released Shart when his mate fell and growled more fiercely. It stalked towards me, so I swung my staff at its head. The wolf caught it in its mouth and tore the weapon away from me, snapping it to tinder between his jaws.

Staggering back a few more feet, I got ready for the inevitable life-ending attack. However, the wolf slowed after a few more paces and then fell to its side, twitching. Grabbing half of my ruined staff, I went to drive it into the creature's heart, but small wisps of smoke were already leaving its flesh.

The wolf erupted in fire, forcing me back several more paces as I scrambled away.

With the wolves dealt with, I moved back over to Shart. He was a bloody, mangled ruin, with over half of his hit points gone. I picked him up carefully, as more blood than he should have been able to hold was streaming everywhere, and began looking at his wounds. He had a bleed effect on him that would cause another 20 or so points of damage, I realized. Still, he was probably okay.

"What happened to the wolf?" I asked, shaking some of the demon's blood from my hands.

"I got him for ya. Stupid animal didn't realize my blood is pure poison."

I dropped Shart.

He took 2 points of falling damage.

CHAPTER 4

BASE OF THE RIDGE

"I'M NOT POISONOUS TO *YOU*," HE INSISTED A FEW MINUTES later.

I was still busy binding my wounds using leaves and anything else I could think of to prevent bleeding. I had dropped to fewer than 10 hit points after the wolf's bleed effect on me expired, which was as close to death as I'd ever come.

Well, discounting my weakness against trucks.

Healing ten times faster apparently meant very little if you had a large, open wound. Any actual injury required first aid, which so far had netted me over 200 skill points. First aid was a common skill and actually provided some benefit even if you were untrained. Unfortunately, it required 250 SP to get to Novice level, and while both Shart and I had been terribly injured, we weren't quite there. Yet.

After I bound the wounds, I found out that you gained roughly one hit point back every ten hours. I was down 33. This would normally indicate that I was due for nearly a week of healing bedrest. However, I had two things going for me: First, my buffed stats, both Strength and Endurance, factored into healing, which would improve my recovery to 2 HP every eight hours. The second thing was my demonic regeneration, which further increased that by a factor of ten. So now instead of just 2 hit points, I'd be at full hit points in just over eight hours.

Magic worked better, but I didn't know any magic and Shart didn't have any mana. Despite his *much* higher hit point total, his stats were utterly terrible. They were all either below average or *way* below average in all cases. Even with demonic regeneration, he only healed about 16 HP per day. His mana was worse; there was no demonic mana regeneration. Due to his condition, he only recovered about one mana per day.

"We draw mana," stated Shart, "we don't regenerate it very fast otherwise."

"Would you having a full mana pool help our current situation?" I asked.

"No. Most of my buff spells won't affect you because of your level. Your Unbound effect doesn't let me do things to you like that. I don't know any healing magic because, when I'm at full power, I regenerate on a per-second basis."

"Must be nice," I said, finishing the bandage on my ruined ankle. I focused on my character sheet to see how long this would take to heal.

- Name: Jim
- Hit Points: 8

- Lingering Injury: Ankle
  -25% movement, 17 HP

"What's a lingering injury?" I asked.

"The wolf has a long-term effect on you," replied the demon. "You have to recover that many hit points before the lingering effect wears off."

Groaning inwardly, I considered the timeframe That was just a bit under the full eight hours for me to fully heal. Actually, it was six hours and forty-eight minutes on the nose. While I'd initially found the ability to count the literal seconds of an effect down, I found the details less disturbing as time went on. I got a hit point back every twenty-four minutes.

"Do the injury penalties stack, or do they all heal at once?" I asked as I tended my injuries.

"They stack; you have to heal each one individually. I have multiple injuries, in case you care. Some lingering wounds have status effects, while others reduce your maximum hit point total. In either case, until the wound fully recovers, those hit points must be spent to clear the wound. Afterwards, you have to regain the hit points again. I have two of those. My maximum hit points are seriously down."

So, if I'd had a 10-point lingering wound that affected my maximum hit points, I'd have to heal the 10 points to bring my max from 30 to 40. Then, I would need to heal those 10 newly-open hit points. That was brutal.

"What happens if I die?" I asked, as I tightened another bandage.

"I don't know, and I don't want to find out," said Shart. "You are my ticket out of here. If you die, the demonic bond should fade from you. My problem is that I can't enter the Demon Door without someone else opening it. That's a pretty rare occurrence."

We sat in silence for a few more minutes as I tried to weave another rope. I'd attempted to skin the wolf, but without anything sharp, I'd given up pretty quickly. The male wolf was a lost cause; it was a smoldering ruin.

The wolf meat was decent, though, if a bit gamey. It tasted of demonic spices, which I was also immune to.

CHAPTER 5

IN THE WOODS

I WOKE UP ABOUT SEVEN HOURS LATER. I'D RECOVERED AN additional 17 hit points, which cleared my lingering wound. However, due to the 17 point lingering wound, I was only recovered to 15 hit points . . . so overall I was pretty miserable. However, I felt much more confident that I'd live. Shart didn't sleep so he'd watched over me the whole time, like a fat ugly guard dog.

Deciding that we'd have to go around even if it did take longer, I started tracing the cliff wall that the gorge had cut through. The wall went on and on. However, because of the change of terrain, the forest was less dense here. It was far easier to move forward, even with the little ball of shit back at his post on my shoulder. Shart could sense wolves if he tried, and I kept a keen eye out for anything as we moved. After a few hours, we came to a place where a road had been obviously cut into the cliff.

"Next time look for more of these," I stated as we walked up the path.

While we were walking, I got the exclamation mark again and checked to see that my staff skill had ranked up.

Staff: Rank 1 (50 SP/250 SP). You can deliver a powerful blow at the cost of increased Stamina. Damage +50%.

I glanced up at Simple Weapons, but it needed 500 SP to level and it was only at 52. This meant Simple Weapons was tied to the sub-skill Staff and gained a SP every time staffs did. Nice to know, I supposed.

I was really hoping hiking would level up, but it was at 15 SP of 200. Examining the Hiking skill further, it seemed that you gained SP based on distance walked and unique natural things that you'd seen. A chart broke it down, telling me that I'd walked 10 miles and seen one natural wonder, the gorge. Taking this long to gain a level kind of sucked, but if I'd been walking on cut trails instead of deep woods, I would have made better distance. Unfortunately, there wasn't a Skipping My Way to Grandmother's skill (even if there had already been wolves), but I'd somehow survive.

Class: Warrior 1 (1459/3000 XP)

The two wolves had been worth 407 experience points, and I needed 2000 to level up again. It was looking like each level cost more than the one before it, but there didn't seem to be a pattern for skills. For class levels, it looked, as far as I could tell, that it cost 1000 additional experience points per level.

In practical terms, that meant that I needed to kill between seven and eight more wolves to level up to 2. Hopefully, that would grant me enough bonuses to make them less of a threat.

"If you see a single animal you think I can take, alert me," I said to my still moaning companion. Shart had recovered more hit points, of course, but still had multiple injuries that were preventing him from healing well. I couldn't count on him operating like a deadly chew toy again. He was really more of a busted squeaker toy, or a whiny ass toddler. An ugly whiny ass toddler.

So, with the village only a few hours away, I started looking for other things to kill. I quickly discovered that my demonic shoulder growth, my lame ass third stick, and myself were limited. Anything small and easily killed, like baby deer and rabbits, quickly ran from me. Shart and I were going to have to make ourselves targets of predators if I wanted something that would actually stick around for a fight.

Briefly, I considered making a spear with a piece of rock, but I didn't have the right kind of rock; I was also more skilled in Staff than

Spear. With no good options, I continued searching the woods for game. Finally, I came upon another wolf.

I walked into the meadow where it sat, messily devouring a rabbit. The wolf, raising its eyes to me, snarled. He began stalking me, his tasty carcass forgotten. I gripped my staff more tightly as I felt the fear sink into me again. My leg suddenly hurt more and I was painfully aware that I had only healed up to 23 hit points.

The wolf lunged, but I blocked his jaws with my staff. This left his massive paws free, however, and his claws scratched against me as I flung him away. If I were wearing even regular clothes, I would have been fine. Instead, I was covered with dozens of small oozing scratches and I was down 2 hit points. Thankfully, the loincloth provided what little protection it could, and I was still in possession of two balls.

As the canine moved to bite again, I swung my staff at his furry body. This managed to only knock him back a pace and further anger him. He growled and got ready to lunge again but I held my staff at the ready. As he leapt, I began to swing the staff. I could feel my energy flowing into the strike, empowering it somehow. As my Stamina bar drained more than normal, the staff smashed into the wolf. With an audible crunch, the wolf's spine shattered.

The wolf thudded to the ground, unmoving. I exhaled and slumped to the ground. Shart said nothing, which was good. If necessary, I had planned on using him as a shield, regardless of his hit points.

I noticed a pop up in the corner of my vision which I quickly selected.

Unarmored Defense (10 SP/100 SP): Amateur. Defensive stance; you can expend Stamina while defending to decrease chance to be hit and reduce damage.

Wondering what that exactly meant, I got back to my feet and moved around a bit. At first, nothing seemed to happen. Yet, when I visualized an attacking enemy in front of me, I was able to move backwards with much greater alacrity. I dodged around a bit more and found that I could easily jump in some ways that were nearly physically impossible. However, every time I dodged, my Stamina bar decreased slightly.

Once I'd gotten the hang of this new skill, I had Shart find me another wolf. It didn't take long, as the woods were thick with them. Brimming with my newfound self-confidence, a brisk five-minute walk brought me to my next target.

This next wolf was about the same size as the last one. Since I was more or less aware of where it was, I did my best to sneak up on it. I wasn't successful; when I got close enough, the wolf looked up from whatever she was digging. She spun around and snarled at me before charging.

Focusing my Stamina, I got ready to dodge. However, I noticed that the wolf seemed to slow down as she closed in. Not tremendously, but a useful amount. The wolf totally missed me. She growled and twisted around before lunging again, and again I easily dodged her. I did that a third time, before I started noticing that the world was getting a bit darker. I focused on my Stamina bar and realized that it was getting dangerously low.

Well, leave it to me to forget that. My wife often told me that I'd forget my head if it wasn't attached. I had forgotten to see how much dodging drained my Stamina. I didn't have enough for another dodge, so instead I swung my staff at the wolf. I scored a weak blow against her as she skipped backwards. As I attacked normally, I realized my Stamina bar dropped even further, just not nearly as much. However, even as I waited a few moments for the wolf to get ready to attack again, my Stamina bar increased by one whole point. Looks like I recovered a point every eight seconds or so. If I could hold out, my full bar would be recovered in a few minutes.

Hopefully the wolf would wait.

It did not.

The wolf lunged again. I stepped to the side gingerly; I carefully succeeded in not using any Stamina and still managed to avoid the snapping-jawed maniac. I bashed her on the way past as well, leaving the wolf battered and bloodied. However, that had expended a few more points of my precious Stamina and the world was starting to become a bit darker. I had gone from feeling normal to seriously winded in a matter of a few moments.

When I realized I had enough Stamina for one more power strike, I rushed forward, bringing the staff crashing down on the wolf's shoulders. They snapped, my staff snapped, and I collapsed to the earth, unable to move.

Winning.

After about eight seconds, I had recovered sufficiently to lie there uncomfortably. About a minute and a half later, most of the exhaustion left me and I was able to roll onto my back and sit up.

"What just happened?" I asked.

"Oh, you ran out your Stamina bar," answered Shart. "If you get to zero Stamina you collapse. Try not to do that."

"Thanks," I said. *Asshole.*

After several more minutes passed, I felt sufficiently re-energized and stood, my precious loincloth flapping in the breeze. Stumbling over to the wolf's now permanently abandoned hole, I recognized a small object that did not appear to be a rock. I dug around it a bit more until I found a small orb attached to something. A few more seconds of digging revealed it to be the pommel of a smallish weapon.

Grasping the hilt of the weapon, I drew it from the earth.

"Da da da DAAAAA," I said triumphantly, holding the item above my head for a moment.

"Don't *ever* do that again," said Shart.

- You have found Dagger. Item class Common. Durability 22/35. Damage 2–5.
- **BONUS EFFECT:** Bleeding (requires Puncture skill)
- **BONUS EFFECT:** Savage Wound (requires Wounding skill)

Going through my skills sheet, Simple Weapons had a new category.

- Small Blades (1/80): Unskilled

Looking further, I could see the Puncture Skill under Small Blades, but it was greyed out. Focusing harder upon it, I could tell that it had a level requirement, which I could ignore, and a skill requirement of Small Blades: Amateur. I knew my Unbound trait could bypass level restrictions, but I still had to have at least Amateur rank to engage the sub skills.

Well, that was easy enough, I'll just go and kill me some more wolves.

"Hey, Shart," I grinned. The demon said nothing, so I continued, "Why does this have durability and the staffs didn't?"

"You found the sticks; they are a junk item and have a default durability of 5. You probably have it filtered so not everything you pick up will give you a status update," chuckled the demon. "Cup of water: durability 4 of 5, cleanliness poor."

"Ah." I considered. That would get annoying really quickly. I guess mundane items would be blocked. Otherwise, you'd just see pop ups everywhere. Curious, I dug into the menu until I found the setting for blocking junk status updates and flicked it off. So many numbers flooded my vision from sticks and rocks that I had difficulty seeing anything else. I reactivated the junk filter and my vision cleared again.

After I had recovered my sight a moment, I walked over to the wolf. "I'm going to skin the wolf now that I have a knife."

"What's your Skinning skill?" asked Shart.

"Untrained."

"I'll be over there," gestured the demon, as he walked over to a nearby tree and collapsed again.

Twenty minutes later, I walked over to where Shart sat, fanning himself with a leaf.

"Wow, that went as well as I expected," he said. "How did you get fur in your teeth and do we need to bury that?"

"I don't want to talk about it."

CHAPTER 6

OUTSKIRTS OF THE VILLAGE

- Name: Jim
- Hit Points: 30/45
- Stamina: 40
- Mana: 20
- Class: Warrior 1 2132/3000
- Strength: Above Average
- Dexterity: Average
- Endurance: Above Average
- Willpower: Average
- Spirit: Average
- Charisma: Average

Combat Skills:

- Unarmored Defense (15 SP/100 SP): Amateur
- Dodge (5 SP): Unskilled
- Mitigate (1 SP): Unskilled
- Light Armor (100 SP): Amateur
- Medium Armor (150 SP): Amateur
- Shields (100 SP): Amateur
- Martial Weapons (10 SP): Amateur
- Simple Weapons (71 SP): Amateur
- Staff (60 SP): Rank 1
- Powerful Blow
- Dagger (1 SP): Rank 0

Non-Combat Skills:

- Demon Lore (2001 SP): Amateur
- Hiking (9 SP): Unskilled
- Stealth (14 SP): Unskilled
- Skinning (1 SP): Unskilled
- Cooking (4 SP): Unskilled
- Perception (6 SP): Unskilled

AFTER A VERY LONG BATH IN A VERY COLD STREAM, I SPENT some time finding a hidden spot and leaving Shart awake as a sentinel. Not that he really slept, per se. He kind of just rested a bit, with a really foul look on his face. Kind of like a constipated baby monkey. Finally, I managed to rest for the night.

Upon waking the next day, I noticed a prompt. This informed me that my Stealth skill had improved. That was good news and I resolved to sneak up on something and kill it today.

Casual slaughter of woodland creatures had never been my thing, but when I was getting scored on it, I found the entire concept fascinating.

So, wearing my loincloth (of which one should not ask the origin) and holding my dagger in one hand and replacement stick number four in the other, I began to travel towards the village again. The village was closer and the road was nearby. I wagered that if I showed up with nothing more than what I had now, I'd get a very cold reception. If I could skin a wolf or two with my new dagger, I would be able to sell it for a bit of silver. Then I could buy things, like a better loin cloth.

With that in mind and a few more hit points restored, I prodded Shart. "You better yet?"

"You can tell by looking at me that I'm not," he replied.

"Wanna go kill more wolves?" I asked.

"You seriously do not like comfortable beds," he replied. "I found you one."

With that, we were off again. The next wolf was just off the road ahead. We quietly stalked it for well over two skill points—er, miles—until we got much closer. The trees nearby had thinned out somewhat, making it less of a dense virgin forest and more like a navigable backyard woods. With less underbrush, I was hoping to get closer and sneak attack the wolf.

I began creeping through the woods, carefully, like a creeping thing. Apparently, I was still untrained in Metaphor skill. My hunting record was getting about ten feet away before the creature would become aware of my presence. This time, I had confidence. It oozed from me. If this was due to me being at more than half health, or the fact that I'd gotten the best of four wolves so far, was anyone's guess.

My target was resting by an entrance to a cave. It was a man-sized hole into the ground, with several trees nearby masking its presence. I'd have totally missed it without Shart pointing me to the wolf. There wasn't as much room to maneuver as I'd like, but if I could get the drop on the wolf the fight promised to be over quickly.

"There aren't any wolves in that cave?" I checked with Shart.

"No," replied Shart sourly.

Creeping closer, I came in from behind the wolf and downwind. I was moving painfully slowly, but I got into position to pounce on the wolf who was still lying there. At this distance I could see the gentle rise and fall of his chest. I could also see a strange pattern on his fur that I didn't recognize. This wolf was larger than I expected, but still not as large as the first wolf.

With a deep breath I pounced, leaping through the air in a triumphant arc, dagger first. My blade pierced his back, driving deep into what I hoped were the vital organs. The wolf's body jerked; the wound was instantly fatal but not silent, as it made the most wrenching yelp as it died.

Several things happened all at once: I noticed a prompt in the corner of my vision, but instead of a skill notice it showed another golden coin. There was also the sound of feet in the grass behind me. I turned just in time to see what could only be described as a goblin charging me with a club.

The goblin closed the distance before I had a chance to react and struck me across the chest right as I brought my dagger free from the wolf. The impact was far out of proportion to the size of the creature;

I was physically lifted off my feet and thrown back into a nearby tree. The strike did 10 points of damage, and my Stamina dropped by 6 as I slipped down the trunk to the ground.

It took the goblin a moment to recover. He was about the size of a ten-year-old child, but built like a grown man. His body was all muscle and his teeth were all sharp points. He was also screaming at me incoherently.

Now that I was back on balance, I rushed the goblin. Had it been two human-sized opponents, his weapon would have given him a reach advantage. My longer arms were an asset, putting us on more equal footing, and I managed to dodge his second strike while I slashed at him. I came out uninjured, but he had a bloody gash to his torso to show for his troubles.

Screaming, the goblin stumbled back. His eyes went wild, looking first at me and then his open, gaping wound. He grabbed at it, slumping to the ground as his stomach fell out of the cavity. He cried at me hoarsely for a moment, then died.

I watched the little creature there for a moment. "Well, that didn't feel very heroic."

"What, did you expect him to fight to the last hit point?" asked Shart. "He was a feral goblin. You attacked him. If it makes you feel any better, they like to pluck out the eyeballs of human children and eat them as a delicacy before they kill them. Goblins are selfish, evil creatures. You won't be finding any of them that are secretly good. That doesn't mean they don't care about anything, though. You killed his dog."

"Oh," I exhaled loudly. The goblin looked like a little green disgruntled child. I'd just killed him. I'd have to live with that.

"Let's get to the village," I said. I hesitated, though, and then walked into the small cave searchingly. I found a second functional dagger, a not inconsiderable amount of poorly tanned leather, and a small pouch of silver coins. Searching the goblin, I was surprised to find how much blood had poured from his wound. Then, I remembered the skill prompts.

- Small Blades: Amateur. You do additional damage with small blades. You gain additional sneak attack damage with small blades.
  - **PUNCTURE:** Your attacks with small blades bypass 2 points of armor per small blades rank, doubled during a sneak attack.
  - **RUPTURE:** Your attacks with small blades cause Bleed, based on attack damage—50% additional Bleed over twelve seconds.
- Stealth (100 SP/2000 SP): Amateur. You are now able to sneak much more effectively. You make 25% less sound when traveling. If you attack a target that is caught unaware you can perform a sneak attack for additional damage.

The sub skills didn't seem to have multiple ranks. There might be a Puncture 2 later on down the line, but I couldn't yet see if it existed. Glancing at my combat log, I'd gained the level in Stealth just prior to the attack with my dagger. Apparently, the extra damage was three times the normal value and I'd scored a critical hit, which had doubled the base damage. That had made the base damage 2–5 times 6 and I'd struck well. The attack had done a total of 30 points of damage and had ignored all of the wolf's defense.

The goblin didn't have many hit points and I'd increased the rank in my Small Blades skill so my base damage had gone up to 3–6. I'd hit him for 4, again ignoring his lower defense, but he'd gained a bleed effect for an additional 2. That wouldn't have killed him if he was healthy, but looking down at him, I could see that he was not. Something had savaged him earlier, so my strike had just pushed him over the limit.

Finally, I saw why the club hit had caused Stamina damage. I had a Mitigate skill that allowed me to expend Stamina to reduce hit point damage. I had ended up spending 6 points to reduce the club's damage by 2. If I hadn't, I would have sustained a much worse injury.

Then, I noticed the level prompt. I hadn't realized that I was going to level from this—I had been several hundred experience points off. I had been figuring on needing to kill several more wolves to gain the next level.

"I leveled up," I said to Shart.

"Again? That's quick," replied the demon, peering at me questioningly.

- Level UP, Rogue 1
- You have selected the Rogue Class. Please choose two stat buffs for yourself at first level!
- You have gained the skills Light Armor and Stealth, as well as all Simple Weapons, and you gain one rank in the sub-skill Daggers.
- You already have skill with Simple Weapons. Please choose another skill or one will be chosen for you.
- You already have skill with Light Armor. Please choose another skill or one will be chosen for you.
- Your Hit Point total is increased by 10. Your Stamina is increased by 10.

"Level of Rogue," I said.

"No, you got basic-bitch Warrior," Shart argued. "Not that Rogue is much better, but you don't get two classes."

"Well, I'm looking at the prompt and it says I have a level of Rogue," I countered. "I need to assign these stat bumps."

Shart glared at me with a questioning expression, but I didn't really feel like messing around. I just selected Dexterity for both bumps, moving me from Average to Good. My Stamina increased by another 15 points from that.

My body changed instantly. With Strength, I got bigger and more muscular. With Endurance, I got . . . leaner, for lack of a better word. The kind of form you see with marathon runners or Olympic swimmers. With Dexterity, I suddenly got a lot more defined and shorter, I think, if only slightly. My body seemed to respond much more rapidly than it did before and much more exactly how I wanted it to.

Shart's eyes went wide as the stat buff hit me. You just couldn't hide that and after a moment I watched the few precious points of mana he had accumulated over the days vanish as he began mouthing words to a spell.

"My spell says you are a level one Rogue," he said, "but I *know* you were a basic-bitch Warrior."

I brought up my character sheet.

• Name: Jim   • Class: Rogue Level 1

"When did I stop being a Warrior?" I asked.

"When did you start being a Rogue?" Shart retorted.

I focused on my character sheet again. There was a Rogue tab there, with the same general outline as the Warrior tab. The thing was, the Warrior tab was still there as well. They were both there. The sheet looked weird with both unlocked, kind of filling up my mental buffer for looking at this sort of thing. It was like visualizing too large of a thing in your head and being unable to keep track of it all, like trying to take in the Grand Canyon all at once. I focused on the various tabs and realized that all of the class tabs were there, too. They were just hidden.

"Oh," I said with a bit of wonder. "I have them all."

"*What?*" asked Shart, sounding very curious as he continued examining me.

"Warrior and Rogue are both there," I said. "I can still select both of them and they are both active."

The demon boggled. "You have *two* classes? That's not possible. The <operating system> doesn't allow for multiple classes. Hell, I only have one class."

"Maybe that's because you just suck. I have two," I said.

At least two.

"I'm going to have to consider this. Let's get to the town." I knew Shart had to be truly confused, as he let the insult go unreturned.

"One second, let me try something."

I went to the skill screen and focused on it. I had three open selections there and I wanted to use them. Several skills I had were starting to become clearer. One of these was Perception, which I selected.

You have achieved Amateur rank in Perception.
You are now much more observant.

Instantly, I started seeing smaller details more clearly. Further, I could process information better. The skill icons were still muddy, but now I could see it was because they were actually writhing around rather than just being hard to look at.

Flipping back to my character sheet, it was easier to process the whole thing. Several of the other tabs were starting to fill out. The Woodsman tab was almost ready to level. I was able to filter the skills better, cutting out unnecessary details until I focused on them. That was going to be helpful.

I was still just wearing a loin cloth and that was alarmingly breezy. I examined Skinning and realized I wasn't anywhere close to leveling it. Still, I selected it, figuring that it would be a good revenue source if nothing else. I instantly saw how to skin the goblin's pet for maximum effect. I set about that task while trying to figure out what my final skill choice should be. My guilt over killing the goblin's dog was offset by my desire for pants.

Reviewing, I determined that I could select any of the random skill icons that were in my list. Problem being that those were all crap shoots. I could get something useful, or I could get something that wasn't going to help me at all. That said, it was only an Amateur rank, I quickly tested and could not increase my existing ranks with one of those buffs, so that wasn't going to be the end of the world.

Searching for something like Leatherworking, I didn't find anything. There were so many icons—over twenty-two hundred that I could see with my Perception skill—that just randomly guessing was out. They did seem to flow in a few patterns, though. All the Simple Weapons skills were more or less bunched together. The Martial Weapons skills, too. I found Skinning again, near a still unknown central skill. I decided to gamble and selected that central skill as my final power up.

The world seemed to twitch again, just for a moment. Shart noticed it, watching me even more intently. "What did you do?"

"I selected Crafting, a world-shattering event."

"What *kind* of crafting?" asked Shart.

"Just crafting," I said. "Good old generic crafting."

"There *is* no generic crafting skill that I know of. Did you take Leatherworking?"

Reexamining my sheet, I saw:

**Crafting 1 (1000 SP/100,000 SP): Amateur.
You have basic crafting ability.**

Shart continued grumbling, but I sat down and cut some of the leather I'd taken from the goblin. I stitched together a not terrible pair of leather pants and a shirt. The shirt *was* terrible in every way, and I decided to remove it after only a few minutes. When we got closer to town, I could always put it back on and not appear to be a savage in hastily-made pants. I'd also made two sheaths for my daggers. One turned out okay; the other one, not so much. I put the good dagger in the okay sheath.

**You have acquired: Shoddily crafted Leather
Shirt, Defense 1, Durability 8/8, and poorly crafted
Leather Pants, Defense 1, Durability 10/10.**

"How do I look?" I asked.

"Well, you don't have the Leatherworking skill," Shart snarked, "but I guess it's better than seeing your mostly naked body. If you are done being lazy, let's go."

I glanced at my skills. My Leatherworking and Crafting had both gone up 4 points. Reviewing, crafting skills were based on two things: First, was the value, in silver, of the items you yourself had crafted. The second factor was whether the crafted item was used to cause or prevent damage. The cool thing was that the crafter didn't have to be using the item themselves; they gained the experience whenever an item made by their hands was used.

We started walking back towards the road and the village. Well, I started walking. Shart sat on my shoulder and muttered strange things about how the world worked. Getting back onto the road, I'd considered that maybe I should have taken Hiking. I was hoping that that would resolve itself soon enough.

Tuning Shart out, I again pondered time in this realm. I was nearly certain that time was moving differently here than on Earth. The wolf hide was the latest example I had. In the time it took for me to stitch the hide together into crude clothing, it had completely dried. I had never been a hunter, but I was relatively sure that curing leather should have taken hours, if not days. I resolved to pay closer attention to time.

Traveling with Perception was different, too. The first thing was that my peripheral vision was almost as acute as my primary vision. That was hard to wrap my head around; it was like I could suddenly see that thing out of the corner of my eye as if I was staring directly at it. Furthermore, I could track multiple objects at once. I watched two leaves fall that were caught up in different breezes and I could have pointed at either at any moment during their fall. When I tried the same trick with three, I found I could do that as well. However, it started slowly draining my Stamina.

All my other senses were likewise improved. I could hear and identify sounds more readily. It would be much more difficult to attack me from behind. My sense of touch was greater as well. I could probably identify my dagger just off the small flaws in the blade. I could smell both Shart and myself; one of us badly needed a bath. I'm certain Shart still smelled like my pee.

This was almost like a low-level superpower. I was quite pleased overall. If only I could find a puddle to throw the stinky demon into.

CHAPTER 7

THE VILLAGE

- Name: Jim
- Hit Points: 36/55
- Stamina: 70
- Mana: 20
- Class: Rogue 1
- Strength: Above Average
- Dexterity: Good
- Endurance: Above Average
- Willpower: Average
- Spirit: Average
- Charisma: Average

Combat Skills:

- Unarmored Defense: Amateur
- Light Armor: Amateur
- Medium Armor: Amateur
- Defense Skills:
  - **DODGE:** Unskilled
  - **MITIGATE:** Unskilled
  - **SHIELDS:** Amateur
- Martial Weapons: Amateur
- Simple Weapons: Amateur
- Staff: Amateur
- Powerful Blow
- Dagger Novice
- Puncture
- Wounding
- Two Weapon Fighting: Unskilled
- Twin Weapon: Unskilled

Non-Combat Skills:

- Demon Lore: Amateur
- Hiking: Unskilled
- Stealth: Amateur
- Skinning: Amateur
- Cooking: Unskilled
- Perception: Amateur
- Crafting: Amateur
- Leatherworking: Unskilled
- Woodworking: Unskilled

THE FINAL LEG OF THE WALK HAD TAKEN TWO HOURS. I'D drawn both of my daggers like a badass twice, until Shart made it clear that I looked like an idiot. Then, I'd turned to whittling. So far, I'd made a bad cat, a bad dog, and a wolf's head medallion that looked less crappy. I'd also found a length of wood that I thought might make a good bow, if I didn't ruin it.

Good luck with that.

We had finally arrived at the village and the results were less than impressive. It was theoretically well placed. It was on top of a hill, and there was a wall around it, although the wall had several large fissures in it that would allow just about anyone to walk through it. There were no guards, or any sort of inhabitants to speak of, and the road outside looked like it hadn't seen a cart in basically forever.

"Well, that sucks," I said.

"This place is so old that I think the village is abandoned," replied Shart.

"I thought this was the noobie area," I groaned. "Isn't the village supposed to be safe?" Most games had a lower level noobie area, where new players could learn the ropes. This area was full of wolves and goblins.

"Well, sort of," stated my shoulder sidekick.

"Sort of?"

"It looks like this is the old starting village. They built a better one quite some time ago. This village should still be protected, but I'm not sensing any of the magical defenses."

"Like, how long?" I asked, dreading the answer.

"A couple centuries," he answered. "And yes, they get stronger the longer they remain undisturbed. But the village should have an enchantment upon it. So long as a single person occupies it, that would render it protected."

"How many people are in the village?"

"None. The village is totally empty of all people," replied the demon. "That explains why six goblins are in there right now."

"You constantly disappoint me," I said, as I started towards the village.

Shart frowned. "If I'm such a disappointment, perhaps you would just prefer to roam around with your head up your ass for a bit."

I sighed. God, I hated that little fucker. However, he had a point. "What do I need to do?"

"Head to the town hall and activate the lectern."

Vague, but whatever.

Creeping into the village was easy due primarily to the giant holes in the wall. The goblins were not paying any attention to the village's boundaries. These goblins were apparently not feral goblins, but rather tribal goblins. That made them a bit stronger, and less prone to having animal companions. Mixed bag there.

As we cleared the edge of the village, we headed towards what I believed to be the town square. As we walked, Shart explained further. Apparently, if I got to this magical town hall lectern, I could reactivate the enchantment that would render the village a safe zone. Shart assured me this was a good thing. I had Shart performing constant scans to see if there were more than goblins lurking about. Our difficulty with this was his extremely limited mana pool. A hard choice needed to be made; he could scan for wolves *or* goblins, but not both at the same time.

We spent a good five minutes with him scanning for every type of monster individually that he could think of, over one hundred in total. Finding nothing, we continued deeper into the village. I slinked between dark, dilapidated buildings that were missing roofs. Many had rotted out walls and several appeared to be collapsing in on themselves. The wind would occasionally blast through the village and, if not for my enhanced senses, I'm pretty sure I'd have bailed even with Shart calling out enemies.

But now that I had my superpower, I had confidence. So, when

Shart told me there was a lone goblin wandering nearby, I changed course towards him. The goblins were all concentrated in a camp outside what appeared to be the village's inn. They had a fire outside, so I reasoned that the chimney inside must be clogged or they could just like the outdoors. It was nice out.

The goblins were all milling about, mostly in twos or threes. Some were in the inn; some were at the stew pot, which was a rusted, battered, iron thing that occasionally hissed and popped. Whatever they were cooking smelled terrible. I'd been sustaining myself on wolf's meat and the occasional berry; I wasn't hungry, but I could eat. Just not that.

My target had decided to be a proper young goblin and relieve himself somewhere downwind of their makeshift campsite. He squatted and started grunting. I was on him before he had a chance to understand what was happening, driving both daggers into his back. With that one furious motion, he died instantly and silently.

My Rogue level had paid off already.

I doubled back to my original course towards the town hall, leaving the body there in a pile of its own shit. I was a badass, and those stupid goblins should fear me. I followed the shadows until I got into the town hall. The door stood open and I brazenly entered. Casting my eyes around the abandoned hall, I searched for the lectern as Shart had instructed.

I didn't have to search long. The lectern was clearly visible in the center of the room. This was mainly due to the giant hole in the ceiling letting in the sunlight. The entire building was more or less destroyed, with massive signs of neglect everywhere. Specks of dust floated in the sun's rays, making my newly sensitive eyes water. The front hall was intact, except for the door, which was beyond warped. It would never close again. Walking over to the lectern quietly, I placed my hands upon it and waited for the prompt.

You have found Windfall Village. There is no current mayor for the village. Would you like to claim the village?

Grinning as the entire town hall lit up in a display of power that must have been visible for miles around, I savored the moment before selecting "Yes."

There are hostile creatures inside the village area. The village cannot be claimed until they are removed. Have a good day.

And the lights died.

"Shart?"

"All five of them are coming here now," Shart started, "and I just found a patrol of another twenty goblins coming down the road. They will be here in about five minutes."

I rapidly moved to the entrance of the town hall and jumped with all my might. I actually managed to get myself almost even with the top of the door frame before hiding in the shadows. I imagined I looked like something of a dark knight, with a little ugly bat on my shoulder. The goblins were approaching, I could hear them. They were all yapping at each other in their language, but I could now catch bits of it. I couldn't understand exactly what they were saying, but I got the basic gist of it: they were not happy goblins. Huh. Perhaps murder assisted with language learning here? I would have to ask Shart about it after these were disposed of.

I knew there were five. Two were coming through the front entryway with their weapons ready. Three more were outside and I could only hear what they were doing. One sounded as if he were running away. The other two sounded like they were just outside the door. I could work with that.

Dropping down on top of the two, I drove each into the floor with a dagger in their backs. They both died instantly as I turned to face the remaining three. One goblin was larger than the other two and had a short sword and shield. The one next to him was more commonly sized and was carrying a short sword as well. The one fleeing had a short bow and he ran faster as I launched myself out of the town hall towards his friends.

Hoping to knock out the big one quickly, I slashed at him with both daggers. He blocked one with the shield and parried my other strike, nearly taking off my thumb. Being a badass, I then literally front-flipped over him to attack him from the rear.

In the movies, it would have worked. Here, the goblin brought his shield up and wildly swung at the only place I was going to be in a few moments. I landed just as his short sword completed its arc, carving through my wolf hide and into my leg for 12 points of damage. I also fell, mainly due to the fact that I think the strike chipped the bone.

His companion went in for the kill and accidentally saved me. He rushed between me and the larger goblin, who had to pull back to avoid striking him. I used that moment to get to my feet, but not before driving my crappy dagger into the attacking goblin's foot. He screamed, reaching down, and I slashed his unarmored throat.

The larger goblin rushed forwards, swinging his weapon. Now that I only had one dagger, I was at a decided disadvantage against a shielded opponent. Just then, I heard a whistling and managed to dodge wide as an arrow zipped past me. The other goblin hadn't been running away, he had been moving into position and now was shooting at me with a short bow.

My Stamina bar was depleting, not quickly enough to be a danger yet, but it was a concern. Dodging arrows was Stamina intensive; a second shot almost hit me. I could probably bail now, but if I left, the local goblins might put a permanent garrison in this town that I'd never overcome.

An idea struck me, but it would have to be timed just right. I moved so that my back was to the archer, causing all the hair on my neck to stand up. I was now between him and the larger goblin. I waited, dodging and striking at the larger goblin. Finally, I heard the whistling again.

Feinting wide to the left, the goblin tracked me with his shield just as the arrow shot through where I was. It buried itself in the goblin's chest. He stumbled backwards, and I used my free hand to grab his shield and pull it down from his now limp arm, before driving my dagger into his eye.

The final goblin stared in horror for a moment before dropping his bow and starting to run. I still had more Stamina and now, with my improved dexterity, I was much faster than him. I caught up to him in seconds, killing him from behind.

After Shart confirmed there were no more targets, I stumbled back towards the town hall. My Stamina was low, and the goblin had a bleed effect on his weapon causing another 6 points of damage. This fight had left me dangerously depleted.

- You have found Windfall Village. There is no current mayor for the village.

Would you like to claim the village? (Yes/No)

Yes.

- You are now the founder and mayor of Windfall Village, Population 2.
- The village defenses have been enacted!

- You have earned a Founder perk for founding a new village!

Great. I slid down the lectern and collapsed.

We only had a few minutes, so I got to work as soon as I could stand. I bound my leg wound, stopping the bleeding and preventing it from breaking open again.

"If the goblin gang gets past the barrier, I need to run," I stated calmly.

Shart just nodded. He was looking apprehensive. The goblins

were moving much faster than he'd anticipated. If I hadn't managed to kill the goblins in the village as quickly as I did, we'd be in trouble. If they had scattered, I'd have had to flee.

Now that my wound was bound, my path was clear and my pants were dry. For now.

As the goblins approached, I found an intact stairwell in the inn. This gave me a higher vantage point to witness their arrival. The faint blue magical barrier that had been newly created tensed. They were all much bigger than average. The smallest one of them was the same size as the large one I had just fought in the hall. That hadn't gone great for me. Also, they were all riding wolves. Big wolves.

If the barrier didn't hold, this was going to be a very short mayorship.

I had grabbed the goblin's shield and both short swords, as well as my other dagger. I found a few other daggers in the inn while we waited. I was festooned with weapons now. I had a veritable plethora of death-dealing pieces. I was so heavily armed the TSA might have even stopped me at security.

- You have acquired goblin short sword. Damage 2–7. Durability 14/15.

- You have acquired goblin shield, Common. Defense 6. Block +3.

The rest of the recently deceased goblins' supplies weren't much to speak of. The stew tasted foul, and I'm pretty sure that what I'd initially thought was a piece of spaghetti was actually a rat's tail. Only further reinforcing my resistance to eating the stuff.

I had also tucked away some chunks of dried meat. These were from other dubious sources at best, but if those riders started chasing me, I'd be in trouble.

A notification popped into my view. It wasn't the usual event icon either, as it filled up the bottom of my vision.

Hostile creatures are approaching the village.

"Almost here. Get ready," warned Shart. He was invisible and in-tangible now, but still sitting on my shoulder, being a real Negative Nancy. If this didn't work, I would have to sneak out to somewhere and go all Minecraft in the forest. I envisioned setting up a semi-permanent camp with Shart and prepared myself for a much more significant effort to avoid that.

The first two goblins and their mounts crossed the line. For an instant, I was confused. Confusion quickly gave way to terror, as they passed through the outer range of the barrier. Then . . .

They caught fire, as did the two after them. Several more behind them were soon ablaze as well. Suddenly, they were all scrambling to get away from the barrier. Well, the survivors at least, because "caught on fire" was probably underselling it. They literally erupted into flames out of . . . well, everywhere. These were not healthy flames either; this was a sort of bluish fire that seemed to make its victims do quite a bit screaming before they collapsed. Seven goblins and six wolves died, and many more were injured. One wolf tossed its goblin aside and ran back over the barrier, leaving his rider to burn to death, one fist raised in anger towards his mount.

The barrier worked.

I was safe.

CHAPTER 8

TOWN INTERFACE

- Name: Jim
- Hit Points: 22/55
- Stamina: 70
- Mana: 20
- Class: Rogue 1
- Class: Warrior 1

- Strength: Above Average
- Dexterity: Good
- Endurance: Above Average
- Willpower: Average
- Spirit: Average
- Charisma: Average

Combat Skills:

- Unarmored Defense: Amateur
- Light Armor: Amateur
- Medium Armor: Amateur
- Defense Skills:
  - DODGE: Unskilled
  - MITIGATE: Unskilled
  - SHIELDS: Amateur
- Martial Weapons: Amateur

- Simple Weapons: Amateur
- Staff: Amateur
- Powerful Blow
- Dagger: Novice
- Puncture
- Wounding
- Two Weapon Fighting: Unskilled
- Twin Weapon: Unskilled

Non-Combat Skills:

- Demon Lore: Amateur
- Hiking: Unskilled
- Stealth: Amateur
- Skinning: Amateur
- Cooking: Unskilled

- Perception: Amateur
- Crafting: Amateur
- Leatherworking: Unskilled
- Woodworking: Unskilled

THE TOWN HAD AN INTERFACE ALL OF ITS OWN. IT WASN'T even attached to my character sheet. Instead I had to focus on a small town icon, which brought up the Noobie Village in my view. I got an overhead map with the various buildings highlighted. Most were showing 0 durability, indicating significant damage. With my Crafting ability, I could tell they were going to require some very extensive repairs to get back to being usable.

The main menu was pretty simple. It just said:

Windfall Village, Level 0. Population: 2. Mayor: Jim.

"Well, that's that then," I declared. "We have a town."

"About that," said Shart. "First off, you have a *village*. I'm a demon; I can't be a mayor or even a citizen. Second, we still have a problem, because when you leave the village, it becomes abandoned. The barrier will fall again. I'm betting those goblins are just waiting around until you try to leave."

"Maybe I could gather up some supplies, equip myself with a bow, and attack the goblins out of range?"

"No," replied the demon. "When you attack out of the barrier from the inside, the defensive properties will fail. The goblins will be able to return the favor. Mind you, the barrier will reset after five minutes of you ceasing an attack to the outside."

"Great," I said. *Well, at least I could gather supplies and make a better trip out of here. Maybe I could find the materials to finish a bow . . .*

Then I recalled something. "You said you don't count as a citizen?"

"No," said Shart. "At best, I'd be considered your familiar in the town interface. I'm technically an Elder Demon, we follow special rules."

"The menu says the population is two," I said, but Shart looked at me like I was an idiot.

Idiot. I opened the town menu and searched for a population tab, which of course existed.

- Windfall Village
- Population: 2

- JIM (MAYOR)
- TOOMEN MASTERBROOK

Before I opened my mouth, I quickly reviewed the tabs and found one that had the city and the population. It showed me . . . but this time no one else. I checked the options and found one for inactive citizens and suddenly Toomen appeared in the church.

"He's in the . . . ," I began, trying and failing to identify which building the church even was. "Destroyed structure," I finished lamely.

Looking around, Shart replied, "You're gonna have to be more specific."

It took us about fifteen minutes to figure out where it was, and that was with me even having a map.

Smashing our way to that particular location wasn't any more challenging than one might expect cutting your way through a destroyed town with like a hundred years of overgrowth would be. I wondered about the newer village Shart had mentioned. Had all the residents of this town simply fled there? How much nicer was this new village? I bet they already had a functioning mayor. And functioning buildings. Rounding a slight curve, the decrepit church came into view.

We made our way into an open area in what might be politely described as the front lobby of the church. Following the next entryway, I walked into what probably once had been a very nice, well-constructed cathedral. However, now the structure was beyond ruined and the walls had collapsed in most places. The great ceiling was scattered all around us on the moss-and-mold-covered floor. Grass and weeds grew through cracks and fissures in the stone floor.

Both Shart and I were utterly unimpressed with this defunct worship center. However, a cursory examination of the room did present a very impressive and well-maintained statue located directly behind the pulpit.

The statute was interesting for a variety of reasons. First off, it was compelling to behold. The marble male wore a very artistically rendered expression of serenity. Second off was the fact that the statue was entirely bereft of any form of vegetation whatsoever. In fact, there was a good three-foot circle surrounding the statue where *nothing* grew.

It was a perfectly circular patch of barren dirt in the middle of a fertile field of weeds. I felt my Demon Lore skill activate, and I became instantly aware of some sort of curse exerting influence on the statue.

"Can you dispel this?" I asked Shart, glancing at my prompts.

"In my present state," replied Shart, "no. By the way, you *break* a curse, not dispel one. That's an important distinction." Again, he shot me his patented *You are an idiot* look.

"How do you break a curse?" I asked, as I looked at the statue really hard in an attempt to will a prompt.

Shart chuckled. "That's easy. Just place your palm on the statue."

I did so. The stone felt abnormally warm, considering I'd been walking barefoot through the rest of the building and all the other stone had been of a nearly uniform cool temperature.

"Now focus. Concentrate. You need to feel into the magic of the curse. Feel it throb in your hand. Feel it harden. It will throb faster and faster and then splatter all over you . . ."

I opened my eyes and moved my hand up about a foot, glowering at the demon. He might not be able to lie to me, but apparently, he could fuck with me a bit before telling me the actual truth.

Shart chortled. "Okay, dum dum. You are trying to feel a synchronicity of magic with the curse. At first, it will allow you to gather more information about the curse. Breaking it is quite a bit harder, but baby steps."

Frowning and closing my eyes, I concentrated on the feeling. There was something there inside the statue, but it was elusive. I relaxed, letting the magic flow through me and into the statue. I could sense the magic and the curse, but even after five full minutes I felt no closer than when I had begun.

"What the hell are you doing?" asked Shart.

"Relaxing to let the mana flow through me," I said. "Like the Force?"

"I don't know what 'the Force' is, but it sounds stupid," replied the demon. "It's a curse. You have to grab that thing and throttle it with your magical powers. Think of it more like a goblin's throat instead of your fragile dick. You want to grip that thing and choke it to death, not give it a casual wank."

"Oh, when you put it that way," I muttered. That was different. I settled in again. This time, instead of relaxing, I began pushing magic into the statue. Whenever I found the curse, I tried to snatch it. Initially, I had no luck. It was like reaching into a dark box while wearing gloves and trying to catch a slippery banana. But if a monkey reaches for a banana enough times, eventually he gets lucky. Somehow, I grabbed the curse for a moment. I instantly regretted that, as the curse throbbed then hardened in my mystical hand. I tried to release it but couldn't and the curse throbbed and finally erupted all over my face.

Black lightning spurted from the statue and all over me. I collapsed to the floor, my mind so fuddled that thinking was nearly impossible. Shart was yelling something at me, but the statue seemed normal and sitting here felt nice.

I don't quite know how long the lightning lasted, but however long it was, I'm going on record as it was way too long. All I could do for the duration was feel pain, and there was so much of it. It was so hard to think that I couldn't come up with a method to get away from the energy. Finally, it stopped and I laid there numb for several minutes. After that time, I replenished a single point of mana.

Mana 1/20

And just like that, everything snapped into normality. My head felt drained, like I'd just studied my butt off for a huge test and that test had been super difficult. Or I just had bronchitis and was still recovering. Even stringing two words together was impossible. I'd have been worried about brain damage, but I couldn't actually collect my thoughts well enough to articulate that for several minutes.

As the seconds slipped by, I began to agonizingly slowly recover mana. Each point caused my mind to become more and more active, until after a few more minutes I could think again. It took a bit longer for me to be able to form my mouth into words.

"What happened?" I asked weakly.

"Your mana got drained by the curse," replied Shart as he examined me. "You'll be okay in a few more minutes."

"I felt like I was dying."

"That's to be expected. You really aren't supposed to go to zero mana," replied the demon. "You can't cast down that low. For example, if you stay at zero mana or Stamina for too long, you'll die. You were only at zero for a few seconds, you baby."

"So, curses can defend themselves?" I choked out.

"Well, yes, but that's half the point of the stupid Curse Breaker skill: to avoid that. Since you have no idea what you are doing, and that looks like a powerful curse, you got blasted."

"Good to know. I'm just going to lie here for a bit," I said, sensing some fleeting warmth. That's when I realized that I'd pissed myself.

I started feeling worse before I felt better. At no mana, it was nearly impossible to think. At just a bit of mana, you could realize something was terribly wrong but not how to do anything about it. The sense of impending dread was horrible, but as you slowly clicked through those moments, you started feeling better. My mana regenerated at about the same speed as my Stamina, and both regenerated extremely faster than my health. I'd be topped out on both inside of three minutes, no matter what I'd done. At least, so far.

It had felt like hours but it should have only been a few minutes. Sensing my mana, I could tell it was regenerating slowly. I had several prompts with a brain surrounded by lightning bolts. I checked my character sheet.

> Mana: 3/20. Regeneration halved due to failed
> curse breaking attempt. Duration: 1 day.

Well, that was harsh, but I didn't really use mana for anything, so I'd survive. Losing health was agony, losing Stamina was beyond exhausting, and losing mana sucked your mental faculties right out of you. Even at 3 points, it was hard to think.

After thirty seconds or so, it was really hard to tell, my mana regenerated up to 6 and everything became much clearer. I checked my health and Stamina, but both were totally unaffected. The statue was still there, so I'm going to call this a zero sum experience.

Rolling onto my back, I looked up into the stars and considered their wonder and majesty. And opened up my character sheet. I had two coins in my view; I realized that I hadn't bothered to level. All of my plans had been contingent on the barrier holding. My skill selection would have changed radically if I was in this town or hiding in the wilderness.

- Woodsman Level 1: You have gained the first level of the Woodsman class.
- Level UP, Woodsman 1
- You have selected the Woodsman Class. Please choose two stat buffs for yourself at first level!
- You have gained the skills Light Armor, Tracking, Survival, and Trapping, as well as all Simple Weapons and Bows, and you gain one rank of the specialty Archery.
- You already have skill with Simple Weapons. Please choose another skill or one will be chosen for you.
- You already have skill with Light Armor. Please choose another skill or one will be chosen for you.
- Your Hit Point total is increased by 10. Your Stamina is increased by 10.

"Shart, does anything increase regeneration?" I asked.

"Spirit governs how quickly you regenerate all resources," he replied.

"I thought that Endurance increased regeneration speed?"

"No, Endurance increases regeneration amount, but spirit increases it quite a bit more. Basically, Spirit reduces the window of time for you to regain resources for all three kinds; Endurance increases the amount. "

That was worth considering. I kept running out of Stamina. Having more Endurance would give me more Stamina, but just increasing my Spirit might do more. It would certainly be handy to recover health faster. I dumped both points into Spirit. My head cleared slightly more.

Spirit: Good

The length of time between my recovery periods dropped from six seconds to about four. That would be handy. I could also tell that my health recovery was similarly reduced from eight hours to six, meaning I'd recover a third more hit points per day.

Glancing at my skills chart, I looked at my three new skills. Tracking allowed you to hone in on opponents and see their tracks if they were fresh. Survival allowed you to operate successfully in the woods, and Trapping gave you the ability to build traps. Traps sounded useful, but I'd get into that later.

I took my two free skills and found Curse Breaker in the skills list. It was at 1 of Unknown, so I purchased the skill.

Curse Breaking (500 SP/10,000 SP): Amateur.
You can now expend mana to break curses
and reduce the effects of failed attempts.

Glancing at my status bar, the duration of the mana burn was down to twelve hours.

That left one more skill. I considered for a moment and then closed the menu. A prompt appeared.

You must select a skill within the next forty-eight hours, or the skill will be randomly assigned.

I could live with that. I might randomly assign it myself.

Standing, I walked over to the statue again. Shart almost said something then quieted down with a harrumph. I placed my hand on the statue's chest and focused. This time, it was easier. I could see my "magic hand" and the "curse" which still wriggled around like an eel. Instead of blindly searching for it, I was able to corner it quickly and grab ahold of it firmly so there was no backlash.

You have discovered a Curse of Stone. You can Break the Curse for 600 Mana.

"Six hundred Mana!" I exclaimed, selecting "No." "Yes" had been greyed out, so it wasn't much of a choice.

"That's fairly normal for breaking a curse that's mid- to high-level," said Shart, who suddenly peered at me again. "Wait, now you are a *Woodsman*? This doesn't make any sense at all!"

"Yes, I leveled up again," I replied, sheepishly.

"How the hell did you take Curse Breaker? It's a higher-level skill," questioned Shart, before he remembered. "Oh, Unbound. Well, that's silly. You took a skill that you can't possibly use, because you don't have nearly enough mana. There is a reason it's a higher level."

"Yes, but six hundred still seems like a lot," I said.

"There are buffs," replied Shart, "and skills for that matter, that either reduce the cost or increase your own mana pool for specific spells or abilities."

"So, I can break the curse later?" I asked and Shart nodded.

"If you want to," added the demon.

He became silent and I was still looking towards the stars. It had been late afternoon when we'd gotten to the church and now it was quite dark. Yawning, I figured it was the mountains, possibly enchanted, turned day into night earlier than should be possible. Then, I remembered the second coin in my menu; I selected that.

- Level UP, Warrior 2
- You have gained one Perk. Please select it from the Warrior menu.

- Your Hit Point total is increased by 10. Your Stamina is increased by 10.

No stat bumps this time. Looks like those were saved for special occasions. The Perk was new, though, so I flipped open the Warrior menu and was greeted with a large series of tiles. It was a Warrior skill tree, and I couldn't read anything past the first few tiles.

There was Dual Wielding, which required above-average Dexterity, though that was blurred out; it improved your handling of two weapons. Sword and Board improved your use of a sword and shield in tandem, but it required above-average Endurance. Next was Great Weapons, which required above-average Strength. Finally, there was Resistance, which increased your base defense by 7.

I had to contemplate that. I had everything but the two-handed sword, so investing a perk into something I couldn't use didn't seem smart. I did have a sword and shield, and the goblin with the sword and shield had seemed pretty effective against my daggers. Then again, fighting with two weapons seemed to be useful, as well.

Above those, several larger tiles could be seen; I just couldn't quite make out what they said yet. I suspected they were some sort of sub-class to Warrior, but I couldn't be sure.

I flipped open the Woodsman page and checked my experience there. I had earned experience points most recently for the two-weapon fighting. Checking the Rogue page, I'd earned experience there from fighting with daggers and through the sneak attacks. Sneak attacking appeared to be far more worthwhile.

Selecting Dual Wielding was the best way I currently saw to gain experience points in most of my classes, so I selected that. I might not try to compound my advantages quite so much later, but right now that seemed to be the best choice. After I locked in the Perk, I suddenly felt askew.

I'd been a righty my entire life. My left hand was my off hand and it always had that slightly noticeable, if you focused on it, feeling of an off hand. That was gone. I tried flipping a dagger in my left hand and it felt identical to doing it in the right. Taking a dagger in both, I started performing flips and spins to the best of my ability, which had grown since I'd gotten here. And if you had to guess which hand was my dominant one, you would have failed.

Interesting.

I reviewed my Two Weapon Fighting. It had advanced from Amateur to Novice. That improved the damage with my main hand weapon slightly. But it also noted that *both* of my hands were considered main hands now. I also had Twin Weapon, but that simply improved my speed and damage when wielding two weapons of the same type.

I grabbed a short sword and swung it while doing the same with a dagger in the other hand. It was impressive to see how easily I moved both weapons, but I also realized that wielding large weapons would still be a challenge due to the weight. Also wielding large weapons drained my Stamina faster. Two longswords would probably not be practical until I was at a higher level, or at least with higher Stamina. Maybe there was a perk that would help with that. Even with those, I was pretty sure two greatswords would have been impossible.

I didn't have a bow to test my archery, so I decided that would be my next project. I also noticed a flashing exclamation mark, so I selected it.

You have been offered a Quest: You have found a cursed statue in your Town. Will you seek to remove the Curse? Reward: Toomen Masterbrook will become active in your town.

"Hey, another quest," I said. "I might even take this one."

"Screw off," said Shart, still upset that I hadn't accepted the quest to find his stupid Demon Door. "You can take a quest and get a reward. The more difficult the quest the greater the reward. My quest has a great reward for you."

"But you are planning on betraying me," I reminded him. "Not to mention, I am nowhere near leveled up enough to even open the door if we found it."

Shart growled, then nodded.

"Yeah, so I'm not going to do that," I said, as I mentally flicked the acceptance prompt.

You have accepted the Quest: End the Curse on Toomen Masterbrook. You will need to find a powerful curse breaker to end the curse!

There were no more details than that. I already knew how to remove the curse; the art was finding enough mana to do it. It filtered into my quest tab and I more or less set it to ignore. I noticed that several other quests were listed there, so I selected one at random.

- **Local Blacksmith <Jim> needs Iron to forge a breastplate. Reward: Breastplate.**

I looked at a few others.

- **Local Baker <Jim> needs Wheat to bake bread. Reward: Bread.**

- **Local Tailor <Jim> needs Cloth to make pants. Reward: Pants.**

Down the list went. I was apparently quite popular in the quest series, with over twelve different kinds of quests related to crafting.

"Why is my name appearing as someone offering quests?" I asked Shart, as he glowered at me for again refusing his Demon Door quest.

"Oh, that. You are the only one here, so any quests that the town would offer related to any skill you possess is going to default to you. Even at your level, there are probably one or two that you qualify for."

"Neat," I said. "So I get bonus experience for that?"

"Probably. Maybe a few items too. This is where you are supposed to get your better starter gear."

I cycled through everything until I found one I was hoping for.

- You have selected <Jim>
  needs Materials for a bow.

"Damn right I do."

CHAPTER 9

TOWN SQUARE

SHART AND I SPENT THE NEXT DAY GATHERING UP MATERIALS, searching for the items I instinctively knew would allow me to make a starter bow. I had the actual bow stave from my trip through the woods. What I didn't have was anything else, particularly decent bow string.

The town was picked clean. Probably picked clean a very long time ago, honestly. Searching for anything useful took quite a bit longer than one would hope. It paid off, though, as I ended up finding something I knew could be fashioned into a bow string, as well as a handful of iron ingots.

Just holding the components didn't do anything, however. I had to find the bowyer's shop and, more specifically, the tools located therein. This was easy with the town map. There, I'd hand over the materials I'd found to . . . myself. As soon as I walked into the door, I heard a ding in the back of my head and noticed that Quest Marker was flashing in the corner of my vision.

You have completed <Jim> needs Materials for a bow. Please select reward.

I could only see one option, the bow I had chosen earlier. I selected it, but nothing seemed to happen. Well, *something* happened; I felt like I should be making a bow. That was impressive, considering how destroyed the shop was. I very seriously doubted that anyone would be making anything here. As I continued selecting the reward and not receiving the bow, I realized that I wouldn't be able to complete the quest without first making a bow, because I needed to reward myself with it.

Great.

Fortunately, the materials left my inventory and were turned over to the town's resident handsome bow maker who took them and attempted to make a bow . . . with several broken pieces of equipment and a dagger. The town's resident bow maker was some sort of idiot who didn't actually have any tools. After a good thirty minutes of flailing around to the hysterical laughter of the town's resident mascot, Shart, and not quite ruining his chance of making a bow, the bow maker had enough and looked back to good old Mr. Skill Tab.

- Crafting: Amateur. You have basic crafting ability.

- Bowyer: Unskilled. You know what a bow is.

Bonus Skill:
- Improvised Tools: Unskilled. You have tried and failed to use improvised tools to make equipment.

Selecting Improvised Tools and assigning my Amateur skill rank to it, I suddenly became aware that I was doing this all wrong. Gathering up a square piece of stone, one goblin corpse, a small piece of a saw blade, a cabbage, and several sundry items, I proceeded to craft one Simple Bow twelve minutes later.

You have found: Simple Bow. Base Damage 1–6. Durability 25/25 (durability -10 due to Improvised Tools).

I held it aloft and smiled, only then noticing the peculiar expression on the demon's face as he tried and failed to comprehend what was going on.

"Why did you do that to the goblin?" asked Shart.

"Well I needed something to keep the bow in place and he was getting kind of rigor-mortisy . . ."

"That's not a word," said Shart.

"Sure, it is. It means something that has had enough time for rigor mortis to set in enough that he can be posed, if one tries aggressively enough," I replied.

"You used that old broom stick and he swivels now," said Shart as his eyes continued to survey the scene. "That's a work of art."

Sighing, I returned to the quest prompt and selected Simple Bow and was rewarded with 250 experience. Not quite enough to level up anything, I thought.

I'd actually kind of expected the quest rewards to apply to all of the classes I hadn't taken yet, but that didn't seem to be the case. Wizard didn't show an experience bar, for example. Neither did Cleric. Those were both caster classes, so I guessed I hadn't unlocked them yet. My Unbound ability only seemed to apply to things if I'd gotten past the initial steps.

"I switched classes again," I said.

Shart nodded. "I noticed when you started playing with your knives. Warrior 2. I wonder how many times you can change classes?"

"Yes, that would be interesting, if I could keep doing that," I said. "I'm curious: How do you gain experience points for Clerics or Wizards?"

"Well, Wizards is easy," he said. "Just start casting spells or using activated magical items. Before you ask, your magic dagger is a passive item. Items like that improve the related skills, while an activated item uses mana and basically casts a spell of some sort."

"Well, I'll have to keep my eye out for a wand," I said. "What about the Cleric stuff?"

"You have to visit the Temple of Light," stated my companion. "Several problems there, as the ceremony is deep inside the temple and I can't enter it. Like, at all. I can't even get close to the place."

"Because you're a demon?"

"Yes, you insufferable moron," replied Shart. "You must have been pretty when you were on Earth, because there is no way your wife was attracted to your brains. Now, there were a few expansions made to this world. One allows you to be a Druid, but you'd need to find a wild grove to have that power unlocked. There was a pirate expansion, so if you get a ship, you'd unlock Swashbuckler. Finally, they added Martial Arts, so you could start punching people until you become a Monk."

"Nope, I want a boat."

"So, you are going to be a pirate," said the Demon.

"Shiver me timbers, and all that." I chuckled.

I spent the next hour crafting several arrows out of nearby trees until I had a small pile sitting next to something I'd found. I was calling it a quiver, but it appeared to be more like a repurposed wrapping paper tube.

It was strange crafting arrows. It wasn't quite like woodworking on Earth, but it wasn't entirely dissimilar. There was quite a bit of actual hand-eye coordination required, as I used an old bowl and a leather belt to sand down the hunks of wood into shafts. That might have been Improvised Tools. I'd been earning skill points there steadily.

I could also see why Improvised Tools wouldn't be a common skill. First, the end-product was always less base durability than a product made with the correct tools. Base durability was important because it was the "base" that other values were calculated from. The second issue was the slow growth rate and high failure chance. Without my Crafting skill, even at the amateur level, I'd have broken one in every two arrows. As it was, I had a few that were flawed, but overall the majority of my arrows were just less durable than normal. However, despite all this building in Improvised Tools, I'd only gained 45 skill points. That brought my Improvised Tools to 5045, and I needed 50,000 to jump to the next rank. By the time you got to the point where you could have enough materials to train to Amateur rank, you wouldn't need it anymore. I'd managed to jump the gun by taking it using one of my free skill boosts. Most players wouldn't have.

However, Improvised Tools applied to every one of my Crafting skills. Furthermore, I had the core Crafting skill, which granted me crafting ability in all crafts. So, my Improvised Tools also assisted me in almost every circumstance. In practical terms, if I saw something that needed repair, I could also see how to best improvise tools and get the materials in position to do that repair. Thankfully, I had the ability to push that back a notch, so I had to focus on things to notice. Until I'd figured that out, I saw ways to repair every building in town using every building in town. It made actually seeing anything challenging.

With my last arrow completed, I sat inside the bowyer's shop and pondered what to do next. I was reasonably confident that I could go back out of town to gather food and other supplies. Aside from that, what else did I have to do? I couldn't go back to Earth. I didn't actually want to help Shart because, like it or not, this was my life now. I was in a whole new world, one with quests and fantastical elements. Just sitting around idly, I kept thinking about my home, my wife, my family, and everything I'd lost. Everything I'd lost and there was nothing I could do about it.

I was truly alone for the first time in my adult life. My wife had always been there for me or needed me. So had my kids, but far more the latter than the former. I had built my entire life around my family and those responsibilities. My loved ones thought I was dead, and now I had nothing but a ruined old village and a stupid gremlin companion bent on betraying me.

I leaned onto my back and looked up at the stars through a hole in the roof. The stars were far crisper than I'd ever seen on Earth. Possibly because I was a city boy, and possibly because I'd never really looked at them. Sitting there in the quiet, I wondered if I could even die in a place like this. Would it matter to me if I did? Why was I here and what could I accomplish? Maybe I should just do Shart's quest and end it all.

I needed my wife. She would have been able to tell me what to do or at least prod me in a more reasonable direction. She wasn't here, though, and never would be. So, I sat looking at the stars and wondering what ideas she would have.

Better ones than me.

Suddenly, a new quest prompt entered my vision.

Quest: Save the hostages. Several Humans have been kidnapped by a local patrol of goblins. Can you save the humans before they make it to their camp?

I selected "Yes" as I stood up with my bow, arrows, and other assorted weaponry.

"The quest is afoot," I declared. Shart groaned.

"So, any quest other than mine you are all for?" he asked.

"Exactly," I said, nodding as we started off towards the edge of the barrier. "It wouldn't be proper to ignore someone in need."

"*I'm* someone in need," replied the demon.

"Your needs involve terrible things happening to me," I noted.

"Well, yes, but what you are doing is still very impolite."

CHAPTER 10

OUTSKIRTS OF THE VILLAGE AT NIGHT

CROSSING THE BARRIER WAS A BIT OF A CONCERN. THE barrier required one living human to populate the village and the only other current resident was a cursed statue. Technically, he qualified, but that wasn't a great hope to put the safety of the village on.

The goblins had spent the last day gathering up a patrol of wolf riders. They would run around the village every few hours, sniffing the ground and howling. This complicated my escape plan somewhat.

My plan was to leave the village and see if the barrier remained active. If the barrier failed, there was no reason to stay in the village; it had been picked clean. The safety of the barrier was essentially the only real value to me now.

If I left and the barrier failed, I would have to get lost deeper in the forest. I doubted the goblins would leave the village almost empty again, and there was a pretty low limit on the number of prepared goblins I could expect to handle.

Everything revolved around the barrier. I would know there was an issue when I tried to cross the border of the village; I'd get a prompt telling me that I had to return to the village or I would lose control. At that point, I'd decided my only option would be to high tail it back to the woods.

In theory, it would take the wolves a few hours to find my tracks. By then, I figured I'd be able to lose myself in the forest. Or at least put so much ground behind me that they'd give up before catching me. I had almost decided to sprint past the border to get just that one bit more of distance before the barrier obviously vanished, but it turned out none of that was required.

I crossed the border and nothing happened. I brought up the town menu and it listed the population as one: Good old Toomen. That man could really occupy a population slot. I was still listed as the mayor, but I wasn't currently in town. Therefore, he was technically the only one there.

Searching around, I didn't see any wolves or goblins. They had a patrol that had run around the village consistently, but that was actually a pretty big hike based on where the barrier faded, almost a mile from the center of the village. Given there were fewer than twenty goblins, they could not adequately patrol over three miles of border. If one were being especially stealthy, they could easily make it out of the town unnoticed.

Five sneaky minutes later, we reached the forest. Okay, forest was a strong word, but I had decided that the trees were thick enough at the five minute point to forgo Stealth and just walk normally. I surmised that the goblins were not going to be able to see me, no matter what I did. Also, I could see their patrol and it was well past me.

Thirty minutes later, I was following the Quest Marker towards the target. The Quest Marker's functioning was reasonably interesting. It gave me a sensation towards the target and what I guessed was approximate distance. I was heading towards one of the mountain walls out west that seemed to surround the town.

My Survival skill kept firing off, too, directing me towards nearby animals, which I shot at with some success. After the first hour, I had to cut back to only firing at rabbit-sized creatures, given that most of my improvised arrows did not survive striking a target. I had several carcasses on me and was sincerely hoping that rabbit meat would be tastier than wolf meat. Now, if I could just find some actual rabbits . . . because I was fairly certain that what I'd shot so far were not. They reminded me more of a certain animated, electric rodent.

(By the way, electric rodents are pikadelicious.)

I encountered one wolf which was very anticlimactic from my previous attacks. I simply snuck up on it and fired at it from about fifty feet. The arrow caused sneak attack damage, which multiplied the damage of the strike. It died instantly.

Damage, I discovered, was different than in Dungeons & Dragons. There wasn't a random roll for it. For instance, my bow had a base damage of 1–6. However, with all my bonuses applied to it, that damage skyrocketed to 7–13. The damage seemed primarily based on both where you hit and how direct the shot was. I could do 13 points of damage on every strike versus a stationary target, assuming I could aim well enough. A glancing blow would do less damage, of course, but I tried to avoid those.

So, when I shot a surprised wolf, I did 13 damage. This was reduced by 3 from his defenses to 10. However, he took additional damage from an unexpected attack, which doubled the damage. He also took additional damage because, as a Rogue, I could perform a sneak attack. That also doubled the total damage. That meant I did around 40 damage per shot, and the wolf had 20 hit points. It got worse—or better, depending if you were the wolf or me. I could aim for the heart, which increased base damage by 50%, or the brain, which doubled damage. Neither was particularly difficult to hit on a sitting wolf at fifty feet.

Another bonus effect of sneak attacks was that if a creature died from the sneak attack, they died silently.

The Quest Marker had been growing steadily closer and at one point had seemingly begun to move. That's when I came to the brilliant conclusion that it *was* actually moving. The hostages had to be very close indeed. I began sneaking across a ridge and my Perception skill allowed me to catch a few whispers of goblin speech.

I'd found the section on my character sheet that dealt with languages, and it wasn't on the skill part. Instead, it was on the proficiency tab, which seemed to be a very abbreviated version of the skill sheet. While languages weren't all or nothing, they didn't seem to fall under the typical skill rules for whatever reason.

I was listed as having 28% comprehension of the goblin language, which meant I could sort of understand what they were saying in general terms. I snuck to a spot somewhat near the road where I could clearly hear the goblins. They were not quiet. While they actually had scouts out, they were not wildly effective. I got behind one of the scouts and got within eyesight of the goblins.

There were around thirty of the greenskins walking down the path. They were a motley assortment, with a few general trends that could be gathered. The bigger ones tended to be the best armed and equipped. In fact, they seemed to be an entirely size-based culture.

"I tired," called the first one.

"No care. We go on ahead."

"Everyone tired. We need rest, here safe."

"Here no safe. Look at ridge, anyone can attack. Move to gully and there it safe."

"Okay, we rest at gully?"

A general chorus of assent filled their column.

I watched for another minute and finally saw a human woman and two children. They looked rough and were all starting to become emaciated, despite the fact that they were being forced to carry all the food. Whenever one slowed, the goblins would smack them with their short spears or pound them with their shields until they got up and continued moving. It was obvious that goblins were not nearly as good at carrying heavy loads as humans were, so the humans were being treated like rented mules.

There was simply nothing I could do to save people here. The humans were in the middle of the column and the goblins were scouting nearby. I could possibly have attacked the goblins, but I didn't think that I'd have done more than trifling damage and the goblins would either defeat me outright or kill a hostage. I needed them to be in a position where I could steal away with the people before the fight started.

After deciding that I *would* save the woman and her children, I started ranging ahead of the group looking for that gully. While I wasn't sure it would be a better location for a fight, I knew that this situation gave the goblins every advantage. The goblins knew where they were going, but their path was somewhat predictable. Maneuvering in front of them, I used my Tracking skill to follow the very old tracks on the obvious path as quickly as I could. I found the gully easily enough. It was only about thirty or so minutes for me, but it would take them longer with their packs and prisoners.

The gully was a good defensive spot, if nothing else. Only two sides were accessible, and those both under cover, with good choke points. The top of the gully was overgrown by some sort of stinking roots, so that the area was all but enclosed. My Stealth skill allowed me to recognize that sneaking around in those roots was a sure way to reveal my position. At either entrance of the culvert, there were rudely constructed earthen walls. These looked reasonably sturdy for the most part and, of course, they went almost up to the roots. However, they were not well made. After some more searching, I found a point where the wall was thinned out and plastered over, so I smashed a hole through it. While I didn't have a plan yet, I figured having an easier way in and out wouldn't hurt. And if the goblins were serious enough to repair the hole—which would have involved using mud, I suspected—then that would tell me something as well.

On the other side of the gully, the pathway continued farther into the valley. Older tracks covered it liberally; I conjectured that this was where they would be going next. The path went through some marshy ground littered with trees and other obstructions. It was also full of frogs and other reptiles, which were anything but quiet. Thankfully, none of them seemed to care one whit about my sudden appearance among them.

My plan came together quickly enough. I would trap the hell out of this path and sneak in to get the prisoners. Afterwards, I'd escape through my own field of traps and then break out into the forest on a trek south back to the village. I had many hours of darkness to cloak me, but best not to put it off.

It was time to Kevin McCallister this place up.

It was almost morning before my plan was ready to go. My traps were set. My path was clear. My hidey hole was sized for four people. Now all that was left was to sneak in and save the mother and two children from the armed camp. Easy peasy. It had taken much longer to get set up than I'd anticipated because I'd had to ensure that the goblin guards hadn't seen me. Fortunately, they seemed . . . less than focused in their defensive precautions.

Okay, one of them had fallen asleep. The other was doing something I hoped was dicing, and also, he had a stomachache. I did not care for goblins.

The most challenging bit was actually screwing up enough courage to go through with it. In the abstract, it was stealing from a bunch of goblins. In reality, I was attacking a heavily fortified camp full of monsters with no backup. They looked like the kind of critters who tortured people who tried to steal from them.

I don't have to do this, I thought, as the scope of my endeavor hit. I was planning on entering an armed camp of monsters and stealing their prizes. If they caught me, they would kill me.

"Second guessing yourself," said Shart.

"Yes," I whispered slowly. I was a coward and a fool. This was suicide.

"That's the smart part of your brain talking, and I must say, I am shocked. Up until this point, I was unaware you possessed a brain, let alone a smart part," Shart smart-assed. I growled as he continued, "You can just leave them. The woman will be killed quickly anyway."

"Yes," I replied, tasting the word. They didn't know I was here; I should just go. "What about the kids?"

"Not so good for them," replied Shart. "Best not think about that."

I froze for a long moment, sucking in air, feeling the weight of the world on my shoulders. Who was I to even attempt this? I was just a simple guy from Ohio. I'd never signed up for this.

But neither had they. They were just people in a bad spot and they needed a hero to save them. I wasn't sure what a hero even was anymore, but I decided I knew what I wanted one to be. I'd already died once. I could die again if it saved some kids.

I bravely snuck over towards the goblins.

The gully's southern wall contained an entrance where I expected them to leave from tomorrow morning. There were two guards again, now that one had woken up from his nap. The hole I had knocked in the side when I went through earlier had not been patched. I snuck over. I could see the small eyeball in the corner of my vision showing if I was hidden or not and it flickered several times as the guards looked this way and that. Ultimately, it was a contest of my Stealth skill versus their Perception skill in the dark night as I crept through anything I thought might give me a bit more cover.

The eye remained closed; I made it to the wall. Soon I was under the hole I had made, trying to avoid stepping on the crumbling pieces of earth that were scattered about. On this side, it was quite a bit higher up so I hunched down and launched myself towards it. I only made it most of the way and had to scramble up the rocks for the last several inches.

Mental note: invest in some jumping skill.

A Note has been added: Invest in some jumping skill.

You have discovered Jumping, but are unpracticed at it.

Every little thing, I thought.

Looking through the hole into the camp, my less-than-silent approach hadn't actually attracted any guards. I then lowered myself down into the camp proper. It was dark, with a single large fire in the middle of the camp, casting poor illumination throughout the gully. The light reflected weakly off the earth and stone walls.

There was a cluster of tents in a rough circle around the fire. The tents were assembled poorly, either due to the goblin's laziness or because the cover provided by the gully made a more serious effort unnecessary. Additionally, there were several outlying tents that were also dimly visible outside the ring of light. The remainder of the gully was dark despite the fire; there was simply too much volume for one poorly tended fire to cover. There were no clear paths to any of the tents and the goblins that were still visible were either watching the main entrances or wandering about aimlessly.

That left me stalking through the darkness and trying to avoid the random goblins. I leapt down from my perch at the hole and began to do just that. After a minute, I ran into my first goblin, but luckily, he did not notice me. He moved farther into the darkness, and finally stopped three paces from me and sighed audibly. He then flipped open his loincloth. As he began to relieve himself, I slit his throat from behind and pushed his body farther down into the shadows. I waited a minute and another goblin came out. He looked around for a moment, sniffing loudly. He also stopped to relieve himself. I killed him and hid his body as well.

I ended up doing that four more times before the supply ran out. I'm not going to kid, I wasn't exactly thrilled with the situation, but a kill is a kill I supposed. Each goblin reeked of beer. My heroic self had been killing drunk creatures that were the size of ten-year-olds. If I ever told this tale again, I was going to keep that part of the story to myself.

With no more easy victims, I began creeping through the darkness in search of the human prisoners. With my heightened senses, it wasn't hard to find them; the smell of human was different enough that, when I got within ten yards of them, I knew right where they were in a camp full of goblins.

The hostages were in a large tent that had been thrown together on the side of the main camp. Their tent was being guarded, at its entrance, by a single goblin that had become visible as I moved farther into their camp. He was glumly standing at what passed for attention for his people. I looked at my interface and checked the stealth icon— eye closed—and noticed that somehow, I still hadn't been observed.

Sneaking closer towards him, I saw the icon start to open, so I backed away. Twice more, I tried to sneak right past the bored guard until I realized that there was no way to sneak right past a guard if they were conscious. As I reflected on that, I thought I saw the icon flick open for a moment, but it was just my imagination.

As I moved behind the tent to ruminate, I discovered the crude dwelling was made of fabric. And I had all these knives.

Groaning inwardly, I cut a slit into the tent, being mindful to keep any light from splashing out of it. Fortunately, the tent was dark inside; the only light coming from the fire through the open tent flap.

Inside the tent, I saw the woman and two smaller figures. As before, I assumed that they were a mother and her children. They looked haggard. The woman had multiple bruises. None of the three looked like they'd had a good meal in some time, but they were not so malnourished that they couldn't move. *So the goblins didn't have to carry them to wherever they were going*, I suspected. Further examination and the awkward way they were all positioned on the ground told me they were all tied up.

The light on the woman's face showed that she would have been pretty in better times. A beauty that had been faded by years or terrible circumstances. I suspected the goblins qualified as "terrible circumstances" as much as anything.

Crawling through the slit, I snuck behind the goblin guard and quietly knifed him in the back. He made a slight exhaling noise before collapsing and I sat him down just inside the door to the tent. He almost looked like he was sleeping, and I hoped that no one would pay attention to him for at least a few minutes, but sneaking out that many people from the tent—even through the back—would have been tricky with him alive.

Moving quietly, I knelt next to the woman, put my hand over her mouth, and shook her arm. That didn't feel quite right but there weren't any better options. Her eyes shot open immediately. Her eyes filled with terror, but she did not scream or try to bite me. I took my free hand up to my lips and made what I hoped was the universal "be quiet" gesture. She didn't seem to understand for a moment, but from her angle she could see the slit in the back of the tent. Then, comprehension filled her eyes.

"I'm going to get you out of here," I whispered.

"Who are you?" she asked. Given that we were in the middle of a goblin camp, that seemed reasonable.

"I'm Jim."

She waited a moment. "Just Jim? Did your parents forget to finish naming you?"

"No, it's just Jim," I stated. "Do you want out or not?"

"Yes," she said. "I'm AvaSophia. These are my children."

"Good to know," I responded, looking back through the tent flap as I thought my stealth icon opened again.

"I won't leave my children," she said with a savagery that I wouldn't have expected, forcing me to turn to face her again.

"I wasn't planning on leaving them, either," I replied, and she relaxed slightly. I began cutting her ropes. The knots were well-tied and the rope itself was tough. It took me several moments before I managed to get the bonds severed; she pulled her hands to her chest, rubbing her wrists.

Handing her a dagger, I said, "Wake your children and cut them free. We have a bit of time, but we will need to leave very soon. I have a safe place outside of this camp, but we have to be very careful walking there."

She nodded and began to wake her children. They were both exhausted, but neither complained. When they saw the dagger and felt their bonds get cut, they quickly gathered themselves up for the great escape. I was relieved to see that both the children, a little girl and a slightly older boy, both still had their eyes. I glanced at Shart, pointing first at my own eyes and then at the children.

Shart, still invisible on my shoulder, whispered, "The goblins were still using them as pack mules. Blind kids would have been less useful and slowed them down."

Gripping my daggers and giving one last look through the tent flap, I snuck out through the slit in the back. I had to be ready for anything. Alas, nothing was there. The goblins still hadn't noticed my movement through their camp. I stuck my hand through the slit and gestured for the now former hostages to follow.

The little boy, scrawny but determined, came out first. He looked around in all directions, as if satisfying himself that it was safe. Only then did he wave for his little sister and then mother to follow him out. In the darkness, it was difficult, but I managed to catch just enough of the moon's illuminating light to direct them to the exit point.

"There is a hole. I'll crawl through, and then your mother will push you up to it. You'll have to jump down, but I'll catch you." This was my entire plan. I didn't mention that if the goblins spotted us on the way to the hole things would end poorly. The trio nodded, for they could see the goblins at both entrances well-enough, and we moved quietly through the gully.

Suddenly my stealth icon flashed to "open" and I spun around, weapons at the ready. The children both dove to the ground and Ava-Sophia's face changed from nearly pretty to fury. With my Perception skill, my senses were heightened to a superhuman degree and the hairs on the back of my neck were all standing on end.

However, nothing was there.

For three heartbeats, I stood ready for murder. When none came, AvaSophia started hustling her children towards the exit. I followed lamely behind them, the feeling of being watched never quite leaving me, even though my icon indicated I was under stealth.

We made it to just under the hole when the goblins sounded the alarm. A loud call rose up through their entire camp, voices calling danger as the camp roused. Guards at the entrances began looking for threats both inside and out. Of course, we were right in a shaft of moonlight.

"Ava, go through," I called as the guards from the nearby entrance started running towards us.

She yelled something, but started climbing, getting through

before any of the guards could get their arrows notched. That left the two goblins that knew where the humans were escaping. Suddenly, I found myself with a partner, as the boy stood next to me with a dagger in his hand. His sister, being wiser, was climbing her way to safety as the inner wall was just rough enough for her small hands and feet to find purchase.

The boy was the size of a small goblin. He might have honestly had a chance in a straight up fight against one of the common goblins, but the guards were much larger customers. Each was the size of the one with the sword and shield I had fought in the village. I didn't want to see the child almost escape just to die here, so I moved forward.

There was a patch of darkness where the light of the fire ended but before the light of the moon began. It lasted for maybe the space of two goblin paces. Inside that pool of darkness, I clashed with both goblins.

The first didn't realize that I was engaging both. He was going for the smaller human, the easier target, I supposed. I cut to his side, getting past his guard and driving my dagger into his eye. In the darkness, it was a critical sneak attack; my combat log showed it instantly killing him.

The second goblin was going after me, however, and thrust with his short sword in a strike that should have driven straight through my chest. I activated my Dodge skill, avoiding the strike, and drove my other dagger into his gut. It was the magic dagger. It pierced his armor easily, tearing into his intestines. He screamed, dropping to his knees. His agony was cut short, as the child jammed his own dagger into the creature's mouth, silencing it. The look of malice from that boy was not healthy.

I glanced backwards. The girl had gotten over the hump and jumped down even as arrows struck the stone egress. Turning back, I saw that nearly a dozen goblins had gotten bows out and another six were charging towards us. *Time to go*, I thought.

Grabbing the boy, I rushed to the hole, even as more arrows smashed against the rocks. I had to use the Dodge skill several times, which was much harder when one was carrying a boy not entirely sold on being carried. I didn't have time for this, so I did something I had been trying to avoid.

I didn't really know how high I could jump after I increased my Dexterity and Strength. I'd unlocked the Unskilled rank with Jumping, though, and if ever there was a case to try, this was it. The sensation was odd. I felt my Stamina pouring into my legs for a moment and then I jumped with more power than I'd ever jumped before in my life. It was high enough to clear the seventy or so inches from the ground to the hole, front flip around, and land on my feet despite the sudden hot pain from my side. I landed just outside the gully, next to a wide-eyed AvaSophia, who had been trying to scramble back in to save her boy.

Sitting the now very wobbly boy down, I turned to her. "Let's go. Follow me *exactly*."

The three of them nodded numbly and followed, just happy to be free of the goblins for the first time in however long it had been. With my Perception skill and the moonlight, I was able to track to the single point in my network of traps that it was safe to enter.

Whispering another word of warning, I ushered the family past me and then we all went into the small safe area I'd found in a rotted tree stump. It turned out to be just big enough for the three to fit, which sounds far more impressive than it was, because I was supposed to fit in there, too. The initial plan was to all hide until the goblins were savaged by the traps.

"You're hurt," said AvaSophia.

I checked the Combat Tracker. A goblin arrow had hit me and my Mitigate skill had automatically activated. This reduced the damage from 6 to 2. I checked my Mitigate skill and found it had increased to Novice; now, I could mitigate up to 4 points of damage. The Stamina cost was still 2 per point of damage resisted, but 8 points of Stamina was much easier to replace than 4 points of Health.

I guess nearly getting killed all the time has its advantages.

I considered looking at the Mitigate skill. My Dodge skill was up to 89 SP, so it had to level at 100 or something. The goblins were about to start shooting at me again . . . maybe I should just stand up and dodge arrows for a bit?

Looking through my screen at AvaSophia, I noticed that despite the time I'd spent on the menu, she seemed stationary. Unmoving. She was still talking, or at least her mouth was open to talk, but she wasn't saying anything. Focusing behind her, which was tricky due to the menus, I could see the first goblin exiting the gully. He was hovering in midair.

Time must slow down when I get into these menus, I realized. I closed them.

"It's a minor wound. Just stay safe with your children while I deal with these creatures," I said, reaching into the cubby to grab my bow and arrows. I hoped I looked heroic, because if my traps didn't work it would be the last time she saw me alive.

I strung the bow while the goblins got themselves together. Several of the greenskins did shoot arrows at me, so I ended up using my Dodge skill repeatedly. With the range, and the cover, and the lighting, the goblins just didn't have any real good shots. The handful of them that got close were luckier than anything. The range reduced the cost of the Dodge to almost nothing. In turn, they also didn't do much for the old skill point level. Ultimately, the attacks were more an annoyance than anything.

On the other hand, with my Bows skill from Woodsman and my Perception skill, I was able to drop two of the goblins before they finally stopped shooting. I waited patiently for a moment, figuring that they were going to rush me at any second. I knew that too many Goblins were going to be an issue. I needed an advantage, so I checked my prompts for gold coins and was not disappointed.

- Level UP, Rogue 2
- You have gained one Perk. Please select it from the Rogue menu.

- Your Hit Point total is increased by 10. Your Stamina is increased by 10.
- Level UP, Woodsman 2

• You have gained one Perk. Please select it from the Woodsman menu.

• Your Hit Point total is increased by 10. Your Stamina is increased by 10.

I flipped over to the Rogue menu, looking for a special kind of skill. One that prevented me from getting murdered, mostly. There were Stealth skills and Stealing skills that all looked useful, but not in this situation. There were some Damaging skills that improved my sneak attack or made it more broadly useful, but killing them hadn't been all that challenging; more damage didn't seem better. There was one called Mobility, and jumping through things had been useful once before . . .

Mobility: Grants you improved movement, increasing the speed that you can travel as well as the height of your jumps. Improves the Dodge skill.

Well, that was easy enough. I'd been using the Dodge skill religiously, so improving it seemed wise.

Next, I looked into my Woodsman perks. One was already selected, it seemed. Dual Weapon wielding was the same Perk in both Warrior and Woodsman. Good to know, I supposed. The placement on it was strange though. It was up higher on the tree, under the branch with two of the larger icons attached to it.

Checking to see if the goblins had moved, I was relieved to see they hadn't. I poked one of the icons.

Ranger: Woodsman specialization. You seek out the enemies of the wilderness and destroy them. +1 Perk, +10 Stamina, +20 Health, +10 Mana.

Nice, but clicking it revealed that I didn't have a specialization token, which was apparently like a Perk point, but awarded at a higher level. That was another effect of my Unbound. I could learn any skill I had access to or take any class perk that I had points for. Additionally, I could take any sub-class, if I had a sub-class token.

Well, that couldn't help me now. Closer to the bottom of the perk list was a largish icon for Lore.

Woodsman's Lore: You gain access to the core skill Lore, which reveals information about enemies. Improved Lore also grants you improvements to your Tracking, and bonus damage against enemies that you have at least Amateur skill with. You can sense targets' Health, Mana, and Stamina if you are equal in level, adjusted by Lore skill and monster specific skills. Additional information can be learned at a higher level.

That was intriguing. It might be nice to know what I was aiming at. Bonus damage was nice, and maybe if I knew what I was shooting at, I might come up with few more tricks.

So I selected Lore and my world changed again. I watched my character sheet adjust, the Lore skill appearing and moving my Demon and Goblin Lore beneath it. I could instantly sense more general knowledge about demons and the goblins facing me.

Even while looking at the sheet, I could see through it and to the goblins beyond. Each now had a Health, Mana, and Stamina ring on their chest. Closing the sheet, I saw that one in more detail:

- Goblin: Level 2
- Health: 10
- Stamina: 20
- Mana: 5
- Skills: Bow: Amateur
- Sword: Amateur

Goblins are small humanoid creatures that expand their population wherever they can find food. They are a wretched race that frequently inhabits the ruins of other races. They hate all races, including goblins,

and will attempt to kill or enslave anything they meet. No goblin can
be trusted to keep his word. Sometimes goblins can be controlled by
a Warboss. Goblin gangs can be deadly to the unprepared.

Casting my eyes over the rest of them, they were all similar, with the larger six in front having 25 hit points and the Shield skill. I didn't see anything about Trap Detection, so I suddenly got quite a bit more confident.

I looked into my quiver. Eight more arrows, which wasn't enough for all of them. I drew one arrow and fired it at one of the larger goblins standing outside the gully entrance. He brought up his shield and the arrow shattered into it. He laughed and started pounding his sword into his shield. The other goblins followed suit, and then the goblins behind them started filing out of the gully.

Setting my bow aside, the lead goblin barked out in his garbled tongue, "He's out of arrows. Kill him!" I could perfectly understand him now. That was also part of Lore I guessed, which was turning out to be handy indeed.

Still, the goblins waited a few more moments, gathering their nerve, while calling out and barking at me. Finally, I stood again, gripping my daggers defiantly. The goblins decided that I actually really must be out of arrows and charged me.

Trap Making is a fun skill. More, it—combined with the generally short construction times in this realm, plus a love of the original Predator movie—allowed me to construct a significant number of traps in considerably less time than one would expect. Or hope, in the goblins' case.

They actually ran right past my outside line of traps. Whether because the goblins decided to charge at an angle, or because one of the outer line didn't go off properly, I couldn't tell. In any case, they got about thirty feet in front of me before the first snare hit. Weighted for a human—because that's the trap I could make—it tried to lift a full-sized human male into the air.

Instead, it lifted a goblin. Said goblin kept right on going, slamming into the trunk of the tree I'd built the trap on with a very audible crack. I noticed a ding from my Trap skill at that point, but it got so much better.

Several goblins found what amounted to be buried sticks that, when they stepped on them, shot up like a rake. Except, instead of a pole to the face, it was a spike to the gut. Others tripped a trap where a wasp nest smacked into their leader's chest. Wasps—like goblins—hate everyone everywhere, but especially when their nest smashes into something.

There were spikes, a pit trap, and several falling logs. One goblin slipped on the guts of his friend and managed to strangle himself on a vine. By the time everything was said and done, only seven of the goblins that had entered into the traps left on their own two feet. Well, some of them left on their own two feet. A few were missing one or, in a particularly sad case, both of their feet.

There were lots of traps. Dutch would have been proud of me. As I reached down to pick my bow back up and shoot the survivors, I heard a slow clapping from behind me.

I was fast, with all my upgrades. When I turned around, it was with blinding speed. I had the arrow nocked before I even faced my opponent. A single goblin was standing not ten feet from me, past all of my traps. His swords still in their sheaths, he clapped with a terrible smirk on his face. At point blank range, I loosed a perfectly aimed arrow at his chest.

His Dodge was so fast, he blurred. The arrow slid through the air, slicing through a tree and causing another snare to fly off into the darkness.

"My, you are fast for level 2," he said, watching me with casual indifference. His swords were in his hands now, but he made no move towards me.

"Who are you?" I yelled. I considered drawing another arrow, but that looked good and pointless. His Stamina bar was totally full again.

"Glak'ilk'sic." He bowed. "Shadow Goblin, and Slayer of Men. You just killed off most of Glak'ilk'sic's servants. Bad form."

CHAPTER 11

BATTLE WITH THE SHADOW GOBLIN

I EXAMINED HIM WITH LORE.

- Glak'ilk'sic: Shadow Goblin Level 6
- Health: 60
- Stamina: 80
- Mana: 10
- Sword: Novice. He gains +2 to damage with swords.
- Dodge: Novice. He is skilled at Dodging.
- Stealth: Novice. He is difficult to spot in the best of circumstances.
- Perception: Novice. Sight-based skill, allows him to see more detail in your environment, grants limited low-light vision.
- Twin Weapon Fighting: He gains a speed bonus when attacking with two weapons.

Shadow Goblins are Elite Goblins who have been cursed by drinking the blood of the shadow god. They are imbued with his power and are much more cunning and capable than normal goblins. They like to keep normal goblins around as servants. Normal goblins will always listen to and follow the orders of Shadow Goblins, due to their magical nature. Many armies use them as assassins and spies.

Note: There is a –level difference between you and the target. Attacks will have a lower probability of striking the target. Defensive skills such as Dodge will be more expensive when fighting against a higher-level opponent.

"You saw me in the gully, when I was sneaking around," I replied, drawing my daggers.

"But of course. Though Glak'ilk'sic's clever mind had you pegged as a Rogue. Out here, you have all of those pesky traps, so you must be a Woodsman, or a much higher-level Rogue with Trapping skill."

With that Glak'ilk'sic started pacing at the end of my traps, forcing me to either close with him or walk around in a circle to keep distance. I chose to keep distance. "Why do you think that?" I asked.

"Well, Glak'ilk'sic used his Lore skill on you, of course. You also have Lore, but your readings cannot be right. They claim you have 82 Health, and 90 Stamina. That means that you cannot possibly be level 2. You must have an item that is making you more powerful. And Glak'ilk'sic would like that item." He smiled. "Glak'ilk'sic would like that very much."

He lunged forward in the blink of an eye. Only my newly enhanced Mobility-based Dodge skill allowed me to leap clear, as both swords would have bisected me. He was still close enough to attack though, so I slashed at him. He easily dodged the strikes, flowing backwards until he was standing where he started only a moment before.

"That is interesting," he said. "You jest. You are pulling the wool over Glak'ilk'sic's eyes. I guessed you were at least level 4, maybe level 5. But ha. You fight like a 2nd level Rogue. Tell me, is this humble servant mistaken? Are you just level 2? Has Glak'ilk'sic erred?"

"Well, come over and find out," I bluffed. "You will see the true power of Jim."

Glak'ilk'sic stood for a long moment. "Wait . . . is that your whole name? Glak'ilk'sic thought there would be more. You must have had terribly unimaginative parents."

Suddenly, he was on me again in the blink of an eye. Every strike he made would have gutted me, if I hadn't been dodging around like a maniac. My own counter blows either went wide or he Dodged with almost no effort. Either way, the end result was bad: I was down almost half my Stamina bar and his was only down about a quarter. Health was important, but if you couldn't move, then you couldn't defend yourself. If my Stamina ran out, I'd die.

After one particularly nasty Dodge, I landed wrong. My foot became pinned by a root and I couldn't manage to break it free. Glak'ilk'sic grinned his rictus grin and lunged at me, forcing me to parry both blows with my daggers. That, coupled with his forward movement, left him exposed. I finally managed to score my first hit of the battle, a slight scratch on his left side.

Unfortunately, that move left me exposed and he jammed one of his short swords into my shoulder before leaping backwards out of my reach. I pried my leg free as he stared at me, his expression growing hotter.

"Please tell Glak'ilk'sic something, human," he started angrily. "Because now you parry. You dodge and trap . . . and parry—all badly—and parry is something a Warrior does or a higher level Woodsman, but never a Rogue. How do you do all Dodge and parry and trap, little human?"

I said nothing, starting to pace around him in a circle again. He was down about a tenth of his Health bar. Mine was as well, but my Stamina bar was at nearly 30%. I noticed my bar filled faster than his. That didn't help much, though, because his depleted more slowly than mine and he had a bunch more Stamina left. I noticed my Trapping leveled up again, but that didn't help much.

As long as Glak'ilk'sic could move, I was not going to be able to hit him. Weighing my options, I waited for him to lunge forwards again. This time, I leapt backwards into my field of traps. With Mobility, I could land pretty much exactly wherever I wanted. I chose to land where a goblin had gotten picked off by one of my snares.

Glak'ilk'sic jumped to my earlier vantage point and stared down at me. He glanced about, seeing the results of my traps, but here was the contest. He had the Perception skill and that certainly had to show him *some* of the traps, but it possibly didn't show him *all* of the traps. Skills had success ratios and some of my traps had been rather poor. However, others had been excellently hidden or quite deadly. He had been busy sneaking up behind me, not watching the traps. As he looked back to me, I deliberately took my left hand and patted my pocket.

The goblin charged, trusting that he could find where most of the traps were. I stopped trying to attack him, a futile process anyway, and just started Dodging. My Stamina was still low, and getting lower all the time, however, so I didn't have long to keep up with this game.

He went all in, tagging me several times. Each hit caused a bright flash of pain and a drop in my Health. Most strikes were doing 7 or 8 points of damage. Stamina was worth more than Health at the moment, so I couldn't even Mitigate them. I lost over half of my Health before he made a mistake.

I had backflipped over a tree and he slid underneath it, attempting to strike at my knee. It was there that he found a trap I'd placed to prevent someone from doing just that. A snare caught his leg, yanking him out from under the tree and slamming him into the ground. Several feet away, the sapling I'd used snapped back into its correct position.

I lunged at Glak'ilk'sic's stunned form, but even before I was halfway through my arc, he had tucked himself into a ball and launched himself away from the trap. The snare had broken when he'd been flung, so he was free. He jumped, but landed on one of the paths the goblins had not used . . . and I had trapped just about everything on his current trail.

He managed to land in another binding trap. This time, he was stuck fast. He had also come down with enough force that I'm pretty sure his ankle would have broken—should have broken, at least—but this wasn't Earth. My Stamina was down to the point where I was having trouble seeing straight: 20%. I walked back over to my bow and picked it up as he struggled to wrench his foot free.

"Glak'ilk'sic was tricked," he yelled, using his swords to try to pry the trap loose, but it was very well-made and his swords did piercing damage. Hard wood was strong against that. Grabbing at the two branches that were both now crushing his leg, he then tried to pull them apart through brute strength, an ability goblins lacked due to their size.

I took aim with my bow and fired. He still somehow Dodged it. Without the Lore skill, I would have ran at that point. Gotten some distance between us. I might have even left the three I came to save, maybe. However, with the Lore skill, I could see how much Stamina that his Dodging drained. Dodging while pinned was possible, but consumed Stamina like sand taking water.

I took aim with my bow and fired once more. He Dodged again. His Stamina dropped to a sliver. It was not enough to Dodge again.

"I curse you, Human," cried the goblin. "You are a trickster. You cheated at an honorable duel."

I took aim with my bow and fired. He did not dodge. He was immobile, so the attack qualified as a sneak attack, causing the vicious wound to bleed heavily.

It took the rest of my quiver before I was sure the goblin died. He died screaming obscenities at me, the world, the gods, and the demons. On the final arrow, he was cursing the shadow god himself for his predicament. Then, finally, he quieted.

As I walked over to search the corpse, I slit his throat for good measure. I grabbed his swords and a ring he was wearing. The rest of the stuff was all non-magical, so I left it. Him, I bound up by another leg binding trap for the flies.

"That was a Shadow Goblin," said AvaSophia, who had emerged from hiding when the screaming started.

"Yes." My Lore ability had already confirmed that. Whatever else a Shadow Goblin was, I didn't want anything else to do with them. Then I noticed her children. They were both looking at me in awe. AvaSophia, on the other hand, looked to me, then the corpse, then back to me.

"You just rescued us to lure him out, didn't you?" she said, then, gaining confidence. "You bastard! You rescued us just so he would come out and you could have your little duel!"

"Mama," said the son, "but he won."

She stared at her children, then at me, then finally at the corpse once again. Grabbing her children in a bear hug, only then did she start to weep.

CHAPTER 12

DEEP IN THE WOODS

"WHY IS IT SO IMPORTANT THAT WE BRING THEM ALONG?" I asked Shart quietly, after figuring out that only I could hear the demon. I had eventually forgiven him for allowing me to be snuck up on by the Shadow Goblin. Shart explained that holding a discussion while trying to remain hidden was tricky and, furthermore, there was always the risk of being seen. According to him, some magic spurts could possibly reveal him unexpectedly. He further argued that, had that happened, the sudden appearance of a demon on my shoulder would have done far more harm than good. I didn't agree with any of it, but he's a demon and had his own priorities.

"You need more people in your village," replied Shart. "Also, they will be safe there, but that's mainly a sop for your conscience. I'm really only interested in her ability to power-up the village. She has two kids with her. Those are worth almost as much as an adult."

After the battle, and when I had finally stopped bleeding, I was down to only 27 of 85 hit points. Everything hurt. Not as bad as falling below 22 hit points would have been, as that would have triggered the final quarter of my hit points "Extreme Pain" feature. But it was close.

And I didn't know what to do with the family. As Shart had noted, taking them to the village at least put them in a safe place. Their caravan had been destroyed, she said, and they had been captured. In so far as I could tell, they had no place else to go.

Additionally, since my village had no supplies and AvaSophia and her lovely children liked food, I had to go into the camp and re-purpose the goblin's supplies. As luck would have it, the caravan her family had been traveling with had gotten raided pretty badly, and the goblins had taken several hundred pounds of supplies.

So, if a random stranger had been walking by wondering why I was carrying about 400 pounds worth of "stuff" through the deep woods, that's at least part of the answer.

JoeClarance, the scrappy eleven-year-old boy, was also carrying a bunch of stuff. More than I thought he could, but he wanted to be strong like me. EveSophia, the little girl, was also carrying some lighter objects, but as she was only nine. I had already picked up everything heavy, so she wouldn't have to. AvaSophia, her mother, had been a little bit pickier when she grabbed as much as she could, but she was still carrying a bunch of food, as well as pots, pans, and other sundries.

All I knew was that my package was heavy. I'd love to make a joke about my package, but the crushing weight of my massive package was no joke.

"Are you sure that's not too much?" asked EveSophia again.

"No, darling. It's about what I usually carry when I'm off on a nature walk," I answered. The girl nodded consideringly, like the evil little thing she was, and walked up next to her mother, her lightweight backpack almost floating away in the breeze.

"How did you find the village?" asked AvaSophia. After she had gotten her cry out, which had only taken a few moments, she had moved from emotional wreck to no-nonsense. It was a talent mothers seemed to have; I remembered my own wife doing the same on several occasions. After gathering the supplies, she had been downright eager to go towards my "safe village."

"I was walking in the woods and I found it," I said. She scrutinized my face but didn't have enough of a read on me to determine the accuracy of my words . . . or to see that I had left out several parts which she might figure out later.

She'd only agreed to go with me to my village because she'd heard rumors that there was a safe village that helped new people somewhere out here. However, no one came into this valley anymore, because there were goblins absolutely everywhere. She honestly had no idea whether such a village really existed, or if the rumors were just that. Her options were fairly limited, though. Which explained why she was following a strange man through the woods.

We continued walking and I finally had a moment to examine my gear.

- You have found: Short Sword of Wounding. 7–10 damage, causes Bleed damage.

- You have found: Short Sword of Piercing. 7–10 damage, ignores 4 points of armor.

The ring was more interesting.

- You have found: Ring of Vitality: Lesser. +10 Stamina, +10 Health.

I slid that bad boy on and my pain dropped a notch or two. It got down to the point where I stopped hating every step, at least.

I also had leveled up again. Apparently. The Battle of Trap Field had given my Woodsman skills enough to level before the fight with the Shadow Goblin had even started. However, that was all considered part of the same battle; I'd topped out on experience for that class until I leveled it and started a new fight.

Warrior also leveled due to the damage dealt. It seemed there was a big bonus when the levels were that badly unmatched. Rogue earned me some more, but not enough to level. Unsuccessfully Dodging didn't earn XP, and Dodging isn't a high value Rogue skill anyway. On the other hand, Dodging did earn SP, so my Dodge skill was very nearly at Novice. So, cup half full, right?

- You have leveled up Warrior 3.
  You gain one Perk. +10 Health,
  +10 Stamina.

I went through the Perks menu again. Past Dual Wielding were several weapon skills that seemed to buff damage, attack speed, and the like. I wasn't really having that much of an issue damaging targets, so improving my chance to hit seemed more important.

I frowned and looked over the menu more. The Resistance perk was still there, so I dialed over it.

- Resistance: Provides 8 (5 + level) Defense to all sections of your body. Stacks with Defense granted by armor.

Defense was some approximation of armor, or at least armor granted defense. There were some possibilities there, and it went up with level. I was very aware that my current defenses were anemic, but when I brought up the menu, it was worse than I thought.

Defense:
- Head: 1
- Torso: 2
- Legs: 2
- Arms: 1

You are lightly armored due to (Leather Pants, Leather Shirt) which provide a total of 2 Defense. Your Endurance provides 1 point of Defense. Your total Defense is 3. This increases the cost of your Dodging skill by 25% and increases your Damage Mitigation by 1 point.

Dialing back through my combat log, I discovered that it would have been better for me to fight the goblin naked than with the shoddily made clothes I was wearing. I was going to have to find better armor. While still wondering how much more effective it would be to take a Weapon skill, I selected Resistance.

Instantly, my skin felt tougher, but maybe that was my imagination. I prodded my body, pulling and poking the skin, but it didn't feel any different. Taking one of my daggers and, using my Perception skill to ensure no one was looking, I slid the point down hard against my palm for a one-point wound.

To my pleasant surprise, nothing happened. Well, not nothing; the skin hardened against the knife point to the degree that it only left a thick mark against my flesh. It was akin to scratching dry skin. Aside from that, the mark did no additional damage and my skin became immediately soft and pliable, again. Well, relatively speaking. As soft and pliable as a manly man's skin ever gets.

Glancing at my character sheet, I scrolled over to the defense tab.

Defense:

- **Head: 9**
- **Torso: 10**
- **Legs: 10**
- **Arms: 9**

You are lightly armored due to (Leather Pants, Leather Shirt) which provide a total of 2 Defense. Your Endurance provides 1 point of Defense. Your Resistance provides 8 points of Defense. Your total Defense is now 11. This increases the cost of your Dodging skill by 25% and increases your Damage Mitigation by 3 points.

That was so much better. Hopefully, that meant that every little strike wasn't going to be nearly fatal to me. Not to mention, wounds hurt. I mean, they really hurt, and I didn't like them; anything to reduce that was great.

You have leveled up Woodsman 3.

The Woodsman perks were shorter. There were improved Tracking and Trapping perks, but I wanted to get a feel for how the Lore skill worked before I committed to more of that. I noticed a few Bow skills that were Woodsman only, so I checked out those.

Woodman's Marksman said it gave an improved chance to hit and damage, but that wasn't actually my problem. In game terms, I had problems hitting enemies that were above my level; that had been a major issue in my last fight. Which is when I noticed the Accuracy perk.

I had almost glossed over Accuracy initially but checked it now just to be safe.

Accuracy: Your level is considered doubled when attacking a higher-level target, reducing dodge chance and damage resistance.

The other abilities were nice, but I kept glancing back to Accuracy. If I fought another higher-level creature, I'd like it to not be able to dodge my strikes with ease. I selected it.

"Hey, I wanted to talk to you about something," said Shart, much to my absolute shock, as I continued flipping through menus.

"The hell?" I yelled, but strangely. It sounded like I was shouting in a very empty, very concrete room, complete with slightly faint echoes. "How can you talk to me when I'm like this? I thought this was some kind of private, slowed-down space."

"I can talk to you when you are doing anything and everything," said Shart. "I can't really see what you are doing very well, but I do so enjoy ruining your day."

"If you can talk to me whenever you want, why didn't you help me with the Shadow Goblin?" I growled.

"Because," started Shart as I slowly adjusted to feeling his presence in the back of my mind, "I couldn't. You already knew he was a Shadow Goblin and what the fuck am I supposed to do about that? I'm as tall as I am wide, and not much of either. I also don't have any mana; that's why I bonded you."

"So, you blustered, but you basically couldn't do anything," I observed.

"Nothing useful. All I can do right now is offer you some occasional advice and peek into your mind," replied Shart.

"Good to know that the privacy of my mind is at your beck and call," I said dryly. I tried to look around to see Shart; after a moment, I found him, sort of. He was not as demonic as in the regular world. He seemed more of a glowing orb of absolute darkness, or an orb so dark that it stood out in contrast with his surroundings at the edge of my consciousness.

"Anyway, the broad might mention something about a Dark Overlord." It took me a moment that "the broad" meant AvaSophia. "You should probably be somewhat concerned about that."

"Why?" I asked, flipping quickly through my menu screens, until I got to the Woodsman one.

"Well, he is who we were setting you up to fight," replied the floating globe of evil.

"Good to know," I said, as I stopped really paying attention to my sheet. "What class is he?"

"Godling, of course," replied the demon. "It's the most powerful class. He has a reality warping attack."

"Does he know where I am?" I asked. I wasn't keen on fighting someone like that, even if I had been a much higher level than I currently was. Still, if the Dark Overlord already had a notion of my location, a near future fight might be unavoidable.

"Not yet. But he might start looking eventually, and I think we need to avoid that."

We definitely need to avoid that.

"How?"

"Well, I can't help you right now because I'm totally out of mana."

"You said that already."

"So we are going to fix that."

"Since, if he finds me, he'll kill you too."

"You are a clever monkey," replied the demon.

Breaking out of the menus, I continued walking. Shortly afterwards, a wave of exhaustion hit me, despite my Stamina bar being nearly full. Probably because I was trudging through the woods carrying an insane amount of weight with me. I had tried to carry everything, but I didn't have the Strength stat for it; instead, I'd carried everything just shy of my limit. The problem there was the difference between a video game and real life. In a game, my avatar would have walked on uncaringly. In real life, I was carrying just short of my maximum load and I could taste bile from the strain.

What happened was that after an interval set by this world, you had to rest or your Stamina started to take damage and would begin to deplete. If it went too long, you'd actually strain yourself and it would cause more significant Stamina damage.

My Hiking skill expounded on this, detailing the time it took for my Stamina to become damaged, and then further expanded how long it would take to become exhausted. Stamina damage most typically resulted in your Stamina recovery being slowed. Exhaustion prevented Stamina recovery at all for some period of time, typically hours or days. One did not want to become exhausted.

Having to travel on my Stamina recovery pattern meant that for every 30 minutes of traveling, I needed to spend 1 minute not moving heavy objects. AvaSophia and her kids had it easier as they were not carrying nearly as much as I was and didn't need to slow down to keep up with me. Shart, of course, was having the easiest time of all; I was still carrying him on my shoulder.

I'd keep an eye on it, and rest soon. For now, I kept walking.

"So how did the goblins catch you?" I asked, as we continued marching through the woods.

AvaSophia glanced around again before looking at me, calmly walking, before responding, "We were ambushed. Is that not a concern here?"

"Not here. Nothing hostile is nearby," I said, figuring that Shart would warn me if that wasn't true. My Perception and Lore skills weren't triggering either, though, so I figured the odds of being ambushed at this moment were close to zero.

She watched her children again, both staying very close to me, and then continued, "We were escaping from the Armies of the West."

"Ah, the Dark Overlord," I said, nodding.

"Huh? No, King Harcharles's army. He's trying to take control over the coastal territories, burning villages, and I happened to live in one of those villages," replied AvaSophia.

"Oh," I answered. Well . . . I looked like an idiot. I doubted the demon was wrong though. I'd never seen him wrong, at least, and I knew he hadn't outright lied.

"The Dark Overlord." EveSophia giggled. "Like in the stories!"

"'The hero would come and rescue us and then challenge the Dark Overlord,'" JoeClarance quoted, laughing.

"Children, stop it," chided their mother. "Jim . . . is a good and nice man who helped us when he didn't need to."

"That's like the stories, too." EveSophia smiled. "And I like Jim, even though his name is silly."

"Thanks," I said.

"Don't worry, Jim," said JoeClarance, also smiling. "No one was expecting Grebthar the Destroyer to rush out and save us."

I learned then facepalming was universal.

CHAPTER 13

WHAT'S IN A NAME

"YOU CAN'T CHANGE YOUR NAME," STATED SHART FOR THE fifth time. "You are stuck with 'Jim.'"

We had gotten to a clearing to rest and recover my Stamina a bit more. I was perfecting the trick of shifting to menu time to talk to Shart, so that the others didn't think I was crazy. I'd gone four out of five so far, and they only thought I was a bit crazy, which I could live with. My minute rest would have been up a few minutes ago, but I kept swinging back into menu time to talk to the demon.

"Could I just lie?" I asked.

"How? Your name appears in the tracker," replied the annoyed demon.

"But I *could* lie," I said.

"And when they looked in their experience tracker, they'll notice they got conversation experience with 'Jim.' It won't be hard to figure out who that is."

"Fine! Explain how to make you less useless, then."

"Further, you were the one who chose—" started Shart, before finally realizing that the argument had finally moved past my name. "Oh, just focus on me and give me your mana."

"That's it?"

"Why would it be more complicated than that?"

"Why didn't you ask me for mana earlier?" I yelled into the vast open emptiness of my mind.

"You wouldn't have given it to me," replied Shart. "Before the battle with the Shadow Goblin, you'd have thought you didn't need my help. Now you know you do, so you will."

With no answer to that, I reverted back to regular time and tried to focus on the demon. Just as my concentration clicked, someone tugged my arm.

"Shouldn't we get going now?" asked JoeClarance.

So, I walked, trying to focus on the demon as well as not falling down. I assumed sharing mana would be easier if I was able to concentrate, but the universe liked to throw me curveballs. After a few minutes I finally felt something click between the two of us, but instantly lost it when I saw what I was connecting to. The demon was revolting!

Moving back into menu time, I growled. "What the hell, man? Your spiritual form, or whatever, is disgusting."

"Oh yeah? Well, then find the bond cord and power that instead. Just don't take any back and it should work."

On we walked, and I focused on the bond string—or more apt, finding the bond whisker. It took longer than I'd like to admit. We had time for a whole one-minute break before continuing. Finally, I found the string and managed to grab it with my mystical "hand."

Then came the second part, which would be even trickier, as I had no idea how to transfer mana. I started to relax, which was problematic while walking, and nearly lost control over my bladder. Eventually, I recognized a different sensation. It felt quite a bit like needing to use the bathroom, but higher in my body. I worked that part of my mind for a moment and then felt the tiniest trickle of mana escape me.

Slowly, the rest of my mana pool flowed out like a drunk relieving himself after a night of debauchery.

I'd suffered another Mana Crash after dumping my entire Mana Pool into the demon. In many video games, that doesn't mean very much; you just get your magic back later. Here, it was the functional equivalent of working so hard you exhausted yourself mentally.

Seriously, I could not concentrate in any capacity. I could not think, I could not form words, and walking became impossibly complex all of a sudden. I tried to methodically move forward, but I couldn't even bring up the emotional will to do that. After a few stumbling paces, I just stopped.

As I was leading this little procession, that did not turn out well. The little girl bumped into me and fell over. The boy drew his dagger, as did his mother, and they all searched the forest for threats. I stood there unmoving for about eight seconds, until I finally regained my first point of mana. Then, I just had a terrible headache . . .

Which is when I fell down, the heavy pack landing on me and knocking the wind from my lungs. It took me and AvaSophia quite a while to get it off because I couldn't catch my breath or get into a position to move it myself. By this time, my mana pool had jumped over the proverbial quarter of my points and my mind was working again. However, I also now had a Mana Crash status effect, which translated into said horrible migraine. Imagine someone having a drill and shoving it into your temple, only to meet a second drill that has already been shoved into your other side, and where they meet stews your brains together.

Flipping to my character sheet, I saw that I had *eighteen hours* of Mana Crash.

A whole day!

The pain did not abate in the slightest while in my character sheet—if anything, looking at it made my eyes hurt—so I closed it. Gritting my teeth, I stood up and continued walking, utterly ignoring not only questions coming from AvaSophia and her children, but also the disappearance of a demon shaped weight on my shoulder.

It was a rough few hours back to the village.

CHAPTER 14

RETURN TO THE VILLAGE

I HADN'T EXPLAINED THE SUDDEN CHANGE IN MY MOOD. AvaSophia whispered to her children that I must have been more injured in the battle than I had let on. We continued marching towards the village. After another three hours, twenty-eight minutes, and thirty-six seconds, we finally reached the edge of the woods and could see the village.

"Your town has a wall," she stated, wide-eyed. From our higher vantage point, you could look down onto the large plain that the village sat upon. Well behind it, the ocean lapped at the beach, though the state of the dock told me no one had tried coming ashore there in many years. There were even a number of taller buildings that were just intact enough that the place actually looked respectable from this angle. In fact, we actually had walls, technically. From this side, the walls even looked mostly intact. There were massive breaches in them, however, from whatever had initially laid the village low.

I scanned the horizon for the goblin riders and didn't see them. There was over a mile between where we were at the edge of the forest and the outskirts of the barrier. Further still, to get into the village proper. If we had a good path and the goblins weren't expecting us, then just maybe we could get across without too much trouble.

I moved to menu time, seeing the outside world slow.

"Shart, where are those goblins?"

"I'm looking. Hold your horses," replied the demon from a spot that was not my shoulder. He seemed a bit put out with me still, for allowing him to be knocked from his perch and left behind when I fell. Fuck him. He had mana now; at least enough that he could fly normally. Which reminded me . . .

"How are you spell-casting with so little mana?" I asked. I had given him all my mana, but to him that was just a drop in the bucket. His mana pool, I could tell, was over 800.

"Oh, it's a Demon Racial Ability. We don't suffer Mana Crashes, but we also don't regenerate mana normally," said the demon off-handedly, while he continued doing his mental gymnastics.

"How can you use your spells in menu time?" I asked. That ability would be really handy.

"What?" asked Shart, as he considered what I'd said. "Oh, this is my regular time scale. Your menu time is my normal."

"It takes forever for anything to happen in menu time, though. This journey would have felt like it took years."

The demon was silent for a moment. Then, "No, just about a month."

Oh crap, and that was just coming back. I'd wondered why the demon's attention seemed to be flaky at times. There was the answer. He must have some sort of trick to keep his mind occupied. Then again, he had almost no mana and was slowly regenerating wounds. The wounds always hurt. That meant he'd been in agonizing pain for months, effectively because he'd saved me.

Well, maybe I *could* help him open his Demon Door . . . if he didn't screw me when it was over.

"I see them," growled Shart. "They are running a patrol around the village. If you move now, you should be able to reach the barrier before they see you."

Returning to real time, I gestured to AvaSophia as a familiar weight landed back on my shoulder. "We need to get to the village quickly. There are more goblins, but they cannot come into town."

Both children quivered. JoeClarance recovered more quickly and held his dagger. AvaSophia looked at me. "Are you certain you can deal with them if they get close?"

"I have my bow," I responded. "And my injuries will not stop me from killing goblins."

She nodded, and we all began to move briskly towards the barrier. I couldn't run with the supplies and no one seemed to want to get too far away from me. For six long minutes, everything seemed to be going well, until JoeClarance suddenly fell, screaming.

I pivoted around, nearly falling due to my burden. The boy had fallen into the grass, but the way he had done so looked wrong instantly. His mother got to him before I did, so I cast about looking for the goblins. The pack that we were avoiding was still a good distance away and, even with my heightened senses, I couldn't make out enough detail to know if they'd changed paths.

As I turned back to AvaSophia, who had already gotten Joe-Clarance back on his feet, I saw a second group of goblins. They were much closer than the first group and also wolf mounted. There were five of the larger goblins, and a sixth who was carrying some sort of staff.

"There are more goblins," I called out, mostly an accusation at the demon.

"Don't worry, I think I see the problem!" replied Shart. "Yup, they had an anti-scrying spell up, so I didn't see them." Very handy to know as they were bearing down on us.

I also learned that Lore had a range, and they were not inside it. I could tell that the wolves had lots of hit points and very little mana. I could also see that the Warriors had similar, but not identical, hit points and Stamina to the previous ones I fought. Also, the one that looked like a spell caster had quite a bit more mana than the rest of them. But that was it; no additional information, like levels or how potent the caster was. I might have been able to take all five fighters, but the caster was a wild card and I had too many people to defend around me.

The protective barrier was painfully close.

"Run!" I called out, waiting to see if everyone responded. I was still faster than them, even carrying this much weight.

EveSophia screamed and started running, but straight from the wolves instead of straight towards the town. I snatched her from behind, holding her like a football. JoeClarance looked miserable as he hobbled forwards, but he clearly couldn't run. He had fallen into a mole hole of all things and wrenched his ankle badly. He was much larger than his sister, but I still managed to pick him up, too.

A small icon saying I was overburdened appeared in the corner of my vision.

Gee, ya think?

We tore off towards the barrier, AvaSophia staying close to me and her children. The wolves were behind and to the left of us but were closing distance quickly. The barrier was temptingly close, a small creek almost perfectly marking its edge. It was going to be a race, a battle of endurance. They might have massive wolves and goblin magic, but I had Mobility and Hiking.

I was counting on Hiking to save my life.

We had been jogging to conserve energy. Now, we spent it like wastrels. I watched as AvaSophia's Stamina bar started dropping. With my heightened senses, I could tell where the wolves' heavy footfalls were behind us. We might just make it, so long as AvaSophia could keep up her desperate running for a bit longer.

An arrow flew past me, and then another. I felt a third strike my pack. Then, came a fourth. The goblins were firing from wolf back and had decided to hit the larger target, which happened to mainly be my pack of supplies. Suddenly, I felt a sharp pain and realized that they'd hit the back of my leg. I didn't have any Stamina to mitigate the damage but, glancing at the log, I was relieved to find that arrow had only done 2 points of damage. That was barely a scratch.

We continued flying down the path. AvaSophia's Stamina dropped lower and lower, as the creek got closer and closer. I moved behind her as more arrows were fired, bringing both children to my chest. This made the already awkward running I was doing even more awkward, considering the supplies on my back. We ran down a slope and a wolf broke out in front of the pack. All we had to do was get to the top of the next ridge and the creek would be right there . . .

AvaSophia abruptly spun around, holding a dagger. I couldn't see her eyes, but I understood her stance. She had become a mother bear, trying to protect her young from the wolves. Standing tall despite terrible odds in an attempt to give her children just a bit more of a chance.

I just wasn't having any of it. I stuck out my arm and grabbed her too, moving myself from overburdened to severely overburdened. My Stamina bar dropped below 25% and running was so much harder; I now had a headache to slay the gods added to the mix. The wolf was so close, I could feel its breath on my back.

Then, mercifully, we were over the ridge. I tumbled with the family, splashing into the water. The supplies flew everywhere as the wolf lunged at me. Lunged and promptly caught fire, from everywhere. I'd seen what the barrier did at range, and I'd seen the aftermath up close, but that was after everyone was already dead. Now I was able to experience it up close, and it was every bit as terrible as one could imagine.

The wolf had been running at full tilt when, quite suddenly, he was engulfed. Not just on fire, because not a patch of his fur was burning. From the inside of his mouth to his eyeballs, he was shooting out hot blue flames that were uncomfortable to me at a few paces away. From snout to tail, he was consumed, with all thoughts of anything other than not being on fire gone from his mind. The wolf bucked his rider, who was also similarly afire. The goblin sailed through the air like a burning comet and landed with an audible screaming crack. The wolf dove into the creek; however, it was a magical fire. Water does not extinguish magical fires. The thrashing wolf was quickly surrounded by blue flame *and* boiling water.

The barrier caused 20 points of damage to Stamina, Mana, and hit points per six seconds due to an effect my Lore skill described as

Barrier Burn. The wolves had less than eighteen seconds of hit points, and goblins only had twelve seconds of hit points.

"What happened?" screamed AvaSophia, as the wolf thrashed in the water.

"The barrier," I gasped out.

"That was real?" she half-screamed. "I thought you just made it up. No village has a barrier anymore."

"Well, mine does," I replied, looking around. "We have company."

My Stamina was almost, but not quite, gone. Unfortunately, being seriously overburdened had done a fair amount of Stamina damage, so it was recovering very slowly. I had just gotten to my feet when the rest of the goblin party came to a stop at the other side of the barrier.

The magical goblin looked even worse up close. The regular goblins were like ugly, green middle grade childen, with drunkard noses and few sharp teeth. This one was more angular, clearer eyed, and had tattoos everywhere. Oddly enough, he was white, or at least I thought so for a moment. Upon closer inspection, it looked like he was wearing some form of war paint that was caked on rather heavily.

My Lore skill activated when I examined him.

- Gerk'Tik'Alk
- Goblin Shaman Level 5

- Obscurification spell active: Lore cannot determine any further information.

Goblin Shaman are the religious centers of any goblin community and, given that they don't typically have communities, many live as hermits in the woods. Goblins have a great deal of clan colors. This one appears to be from the Ghost Path sect of goblins, known for their spiritual magic such as Obscurification spells.

"You seem to enjoy hassling travelers," I stated coolly, as I plopped down onto a large rock at the edge of the creek, just inside the barrier.

"We will kill anyone who trespasses in the Shadow Lands," called out the shaman. "I do not know how you reactivated the town's barrier, but I will break it down and slay you."

"You are welcome to try," I said, turning towards the town. I heard an audible crack behind me. One of the goblins bellowed as his weapon flew away, now nothing more than a flaming hunk of smoldering metal.

"Gerk'Tik'Alk will not be ignored!" cried the shaman as he pointed towards the barrier and a blast of ice shot from his staff towards AvaSophia. She jumped down too late, but the blast had already deflected off the barrier.

I turned to face her. "He's not nearly powerful enough to hurt the barrier."

"You dare ignore Gerk'Tik'Alk?" he screamed, though in truth it was so high pitched by this point it was hard to make out. "I will eat your eyes!" He began waving his hands high over his head, gathering up a much larger orb of magic. It took him nearly twenty seconds before he was ready and the orb flashed down quite impressively.

The orb hit the outside of the barrier in a manner that I would describe as "soft boiled eggs hitting a windshield." His mana bar was greatly depleted, but the barrier was not. He started cursing under his breath. I signaled to the group that it was well past time to get going, so we recollected our supplies. Mine had gone everywhere and were drenched. I started gathering it all up while the goblin got himself back under control.

"What is your name, human?" called Gerk'Tik'Alk. "I would know who I kill."

"I am Jim."

The goblins all paused, then looked between each other. Finally the shaman said, "Just 'Jim'? Did your mother know you were a foolish dog from birth, so she didn't waste words on you?"

That was getting old.

I managed to get my pack properly piled so that it could be placed upon my back again. The goblins stood there glowering for a few more moments before two of their number started walking away and the remaining warriors looked to follow. Gerk'Tik'Alk stared daggers at me for another moment before he, too, finally started to follow his companions.

That had been a close one, I thought. Had it gone another way, it might have ended badly. I reached down to start lifting my pack when I heard the audible smack of a wet rock against the back of someone's head. JoeClarance had a good arm; the throw had caused one point of damage with an improvised weapon.

Which, of course, negated the barrier.

I could tell not only from the blue light fading, but also because I got a convenient popup informing me that the barrier had failed and that it wouldn't be restored for just under five minutes. That was assuming that no more attacks were forthcoming from inside the failed barrier. I hissed a quick warning to the former hostage family about any further attacks to the goblins.

I was very proud to restrain myself from making either child cry with my words.

Gerk'Tik'Alk twisted around on his wolf, snarling at me. "Gerk'Tik'Alk will not take such insolence! Your deaths will come as soon as your accursed barrier is . . ." He trailed off, finally truly looking. There was a slightly visible difference in the barrier now; I could tell due to my Perception skill, which I had ardently hoped he might not have.

"The barrier is down!" called Gerk'Tik'Alk, and his warriors returned to him, suddenly interested. Just not quite so interested as to check it themselves, as they glanced at the scorched ruins of what had been an expensive weapon or the smoldering carcass of their former companion. Several went up to the edge of where the barrier had been a moment before and paused.

"It's totally down. Just one more step," I called out, sitting down on my pack and obviously preparing for defense. Well, trying to obviously be not obvious, as I got my daggers ready. I wanted them to think that this was all part of some stupid plan to get them to cross the barrier.

The goblin warriors noticed and several backed off a pace. Gerk'Tik'Alk glowered and walked right towards the barrier. "You fools! Don't you see? If he attacks from the barrier, the barrier will not protect him."

"Sure. I certainly attacked him while your backs were all turned. Make sure you attack me when you cross the barrier, otherwise you'll catch fire," I said, glancing over at the burnt ruin of their former team member.

"That was a river rock, one of those three threw it," called one of the other riders. "He's still protected."

"That's not how barriers work," growled Gerk'Tik'Alk. "He's bluffing."

I stood up and walked right over to the edge of the barrier. Three of the goblin warriors stepped back, only leaving the shaman and one warrior. Stage-whispering conspiratorially, I said, "They know you are almost out of mana and you can't know about the barrier for certain. How about this? I'll let you tap me with that staff of yours . . . if you aren't afraid to lose it when the barrier incinerates it."

The goblin warrior twitched, looking at me and then Gerk'Tik'Alk. He seemed to be edging towards the wrong conclusion, so I said quietly, "You must really trust the shaman?" He looked at me and the shaman again. He thought for a moment before deciding. Snorting, he walked back to be with his clansmen.

"What's it going to be?" I asked Gerk'Tik'Alk, looking at him evenly, as his enormous wolf growled at me. I spared a moment to truly look at the wolf and realized that wasn't actually what the creature was. It was a much larger beast and its eyes showed an intelligence far greater than a wolf should have. As it seemed to be disinclined to attack me, I pushed it from my mind.

"Gerk'Tik'Alk knows . . . I know you are bluffing," muttered the shaman, collecting himself. "I know that this barrier is down and I have full confidence in my own conclusions." He walked his wolf, who carefully avoided the spot where the barrier had been, sidelong towards me. He was facing me with his right arm pointed fully at me.

This was the easiest position to tap me with the staff, but still leave his wolf a path of retreat if the barrier was intact.

That was just what I had been hoping he would do. As the shaman moved to touch me, I launched myself at him. I propelled myself over him in an acrobatic leap, a front somersault that would end up with my feet against the wolf's back. As I launched, I drew my dagger with my left hand and jammed it into my opponent's eye. With my right, I grabbed his staff. As my feet hit the back of the wolf, I used it to propel myself backward. Rotating in the air, I landed where I started inside the barrier. The body of the shaman fell backwards off his now-fleeing mount.

"Anyone else want to test the barrier?" I called out, as I flicked the blood and brains of their former leader off my dagger.

It turned out that the other goblins didn't. I sat watching them for five whole minutes as they rapidly fled the area. My head throbbed like a particularly obnoxious Christian death metal beat. I was exhausted, but afraid to show a moment of weakness. Finally, the countdown faded and the barrier resumed its former shade of protective blue.

The headache was so bad, afterwards I threw up. I mean I held it in until the goblins had gotten out of sight, but then, I threw up properly.

I don't recall eating carrots.

After I had recovered sufficiently and rinsed my mouth out with the cooling water of the creek, it was time to loot the bodies. Well, body. I was pretty certain I wouldn't recover anything from the wretched, smoldering remains of the first one. I went over to the goblin shaman and searched his corpse. He had an amulet and a pouch full of crystals, wadded up in some paper. Adding those to the staff I already had in hand, it seemed like a good haul.

Next, I picked up my pack and started walking over a ford in the creek back to my village. I tried not to glare when I passed Joe-Clarance, but it was so damn hard. It hadn't been his fault, but he'd almost gotten all of us killed. I stomped back towards the town, still with a throbbing head making me slightly dizzy. AvaSophia and her family followed me wordlessly. As the barrier was almost exactly a mile from the town center, it would be a while before I could stop and rest properly.

I walked straight into the least destroyed house that was serving as my campsite and found where I'd been keeping my bedroll. I promptly collapsed into it, wishing for sleep or death. Either was fine. The cloud of flatulence that followed me everywhere was able to keep up using his increasingly functional wings. He landed nearby, still invisible to all but me.

Good shit, I hope he isn't expecting a cuddle.

When AvaSophia came in a few minutes later to check on me, I sent her away with orders to leave me alone until tomorrow, unless there was food. I groggily recalled briefly stirring awake to a plate of beans with bits of unidentifiable meat some time later, though I could not distinctly remember eating.

I slept until the next day.

CHAPTER 15

A WEIRD VILLAGE LIFE

SLEEPING IN A TOWN HAS A NUMBER OF BENEFITS OVER sleeping in the wild. You gain double hit points back; certain injuries recover at improved rates, like Stamina Crashes and Mana Crashes. When I woke up, I felt great. I was no longer dizzy or exhausted. I also didn't have a headache to wake the dead.

I yawned loudly and stepped out into my village. The village square was a largish field that was chock-full of weeds and some decent-sized trees. It was clear you could probably have played football in it, with only a slight change of rules. The few respectable-sized trees had grown up since the town had been abandoned. There appeared to be a fountain in the center, if one looked past all of the weeds and things.

My house was right off the square. I was fairly confident that my house was an old shop of some sort, but I didn't really spend too much time thinking about that. Next to my home were a few of the crafters' shops. There was a blacksmith, with all the equipment mostly rusted, the bowyer, complete with a grotesquely posed goblin corpse that had started to rot, and several more mundane buildings. The actual town hall was nearby, on the square. The church stood on the opposite side. Neither were in good enough repair that I'd wanted to camp in them overnight, as the portions with roofs were limited.

That was actually the main issue with most of the town, honestly.

It was in pretty dire straits and, barring tearing it down and rebuilding it from scratch, I didn't see how this whole place could be salvaged. The only thing the town had going for it was the magical barrier, which I had gleaned from AvaSophia's surprise was rare for a town these days.

Also, I didn't see any other people. The statue dude was probably still in the church, but where were the town's three newest residents? I was about to start searching the town, figuring that the two small children would be easy enough to hear, but then I remembered the town map. Bringing it up, I found the small family had taken up a house that was on the outer edge of the town, near the meandering creek. There was some clear land, or at least land that could be cleared of weeds and debris, nearby.

As per usual, I had several prompts. The first was the simple exclamation mark that told of a quest.

> **Quest: Defeat the Goblin Menace 1: You live in a land of danger; your town is surrounded by goblins. Slay the goblin champions, their captain, and their chieftain, so your town can be saved. You will gain a reward each time one of the goblin heroes is slain.**

> **You have slain: Gerk'Tik'Alk, Goblin Shaman. The enemy tribe are now leaderless and many will desert. You gain a 500 experience points bonus.**

So, the more goblin "heroes" I killed, the easier it would get outside town. That sounded promising.

Another prompt glowed at the bottom of my vision that looked a bit like a Silver Town icon.

> **AvaSophia has requested ownership of "Creek House" and the surrounding fields. Will you grant this request?**

I selected "Yes," of course, and noticed that the population of the town jumped by three in the menu. They had been listed as guests before, and their icons changed from blue to green on the map.

As I walked down the lane, Main Street I supposed, I didn't hear the sounds of children playing. Instead, AvaSophia was standing in front of the house she had claimed, with both her children behind her. JoeClarance was trying to look brave and EveSophia's face was buried in her mother's skirts. All three were staring at me. I checked behind me just to make sure there wasn't a goblin or something sneaking up on us.

"That's far enough," she called out as I started walking up the short path to her new home. I raised an eyebrow. She watched me carefully for a moment. "What are your intentions?"

I considered replying "breakfast" but answering that flippantly with my wife always had about a 50/50 chance of making the situation much worse, so I took a moment to collect myself. I chose to respond to her question with one of my own. "What are you expecting from me?"

With that, JoeClarance broke free of his mother's grasp and moved several yards off the porch. He held his dagger in his fist, as it was a confidence-granting talisman, before yelling, "I'm sorry about attacking the goblins. I know it broke the barrier and we could have died; I'll accept any punishment, but don't hurt my family."

Oh, that was it.

From their perspective, I'd gotten very surly for most of the trip for no apparent reason. Then, I had to repeatedly save their necks when worse came to worst. AvaSophia had thought I was lying about the town; she hadn't believed the barrier even existed. She'd turned around just before it, thinking I was lying and they were all going to die. Up until this point, I assumed she was following me because she had no better option. Now, it dawned on me that she was following me with her family—when she didn't trust me—because she was scared of refusing me.

She'd been ready to fight off the goblins to buy her children a few more moments, fully thinking it was a desperate last stand. They probably had only stayed because they knew the village was safe, but did they think I was? Standing before me, it seemed obviously not. I wondered if me stirring when she brought me food was the only reason she hadn't slit my throat last night. Looking into her eyes, I became quite sure that, if I'd been totally unconscious, she'd have done it to protect her children.

Hard woman.

"Well, no harm, little one," I said carefully. "You didn't know any better and you did what you thought you had to do. I was there to protect you and I'll always do my best to keep you safe."

He seemed to deflate. "Really?"

"Yes. We Mayors need strong, healthy citizens in our decrepit ruined towns." I smiled as he started to sniffle. All the courage he'd gathered poured out of him now that the need was gone. He had believed me when I initially told him about the town, and he believed me now. Apparently, I was able to convince children easily. Adults, on the other hand . . .

Mental note: Bump Charisma stat.

A Note has been generated to "Bump Charisma Stat."

Oh, more notes. This place is weird.

"So, have you made breakfast?" I asked, and AvaSophia nodded stiffly, then invited me onto her property.

After a breakfast of beans and what I prayed was the equivalent of pork, AvaSophia walked me around her home. The glass was all gone from the windows and several were shuttered, though the shutters themselves had gaps and holes. The second story was actually still usable. The roof was in pretty good condition with no apparent leaks, despite the passage of time. The house was essentially a slightly modified A-frame with a few rooms cut into it. A porch completely wound around from front to back.

"Thank you for giving me the house," she said, after we completed the tour of "the fields."

"Well, I'm happy to have helped," I said. "Do you have the proper tools to work the fields?"

She shrugged. "Mostly. We are missing a plow horse, which is going to make plowing the fields difficult, but with enough effort we will manage."

You have been offered a quest: Find a
Draft Animal for <AvaSophia>.

I selected "Yes," of course.

I left the family and walked to the center of town again. Ava-Sophia had some supplies and some seed. Fortunately, she had her Farming skill up to a high enough degree that she could technically get the plowing done. Eventually. According to the Farming tab in the town's menu, year round planting and fertile soil had earned the town an excellent rating in agriculture.

Apparently planting certain crops at certain times was better for the crops and soil. Who knew?

Farmers, probably, of which I am not.

With that out of the way I tried to figure out what the rest of my day looked like. I had several items to analyze and I was tossing around the idea of making myself some proper armor. I wondered if there was any kind of draft animal that could be used for farming. I considered my options for protecting the town. There was quite a bit on my mind. I also briefly wondered where my little demon atrocity was, but decided quickly that I didn't care enough to locate him.

Bringing up the quest menu, I noticed that there was a mental tug towards something north of town, where we'd entered. It was reasonably strong, so it must be close. I walked back to my shop-turned-campsite, and gathered up my belongings, including the magical staff and amulet.

Staff of Frost: 3–12 Frost Damage.
Requires Mana. Charge 2/10.

I held the staff in one hand, then both, trying to use it. Shaking it didn't work, neither did yelling at it. Finally, I just held it and concentrated, focusing on the staff like I'd focused on the demonic bond. Feeling that tenuous connection, I carefully tried to give it just a bit of mana.

It sucked away 8 of my 20 mana and I recoiled as if someone had thrown a bucket of water into my face. I waited for the headache to start, but after a few seconds, I felt the sensation of my mana topping off and I realized that I'd done this task properly, at least. That was something. It still felt like pouring myself into an invisible container, but at least I didn't end up on my knees this time.

Once again, I had to focus on the staff like I did with the bond. Then, it was just point and think about blasting stuff. An icicle the size of a finger formed and blasted forwards into a nearby tree. The ice shattered on the trunk, but not before knocking out a pretty large divot in the wood.

Checking, the charge had dropped by one. Made sense: I got ten shots with it before having to recharge. I took aim at something farther away and fired again. It hit, but did much less damage. It seemed that distance reduced the damage of spells, or at least this spell.

Unfortunately, the staff was a goblin staff. That meant it was just slightly longer than a baseball bat, but only about as thick as a broomstick. Covering the staff from top to bottom were black runes; I had never seen anything like them before; I had no chance at being able to read them. To finish off the garish item, it was adorned by several electric rodent skulls, limiting where one could grab it. It was too short for a walking stick and too contorted for a cane. Also, despite being baseball bat–sized, the staff didn't look sturdy enough to be used as a melee weapon. The cherry on top was that it just looked evil and ugly.

I focused and fired out spells as quickly as I could into the trees at the center of town. The results were not terrible, but they weren't great, either. I could only fire once about every three seconds, which was about the same speed as my bow. Worse, my bow seemed to do more damage, probably because my Archery skill had advanced. If I kept firing, maybe my Staff skill would increase and I could fire this faster or more powerfully. For the moment, the goblin's staff was a poor second-choice weapon. Setting it aside, I vowed to figure out what to do with it later.

Checking my prompts, I saw I had a bunch of skill notifications, but I wanted to look at the amulet first.

Amulet: Properties unknown.

I'd played too many RPGs to just put on an unidentified amulet. It felt warm when I ran my fingers over it. As I held my fingers on it, I recognized that it wasn't true warmth, but a magical power contained in the amulet.

Now, I might actually need some help or, at the very least, some information. Who did I know that understood curses and magic in this realm? I mean, yeah, I knew Shart . . . and to my utter chagrin, that was all. I didn't really believe AvaSophia or the kids would be any help. Shart would have to do. I didn't know where he was, though. I wondered if there was a way to use the bond between us to contact him.

"Help me, Shart. You're my only hope," I called. To my complete surprise, he appeared in my field of vision rather quickly, flying from somewhere behind me.

"You called?" Shart drolled. He seemed cranky and I wondered what I had pulled him from. I was too curious about the amulet to tease him about being at my beck and call. I did find it amusing, though, until I considered the possibility that it might be a two-way street. Then it turned slightly horrifying.

"Shart," I asked, "can you identify a magical item?"

"Identify an item? It's a freaking amulet," replied the ever helpful demon.

"No, I mean analyze its magical properties?"

"Analyze? It's not a plant," he said. "Oh . . . you mean Scan. Yes, I can Scan items. I forget you don't know what you're talking about most of the time."

Calm.

"Can you Scan this for me?" I asked, holding up the amulet.

"No. I have five mana left and that's not enough to Scan anything," he said testily.

"I gave you ten yesterday," I responded, "and you had at least one before that."

"I had three and I used all three, plus five of the mana you gave me, to search for bad guys so you weren't killed," he growled.

"We were *ambushed* right outside the town," I growled right back.

"They were magically concealed. You gave me only a trickle of mana and I couldn't do very much. If I'd had more, I'd have been able to help you more."

"Fine, I'll give you more."

"Woah," Shart said as I started to focus. "You suck at this. Try to only give me a little mana this time."

"I thought you wanted more mana," I replied, frustrated.

"Yes, but if you give it to me all at once, you get a headache. Then, I can't get what I want from you anymore. I have needs and if you keep getting headaches, I can't get fulfilled."

I stared at him blankly for a second. "Fine, I'll focus on giving you only a little mana this time and we'll see how that goes."

Calming myself and feeling around mystically until I'd grabbed the bond, I carefully pressed on it as lightly as I could. After a few seconds, I felt a single spurt of mana flow away. I immediately cut the contact. My mana meter dropped by 2, but half of that was lost to the bond. All that effort had only granted Shart one point of mana.

"How much do you need to Scan the item?" I asked.

"Looks like that's a pretty rare item, so I would say fifty."

Giving Shart that much mana took over an hour of careful poking and prodding at the bond. After the tenth time, it got easier; I was able to hand off more mana at once then. First, five points. Then, ten. Finally, at the very end, I could feel the link much more solidly. I was able to hold on to my own mana better. That let me hand off mana right up to the point where I'd fall below the 25% margin. I'd describe it as the slightest raised mark on a page and I could just feel it if I tried really hard.

Mechanically, each time I used the skill, I got better at it. What had originally been nearly a 100% failure rate eventually dwindled to about a 60% failure chance after ten tries. Further, if I went slowly, it was easier to find the "grooves" in my mana pool to stop at. By the time I had done it twenty times, the failure chance had dwindled to 20% and there was a 5% chance of a better result.

What that equated to after those twenty tries was that I had a 20% chance to fail. That cost me mana but gave no benefit. I had a 75% chance to get an unskilled result, which gave Shart 7 points of mana and cost me 14 mana. Then, I had a 5% chance to get an Amateur result, which gave Shart 10 points of mana and only cost me 15 mana. When the skill actually activated, you could feel it working and tell how much mana to dump into it. The problem was that failures seemed to eat up about 10 mana each time, despite my efforts to the contrary.

All this I determined after the fact. I initially had not intended to spend as much time on giving myself a headache, but Shart had other ideas.

"Fifty mana," I said, proud of myself, about an hour after noon.

"Now fifty more," demanded the demon. "I'm not running myself down to 5 again just so you can see what your trinket does."

I glared at him from my sitting position. "That wasn't part of the deal."

"There was no deal. You asked if I could do something for you. I can, but I'm not doing it for free. The deal is you give me one-hundred mana and I cast Scan for you."

Sighing, I agreed, I didn't have any leverage over the demon right now. Furthermore, Shart having extra mana might improve my odds of survival. He was going to kill me after I got the Demon Door open, not before.

The whole process took hours, primarily because it took around three minutes to get my mana pool back to full after each donation and the process to donate wasn't instantaneous. It also required a bunch of concentration. I basically spent four hours trying to focus my mind enough to pour my magical essence into an ungrateful demon.

I spent quite a few breaks here and there, reviewing my character sheet.

Combat Skills:

- Unarmored Defense: Amateur: You are skilled in fighting unarmored— clothing and robes are considered unarmored.
- Light Armor: Novice: <Rank Up> You are more skilled when wearing light armor. You can dodge as if unarmored.
- Medium Armor: Amateur: You are skilled at wearing medium armor without penalty.
- Dodge: <Rank Up> Amateur: You are skilled at Dodging. You suffer smaller penalties when dodging attacks from higher level creatures.
- Mitigate: <Rank Up> Novice: You can Mitigate Damage from an attack, up to 4 Damage modified by defense, at the cost of 2 points per Damage so Mitigated.
- Parry: <Rank Up> Amateur: You can Parry with weapons. Each weapon is better or worse at Parrying. Parrying costs Stamina.
- Shields: Amateur: You can defend yourself with shields.
- Martial Weapons: Amateur: You can use any martial weapons you find.
- Swords: Amateur: You know which end of a sword to point at an enemy.
- Bows: Novice: You know how to target an enemy's vital spots. Focused aiming will bring up an aiming guide.
- Simple Weapons: Amateur: You are a violent person at heart. You get a bonus to hit with all simple weapons.
- Staff: Amateur.

- Powerful Blow: You can utilize a powerful blow, expending 4 Stamina for 4 extra Damage.
- Small Blades: <Rank Up> Novice: You are skilled with the many uses of a small blade. You gain extra damage when making a Surprise Attack.
- Puncture: Rank 2: Your attacks ignore 6 points of Defense, doubled during a sneak attack.
- Rupture: Rank 2: Your attacks cause bleed, based on attack damage, 50% additional bleed over 6 seconds.
- Wounding: <Rank Up> Rank 0: Your attacks can wound a target causing a Stamina wound: base damage equal to weapon damage. Effect lasts for 30 seconds.

- Two Weapon Fighting: Novice: You gain +2 points of Damage on your primary weapon.
- Twin Weapon: Amateur: You gain +2 points of Damage when fighting with the same weapon type.
- Hiking: <Rank Up> Novice: You travel farther and suffer less Stamina loss from long travel. Your overburden penalty is reduced.
- Jumping: Unskilled: You know how to jump and put some force behind it. Practice makes perfect.
- Stealth: Novice: You are quite sneaky. When holding still in shadows you become almost invisible.

Non-Combat Skills:

- Skinning: Amateur: You can skin and prepare animal hide.
- Cooking: Unskilled: You can cook and prepare simple dishes without burning them.
- Perception: Amateur: You are far more aware of the world around you.
- Crafting: Amateur: You have basic crafting ability.
- Leatherworking: Unskilled: You can make very simple leather goods.

- Woodworking: Unskilled: You can make very simple wooden goods.
- Bowyer: <Rank Up> Amateur: You can make simple bows. Weapons you craft do additional damage.
- Improvised Tools: Amateur: You can improvise to build almost anything. Items created from Improvised tools will have a Durability penalty.
- Improved Lore: Amateur: You are granted the ability to see

Health, Stamina, and Mana bars on all non-obfuscated creatures. You gain a bonus to all Lore checks.

- Demon Lore: Amateur: You know more about demons and their race.
- Goblin Lore: <Rank Up> Amateur: You are knowledgeable about the goblin race.
- Animal Lore: <Rank Up> Amateur: You are a skilled hunter, who knows much about the animals of the natural world.

Magical Skills:

- Infuse: Amateur: You can grant mana to willing targets. For every 2 mana spent, they will recover one mana.
- Empowerment: <Rank Up> Unskilled: You know the enchanting Empowerment skill. You can infuse mana into magical items. Every time you do this, there is a chance that the charge is permanently reduced by 1.
- Mana Control: Unskilled: You have learned the basics of manipulating your mana pool. You can attempt to resist with Stamina any efforts to over drain your mana.
- Magical Blast: <Rank Up> Unskilled: You have handled a magical implement and can use it to cast prepared spells at a target.

Well, that was a lot. Several things interested me.

The rank ups in Goblin and Animal Lore were nice. Animal Lore was at 88/100 SP for another rank up. I was due to go into Novice soon, which would tell me what Novice meant for all the other Lore skills as well. I moderately disliked having to look into the individual skills to see their total skill points, but there were just so many numbers otherwise.

Light Armor had also increased. The Dodge, as if unarmored, was handy because that 25% increase to my Dodge costs was problematic. Of course, that meant I'd leveled up Light Armor while wearing the least amount of light armor physically possible. I'd definitely have to correct my armor, and hopefully before the next battle.

Dodge and Mitigate had both ranked up since I'd last looked at the skill sheet. I already knew that. Their improvements were helpful. The cost to dodge against the Shadow Goblin had been 8 per dodge, as opposed to my usual 2. They hadn't been nearly as effective. If I'd had a normal Stamina pool, I'd have run out quickly.

Parry was another useful skill, but glancing at my Parry percentage, it was too low to be useful with daggers. Or, at the very least, with the daggers I was currently using. I trusted them; they were helping me earn experience for three classes. I just felt that if I'd been fighting with a sword, I could have Parried and Dodged attacks much more efficiently. Also, the Parrying cost with daggers was much higher than with a larger weapon, so it was really not well suited to the task.

My Bow skill now had Focus Aiming. I took up my bow and readied an arrow but didn't notice any difference. I concentrated or, I guess, *focused* on a target. As I did so, a small circle appeared in front of me. I drew an arrow back and the circle narrowed into a much smaller circle. I fired five arrows, each one landing within the circle. This made it effectively a crosshair for my bow. I found that the aiming point got smaller if I held the bow more correctly, to my eye instead of just shooting from the hip. It got bigger when I moved and very big when I attempted to run. So big, it was almost rendered useless.

I could see the targeting circle being very handy, but it just told me where the arrow would hit. There was no predicting where the target would move; a long shot would still be a combination of aiming and intuition. Regardless, it was still very useful.

- Simple Bow: Damage 10–14.
  Durability 7/25 (durability –10
  due to Improvised Tools).

My bow was getting pretty ratty from the earlier battles, but they were simple to make. I'd have to make a new one before I next left the village.

My Novice Dagger skill was also nice. The extra Damage from a Surprise Attack might have been what finished off the last goblin. Or not. Rogues and Casters never had the best relationship in any game, and he'd walked right into knife range, all fat and happy. It had been like a lamb to the slaughter.

My secondary Dagger skills had both improved, too. I noticed that they both applied to all of my dagger attacks, despite only one being magical. As I examined them, I realized both had a level requirement, which I couldn't see; it was zeroed out. So those were both higher level skills that I had picked up for basically nothing. I idly wondered what other Weapon skills I could learn like that.

- Dagger of Wounding: Item class: Common. Durability 7/35. Damage 8–15.
  - **BONUS EFFECT:** Bleeding (requires Puncture Skill) Bleeding: Your target will suffer Damage equal to 50% of weapon damage over 12 seconds (Active).
- **BONUS EFFECT:** Savage Wound (requires Wounding skill) Savage Wound: All wounds caused by this weapon's effect are increased by 50%.
- Goblin Dagger: Durability 3/15. Damage 7–11.

The second effect hadn't been Active before, because I'd just gotten the Wounding skill. That was nice. It meant that I could do up to 30 points of Damage in a sneak attack, and up to a 45 point Stamina drain.

Impressive, until you counted on Defense, which was generated from your Armor and Endurance stats. I was running around all but naked with a Defense of 9, and I could Mitigate 4 points of Damage on top of that. Even ignoring 6 points of my Defense, I'd only take 5–12 from a strike as powerful as my own. I could mitigate that down to 1–8 before the sneak attack effect was applied. That turned a hypothetically lethal wound into something that was downright survivable.

Which is what I was running into now. The smaller goblins were not even attacking for 12 points of damage and, with my Defense and Mitigate, I'd been able to all but ignore some of their attacks. However, there was quite a bit of room for someone to be able to do much more damage than I could resist. For the third time I realized how imperative it was to find better equipment.

In my current circumstances, my dagger was a great weapon. That use was going to dwindle quickly. Further, the Durability was dropping dangerously low. Even now, the blade looked badly dull. I didn't even pretend to know how to repair it. The metal it was made of, I could instinctively tell, wasn't steel, which is all I had for repairs.

My other dagger was mostly junk. I actually had a third dagger in my pouch that I'd looted off of a goblin; it was in better shape, but I just hadn't bothered to switch over. I ideally wanted to see if I could repair or reforge either of my original daggers.

I also had found some short swords. They did a base of 2–5 damage, which was improved by one due to my Strength, so 3–6. However, if I grabbed two of them, their damage improved by 4 points because of my Dual Wielding and Twin Weapon skills. So, with all of my skills and abilities applied, the short swords ended up doing between 7 to 10 points of Damage. The Shadow Goblin's short swords had not been magical, just finely made. That granted them +1 damage and +10 durability. They were going to be my backup weapons, if I ever got around to needing them.

Next was Hiking, which had improved to Novice. It increased what I could carry before becoming overburdened. The supplies I had lugged around all day yesterday had been pretty well deconstructed while I slept. This prevented me from using them for a comparison, until I remembered there was a menu option for that. I could carry 200 pounds in my pack before, 140 base plus 60 for the Strength boosts I'd taken. After the skill increase, I could carry 400 pounds. Lifting it was still a chore but, when it got onto my back, I could essentially go for miles without issue. I could go over 400 pounds and be overburdened, which I already had. I'd even gone beyond overburdened while carrying all three members of AvaSophia's family. Carrying half your capacity didn't really have any negative Stamina effects, except for slightly slower Stamina recovery.

That encumbrance system was much more natural than a video game, I thought. In most games, if you went a feather over your Encumbered stat, there were nothing but penalties. Here, I could go over, but the penalties got progressively worse the more weight you added. A little hardly mattered, but the flip-side was also true. If I was playing a game and there wasn't a hard cap, I could basically lift the world and just suck up the penalty.

Next, my Perception was something I had been using quite a bit. However, a quick examination of the skill revealed that it required over 5000 SP to go to the next level; I was only at 800. That meant that after another week, I'd jump to Novice, because I effectively always used that skill. I'd have to see if there was some way to level it faster. I had learned that while it was handy in menu mode, it didn't actually gain any skill points here.

The only way to increase a skill in menu mode is if you had a skill boost saved up.

My general Crafting skill was still there, and it wasn't going anywhere soon. It effectively granted me one additional level of skill in all of the sub-skills for crafting. These had been made into their own skills sometime after the rules of the world were written, and then adjusted. It made sense, from a certain point of view, but was hard to reconcile with my earthly sensibilities. In any case, I had the old Crafting skill and it was in some ways better than the new one, but also horribly expensive to level.

Leatherworking I had earned from my abortive attempts at bad pants, which I was currently wearing. Woodworking I think I earned while I was making some of my contraptions for Bowyer. And Bowyer had been at unskilled when I left, so I had to go through the skill log to figure out what happened there.

It didn't take long to find.

You earned SP in crafting for both making the item, and then if the item was used, I thought. I'd gotten leatherwork SP for my armor, but the stuff was so poor it hadn't really done much. My simple bow, on the other hand, had earned me enough additional SP that, when combined with my arrow making, I'd leveled.

Apparently, I needed to get blueprints to learn how to make any new bows. I could still make another simple bow, but nothing more complex. *Hurray.* The extra damage I could craft into the weapons might be interesting though. I resolved to make that another priority.

Lastly, I checked on my magical skills. I still hadn't gained any levels in any of the Wizard classes; I had no idea what was going on there. I had a feeling if I could see their tabs, I would have seen some earned experience. Unfortunately, I couldn't, so I didn't know how far I'd progressed.

Infuse allowed me to keep granting Shart more mana, slowly. I only had a pool of 20, but I'd finally figured out the trick of stopping at the three-quarter mark. I could just give him 15, which dropped to 7, and then recharge over the next three minutes before I repeated the cycle. It hadn't changed since last time I reviewed it, so I moved on.

The Empowerment skill was the item version of that. It let me put magic into staffs, wands, and the like. I'd used it to recharge the staff but, apparently, I was bad at it. There was a chance to damage the item permanently, which I didn't know how to overcome yet.

Mana Control was interesting. Before I'd started using Infuse, I couldn't really tell you very much about my Mana Pool. Now, I could distinctly feel it when I thought about it. I could tell you how full it was without checking my menu. Also, I could apparently resist if someone tried to over drain it, which I didn't understand. I was tired of dealing with Shart by this time, so I hadn't asked.

My final new skill was Magical Blast, which let me use magical staffs and wands to blast people. I had an Unskilled rank there because I had to be shooting at people; I had been shooting at trees. It presently sat at 1 SP, which was the system "give me" rank for that skill, apparently. No matter how many trees I blasted, the SP didn't go up.

Unless the trees were planning an uprising, I'd leaf them alone. Even though they were all bark and no bite.

I smiled a little melancholy smile at that. My son had loved bad puns. This was too much at times. I could still feel the heat on my body as the car burned around me. My last thoughts had been of my wife. Now, I was here.

Suck it up, Buttercup. You got shit to do.

The amulet was Scanned by Shart after I'd given him 121 mana. I knew I'd given him too much and he knew I knew. I'd been practicing my skill, though, which was still nowhere near Novice rank.

You have found Amulet of Non-Detection. Item class: Uncommon. Charge 19/20 (Passive). Grants the effect Non-Detection. You are considered 4 levels higher for a Lore user and any Lore check can only learn basic information. Also defeats basic scrying. For 1 charge, you can expand this ability to cover a ten-yard radius. Also grants +20 maximum mana.

I slipped the amulet on and immediately felt the funny sensation of having my mana go from full to not full. It took a few more minutes for the newly expanded Mana Pool to top back off, so I didn't recover as a percentage but rather as a whole. 40 points of mana took twice as long to recover as 20. After my pool filled almost fully, I threw another 30 mana Shart's way, giving him 15 more mana to play with.

He didn't bother thanking me. *Ungrateful twerp.*

Dismissing Shart, I began walking back to the bowyer. The closer I got, the more aware I was of a truly horrendous stench. There seemed to be an abundant amount of flies around the door and in the workshop. I quickly discovered the reason: the goblin I had used as part of my bow making tools had indeed begun to rot. Removing the goblin, which was actually a little moist and squishy by now, I "disposed" of the body. That problem solved, I found some other contraptions that allowed me to work on my Bowyer skill and slapped together a simple bow. I called it Mark 2.

Improved Simple Bow: Damage 12–16. Durability 30/30 (durability -10 due to Improvised Tools).

Extra damage was always nice. I also made two quivers full of arrows and those also did additional damage. In total, it increased my Damage up to 13–17. My minimum Damage was now almost as good as my previous maximum Damage had been.

It was only early afternoon, by my reckoning, and I chewed a piece of hard tack while I considered what to do next. The leather working shop was in shambles and missing about every single necessity. It had taken everything I had with my improved tools just to get the two simple pieces I was wearing. I was also painfully short on additional leather due to my inept skinning earlier.

Then again, those goblin wolves were pretty big and I bet they could be skinned fairly easily. Of course, they seemed kind of smart, so I glossed over that idea. I'd kill them if I had to and skin them if I could, but I wasn't going to go out intentionally hunting and skinning intelligent beings that weren't necessarily evil. Plus, there were dumb wolves out in the forest.

However, even if I did skin those, doing anything with that skin was going to be tricky without tools. So I headed over to the blacksmithing shop. It, like everything, had seen better days. Behind the counter, there was what you'd expect from any TV show you'd ever seen. There was a large furnace for heating the metal. Several anvils were still there and, after attempting to lift one, I could see why. However, most of the tools were gone and what was there were ruined. There was a vice on one of the counters, but it had rusted solid. Technically, the anvils were rusted solid too, but I figured if I beat on them enough times, the rust would clear off.

As I didn't think you could blacksmith without a hammer or any charcoal, I got ready to leave. That's when I noticed a thin line of light coming in from a vent in the ceiling. It crossed the floor but, in one spot, the light had a slight ridge that looked unusual in the dust.

I walked over and cleaned the dust away to reveal the floorboards underneath. The smell was wrong; it was an out of place kind of smell for a workshop in the square of an abandoned town. This was a far more earthy smell. I grabbed at the floor with my hand and pulled. Not much happened, so I wisely moved to the other side of the crack and tried again. This time, the floor shook slightly. It was some sort of trap door.

Cleaning the rest of the door off took several minutes, but in the end, I managed it. Finding the handle was a bit more difficult as it had been ingeniously hidden. It was also rusted solid. I took the haft of some old piece of equipment and managed to lever the handle to a position where I could get my hand into it and lifted. The door was heavy, but not terribly so. Underneath was a staircase into the unknown.

Of course, there were no torches, and the light was abysmal. Then I remembered the staff. When I powered it up to cast spells, it glowed blue pretty brightly. That would either be sufficient or it wouldn't and I'd have to find something better. But it was worth a shot. I walked next door and grabbed it, ready to explore the dungeon.

Focusing on the staff, I made it glow blue and walked down the stairs. It was a small room with several trunks that all looked to be exceedingly well made. Also, they were locked with large, sturdy looking locks. They were also all bolted to the floor, because why wouldn't they be?

Being a Rogue—among so many other things—I figured I could just pick the locks. Unfortunately, I didn't have any lock picks. Luckily, a quick search upstairs with my Improvised Tools skill netted me several bent pins that I was sure would work.

And work they did . . . after about thirty minutes. Thirty minutes in the dark, smelly, annoyingly cramped space where I couldn't get at the lock properly. The space was so small you couldn't sit in front of the low lock to work on it; you had to crouch at a strange angle, which I'm sure was the intent.

You have learned about the skill: Lockpicking. You are Unskilled. You can sometimes open locks.

Fortunately, or unfortunately, the lock was tricky. I earned 40 SP of 80 SP just for getting through it. I opened up the chest and revealed tools. Not all the tools a smith would want, I could tell though my Crafting, but enough to do the job. Certainly, more than enough to make a dagger. A large Smiths' hammer sat on top of the pile, lovingly wrapped in an oiled rag.

I sniffed the second box and could make out the smell of coal or charcoal, so that was fuel. The other chest must have had some ingots in it, I hoped, so I attempted to pick the second lock. After thirty minutes, I could tell this lock was even trickier than the first. After another thirty minutes, I brought up my skill tabs to see how much longer until I leveled.

Lockpicking: 40/80 SP.

"What," I cried, "but, but . . . I just spent an hour."

"Oh, lock's broken," said Shart. I wasn't certain when he had rejoined me; my full attention had been invested in my task. "You can't earn any XP from a broken lock. Use that big hammer to knock it off. It will only take about three seconds."

As much as it pained me to admit, Shart was both right and helpful. I was quickly able to knock the two remaining locks off. The second chest contained charcoal and the third contained ingots. Most appeared to be made of iron. I took what I needed upstairs.

Actually, forging something was a bit of a letdown. When I got into the room and set the tools out, I got a prompt:

You are in a Blacksmith's forge. Quality: Terrible.

Apparently the "Terrible" was due to the anvil.

I looked at it. I could instinctually tell that it could be repaired with the proper chemicals and scrapers, which I had. I went to work, de-rusted them both, leaving them both looking like new. That was odd; I suspected that they would have had scuffs and marks on them, but instead they were both like they'd never been used.

Your Forge has leveled to 1. Quality: Average.

A prompt appeared that looked like an anvil, which I clicked. It brought up another menu, showing the shop as it was now. That was a bit creepy, because it showed my tools and materials. There were also a few quests, such as "Make a Dagger." Also included was a list of items I could forge.

Quickly doing the math, I didn't have enough iron to make a suit of medium armor. The town menu did have a Mine listed, but it carried a population requirement to render it fully operational. As the town only had a miniscule population, I wondered if I could even personally go mine ore in a non-operational mine. If I could mine a small amount of ore, I could then smelt it into ingots. That would provide me with enough iron for the armor, but even if I was allowed, I was willing to bet that an abandoned mine had monsters in it.

The tools required for Leatherworking were also listed. It should not have been feasible for me to craft the tools that I needed, but with the general Crafting skill, I was listed as being able to try. I even had enough expendable materials to fail a few times.

This turned out to be fortunate, because fail I did. I actually ran out of metal, until I remembered having tucked away some of the goblins' weapons; I used those to make up the difference.

You have learned about Salvaging. You are Unskilled,
but know how to convert existing equipment
to base parts for use in other equipment.

What was weird was that it took two ingots of iron to make a dagger, which weighed considerably less than one ingot. When I then salvaged that dagger, I got a whole ingot back. I tried not to think about that stuff.

With all that effort, I managed to craft one set of basic leather-working tools.

I also figured out how to repair an iron dagger. Thus, I was able to repair my preferred trusty weapon. Unfortunately, my special goblin dagger was not made of iron and I lacked the unrecognizable metal required to fix it. Just fixing my iron dagger gained my Blacksmithing enough skill points to level up to Amateur.

As I worked the new smithy, I noticed a prompt.

Your smithy has achieved level 1. Please choose an affinity.

There was another skill tree with several branches. One led to weapons, another to armor, and a third led to a horseshoe. That one was the Mundane affinity. I glanced at it just to see what it was and noticed a tool list next to it. Several items were in white, but most were greyed out.

I knew instantly that I'd be awarded that ability if I possessed all of those items. It wouldn't have even been that difficult; I would just have to craft or find the items later. Glancing at the Weapon and Armor Smithing, both had similar requirements. The affinity apparently bypassed those and granted you the ability without having to meet the requirement, interesting concept.

I selected Weapon Smithing, since I knew now how to work towards acquiring the others.

You have selected Weapon Smithing. All weapons gain +5 Durability and +10% Damage.

Not bad. I had just enough material to make one more dagger.

Simple Dagger: Durability 30/30. Damage 8–15.

It was on par with my enchanted dagger, but the enchanted dagger had much better secondary abilities. Well, that was something. I still needed to repair it, but I would first have to learn more about its magical properties; as it stood, I didn't even know what it was made of. I sheathed it and took my newly forged dagger and the undamaged goblin dagger with me.

Time to find some wolves.

- Jim
- Hit Points: 105/105
- Stamina: 115/115
- Mana: 40/40

Shart wasn't responding to me, at all. After going into map mode and yelling until I actually watched a leaf fly across my entire field of vision with no response, I gave up on the demon. He was sleeping or something and I didn't necessarily need him to go hunting for wolves. It was entirely possible that he was just as annoyed with me as I was with him. There was also his ever-present anger towards my lack of acceptance of his epic quest of my destruction. He was around somewhere and ignoring me. I could live with that.

I had forty arrows, my simple bow, and other gear ready to go. The trip into the woods was uneventful now that I could find and target the goblins from increasingly wider distances. The goblins had, meanwhile, decided to get farther and farther away from the town, leaving me a nice clear path to get to the forest.

Taking a different, slightly longer route, I ended up near an abandoned farmhouse that lay just inside the outer border of the forest. From there, I trekked farther into the forest and started using my Lore and Perception skills to look for wolves.

It didn't take long. Within the first thirty minutes, I'd found a wolf, skinned it, and started off towards the next beast. By the end of the day, I had enough leather for several suits of armor. I was tired, but content. I'd even earned the title Wolf Slayer, which made it much easier to gather up the skins. My trip back had me carrying a double armful of sticky, smelly leather that I would have to properly tan overnight back in the village.

I was still well away from the town. Perhaps I was too involved in searching for wolves. Maybe I was assuming too much regarding my Perception skill. Whatever the reason, my guard wasn't fully up. So, when the sizzling black orb flew straight towards my chest, I was surprised, to say the least. I was so heavily overloaded that my Dodge skill didn't work correctly and the orb exploded between my hands. The only thing that saved me was the day's worth of leather that I had been carrying, which blocked the majority of the force of the bolt.

There was still enough of a jolt to lift me off my feet and send me flying backwards into a tree branch.

I blacked out entirely for a few seconds. 59 hit points, more than half of my health, were gone and my Stamina bar wasn't filling properly. I heard a voice approaching me, but I wasn't even sure my limbs worked due to the status effect. I decided to stay still for a moment, while I tried to catch my wits.

"A tough one, they said," stated the first goblin.

"The tough one is dead," said the second.

I opened one eye a sliver and saw the two goblins approaching me. They were slightly shorter and thinner than the other goblins I'd seen, and feminine in appearance, if that was a thing for goblins. They were still hideous, with bulbous noses and several large warts each. Both wore earrings, large hoop ones that clattered slightly as they walked; they held a single larger staff between them.

They were getting closer. Almost close enough for my plan when one screamed, "Alive he is! Bind him we must!"

Not wanting to see what that entailed, I rolled forwards, grabbing at my bow and drawing an arrow in the same motion. The two goblins looked shocked, but as my first arrow shot towards the one on the left, a black barrier flickered into existence. The arrow dissolved into smoke as it passed through.

Charging towards them, I leapt, trying to get enough distance to completely hurdle over both of them. At the apex of my leap, I released another arrow, which hit the barrier as well. The shocked goblin recovered and swung the staff down, causing the head to catch fire for a moment, before a stream of flame shot from it.

I narrowly jumped behind a tree while fishing out another arrow. My bow's Durability had been reduced to 1 by the full day of use and then me violently bouncing off the tree. I didn't know how many shots a Durability of 1 equated to, but it couldn't have been many. Twisting back around the tree the way I'd come, I fired another arrow.

The goblins assumed I'd continue running, so they had moved to face that section of the tree. The stream of fire was already roasting towards the space I wasn't, and my arrow struck the barrier with an audible crack. An instant later, the entire thing shattered with a pop.

Drawing another arrow to fire, one of the goblins let fly with a dozen glowing white orbs that streaked through the air towards me. My arrow missed the targeted goblin, instead striking one of the orbs as I tried to dodge away. Even my Dodge skill was useless against that barrage of blasts and I was struck several times. Fortunately, my Mitigate skill worked, though I noticed that the Resist skill didn't. The orbs were not affected by any of my Defense and caused me another 6 hit points of damage.

Both goblins were chanting, but whatever magical effects they were doing were not ready yet. I quickly brought my bowstring back to my ear and took aim at the one generating the barrier. She glared at me, chanting and gesturing as fast as she could, when I heard the twang as my bowstring snapped.

For a terrible instant I was standing there without a plan in the world. One of the pair finished her spell just as the other stopped casting hers. A glowing gourd—seriously it looked like a butternut squash or something—of flame appeared in the goblin's hand. Much like a professional pitcher's windup, she prepared to throw the strange object at me. The other goblin dropped to her knees and placed her hands on the ground as I used my Dodge skill to fling myself behind the tree.

Intuitively, I realized it would explode. I jumped, grabbing the highest branch I could reach, then hauled myself even higher as the brightly glowing orb landed at the base of the tree. It exploded into a fireball. I took another 3 points of damage as the branch I was on suddenly erupted into flame, but I was high enough to avoid almost all of it.

Strangely, the fire died much more quickly than I expected. One moment, there was a glowing fireball underneath me. The next moment, there was simply smoke.

I resolved to not be in that tree anymore and attempted to leap away, only to find my ankle had caught itself in the branch. No, strike that. The branch was *wrapping* itself around my ankle. I pulled against the branch with all my might, but I was stuck properly. I had a hatchet with me that I'd stolen from some dead goblin and I attempted to hack away at the branch. Somehow, despite it only being around the width of my finger, it was incredibly tough.

With the smoke, they couldn't see me quite yet; I had a few more precious seconds to think. I focused, activating my inner eye, and found the strand of magic that connected the goblin's spell to the tree. Instead of putting more power into it, I attempted to draw the power out of it.

"He tries to counter the spell!" cried one of the goblins.

"He tries to be a Rogue as well," replied the second. "We shall find him and kill him."

It was like trying to empty a pool with a cup. I was draining just enough power to force one goblin to do nothing more than concentrate on the spell. Unfortunately, that left the other goblin to hunt me down; she started off towards me.

I was still trying to cut the branch with the hatchet and draw the magic out of the spell when she came around the corner. A few times, my draining and cutting had allowed me to get a good whack in on the branch. If I could have kept it up for an uninterrupted period of time, I would have been able to get myself free. However, the approaching goblin had other ideas. She drew a wand and pointed it at me. Suddenly, I felt my body warp.

My Mana bar started twitching. I instinctively applied Stamina against it, causing the other goblin to shriek in pain.

"Fights hard, this one little wretch," she cried.

"The tastiest fish is the hardest to catch," replied the other.

Taking my hand from the branch, I drew a dagger and flung it at her. Unfortunately, with me balancing on the branch while trying to resist both spells, my aim wasn't good. It thudded into the ground next to her. She looked at it for a moment and then grinned up at me, now holding a second wand.

"Nettles, a supper for thee," she cried, pointing it at me. This spell affected health. My skin felt like a thousand biting insects were upon it. It wasn't even doing damage; it just hurt. It did succeed in ruining my concentration, however, and the branches of the tree started wrapping around me more, grabbing both legs.

Tethered to the branch in agony, I still tried to struggle free when an errant breeze blew away a patch of smoke. Only then did I clearly see a bees' nest. Figuring it couldn't get worse, I used my free arm to hurl the hatchet at it. With a secure grip on the branch, my aim proved much better this time. The hatchet struck true, splitting the hive.

Half of it landed on me, covering me with a thick, sticky honey and hundreds of angry bees. They launched themselves at me, stinging me hundreds of times. However, that was physical damage and my Resist skill ignored each strike. The second half of the nest landed next to the goblin beneath me. She was less than impressed.

A high-pitched scream alerted me to the incapacitation of the foe underneath me. The nettles stopped. The bees hadn't been able to hurt me at all. Suddenly, free from pain, I tried desperately to drain the magic from the branch around my lower torso.

"This spell takes all my might," cried out the second sister, as my Mana Drain cut deeply into her mana.

"They bite, they bite!" came the reply, as the goblin beneath me was stung over and over again.

For an instant, the spell-casting goblin and I struggled. Her attempting to keep the branches intact; me attempting to drain the mana from them. I realized she'd stopped at my feet because they'd basically been hardened into place, but not well enough. I could totally get my feet free if she stopped now. Then, all of a sudden, she shouted, "You fool, you bring them to me?"

In that moment, the spell broke. The branch, which had been gripping me like steel, slackened enough that I was able to wriggle free. I kicked off the branch, falling down to the earth below. I landed hard on my hands and knees, causing 7 points of damage. I saw the hilt of my dagger and snatched it up.

Maybe I can end this.

Cutting through the smoke, trees, and underbrush, I moved to an area that had yet to see combat and laid eyes on both goblins again. Both were still hideous, one even more so since she was covered in bug bites on every exposed portion of her skin. I watched as she poured the contents of a vial down her throat and the wounds started healing instantly. Great, she had a healing potion. The other sister had one as well, but seemed loath to use it, despite her own wounds.

I need healing potions! Who else has those? Can I make those?

Both were scanning the forest, now with either full or mostly full health. Neither of their magical pools was super depleted; all of my reserves were. Abruptly, one turned her head towards me and pointed.

"He hides in the trees!"

"Cut him off at the knees!"

Both sisters began gathering up their magic for round two.

CHAPTER 16

AFTERMATH OF THE WEIRDNESS

I DID THE ONLY HEROIC THING I COULD THINK OF AND RAN away from the goblins and towards my town, sprinting the whole way there. Unfortunately, they came after me. Thankfully, these goblins didn't have wolves, so it was just me running away as fast as I could from two horrible little creatures.

Whenever I thought I'd lost them, they would appear, blistering the air around me with spells. Now that I lacked a ranged response to them, they concentrated far more on offense than defense. The only reason I survived was that I had longer legs and could therefore run faster.

What had taken me hours to walk took considerably less time to run. I used every bit of my Woodsman skill to my advantage, darting through trees and avoiding dead ends. At long last, I saw the barrier in the distance. I managed to make the final sprint across the field that separated the forest from my village in record time. I crossed the barrier and collapsed into the creek.

• Jim   • Hit Points: 31/105

I lay face up in the creek, letting the cool water wash away the sting of bitter defeat.

I had lost and I had nearly died. I had nearly died and it hurt.

Both mentally, because it struck at the illusion of invulnerability I had gathered up around myself since the first fight with the larger wolf, and physically, because they were casting spells that hurt for the sake of hurting. Involuntarily shuddering from the spell, I tried to focus and calm myself, but the feeling of insects biting every surface of my skin still clung to my mind.

- Quest: Defeat the Goblin Menace 1: You live in a land of danger; your town is surrounded by goblins. Slay the goblin champions, their captain, and their chieftain so your town can be saved. You will gain a reward each time one of the goblin heroes is slain.
- You have discovered the "Weird Sisters," magical champions of the Goblins. You have not defeated them. Defeating them will cause damage to the goblin army!
- You have learned about Sprinting. You are Unskilled. Merrily they ran away!
- You have learned about Counter-Magic. You are Unskilled. Abra can't dabra.

I had learned how to run away faster. That was glorious. I hated spellcasters.

I needed to learn how to cast spells.

It took me a full day to recover from the ordeal. Being able to rest in town seemed to speed that up somewhat. In the meantime, I reviewed my combat tracker to see what they had hit me with. The initial attack was a spell called Dark Orb, which caused Dark Damage. It had been powerful enough to kill me outright, except they'd targeted my chest, which was covered by my day's gathering of hides. They had absorbed the majority of the otherwise fatal blast.

I'd lived and that was the important part, I guessed.

The rest of the day I spent searching the town for anything of value. I was hoping for another cellar find like I'd made in the forge. If I could find some leather or other materials, I might be able to make some sort of armor.

I searched through one row of old houses and found a silver fork and knife, as well as a rusted candelabra, to add to my ever-growing pile of metals. As I looted, I noticed one of my quest markers moving. I selected the quest log:

Find a Draft Animal for <AvaSophia>. Quest updated: You see a possible draft animal.

I looked around, first broadly, and then in line with the direction I felt followed the quest marker. Even with my Perception, it took me several seconds to find what I was looking for. A large furry back was just visible over the grasses in the meadow, beyond the barrier. As I watched, the wolf that had previously belonged to the shaman rose up, looked around, and then dipped its head back into the tall grasses.

I guess that works?

Taking my newer bow and my daggers, I started moving closer to the edge of the barrier while I checked my pouch for something to eat. As I got closer, the direction got fuzzier. I could still tell generally where the target was, but I could no longer point to the exact location of the wolf. That made sense; any Stealth skill would have been rendered worthless otherwise.

I contemplated that for a moment, calling out mentally to Shart, who ignored me. I stepped out of the barrier, into the lands south of the town. The area north of the town was forest, starting off with light groves, and then moving into deeper woods. To the south was the beach. However, between the beach and the town was an open grassland. If you stood and watched for any period of time, a massive blast of wind would slash through it. That explained why there were no trees out here. The only thing saving the town from being buffeted by winds constantly was the thick stone wall around it. That wall provided amazing protection, muting the harm the wind would otherwise cause.

Out here, however, it would occasionally hit me full blast. It wasn't enough to knock me off my feet or anything, but it did add a certain challenge to Stealth. Every so often, your nearby cover flattened, leaving you exposed. It wasn't impossible to predict, though, if you watched the distant grass. It actually made tracking the giant wolf easier.

Finally, I caught up to him. I had noticed several scurrying creatures in the grass, mostly rabbits, prairie dogs, and small rodents. My Animal Lore skills detected even more critters that I couldn't physically see. Much of this skill was based on scant evidence, even bits of spoor registered with my Tracking ability. The wolf had been here for a few days and had several sets of deeper tracks that I'd found.

At a range of thirty yards, I'd finally gotten a good look at him. It was a huge wolf, far larger than any dog I'd actually been in the physical presence of, including St. Bernards and a Great Dane. He came up to my shoulder when he stood, and I was once again overcome by the intelligence he seemed to exude. He didn't look hungry. In fact, I'd found the remains of quite a few small animals, indicating that he'd been successful in his hunting. He did, however, look messy for a dog.

I used my Lore ability.

- Kappa: Warg, Level 5
- Health: 80
- Stamina: 100
- Mana: 10

Wargs are the trained hunting mounts of goblins. They are magically enhanced wolf pups that are given a special alchemical diet that causes them to grow larger and tougher than the usual breed. The diet also reinforces them, allowing them to be ridden by small humanoids. Actual abilities vary depending on the breed. This one is based on a Valley Wolf and is unusually intelligent.

Hmmm, well that's interesting.

I briefly remembered that you could harness a dog for pulling things and wondered if this guy was big enough to pull a plow. Figuring that I could take him, I stood up obviously, causing him to whip around.

"Who's a good boy?" I asked, as his fur shot up and he began to growl. I knew it was just his fur expanding, but man, did that make him look bigger.

Neither of us backed down. He kept growling and I kept calling him a good boy. He took a step towards me, I took a step towards him. This made him pause. He probably assumed I'd back away and run or something, but I didn't. That ruined his plan.

"Kappa's a good boy," I kept saying, and to my surprise, he responded.

"How do you know that?" he asked, in a growly sort of way. My eyebrows shot up and his ears flatted more. It was not a good look.

"I can tell your name is Kappa," I said and the Warg snorted.

"All call me Kappa," he replied. His speech was a combination of growls and ear movements, of all things.

"Well, okay, Kappa, I don't want to fight you."

"You killed my rider," he responded. His fur sat back down, but he didn't sit or make any more movements in any direction.

"Yes," I said, choosing my words carefully, "but he was stupid and let me get close to him, knowing that I was his enemy."

Kappa snorted. "He was always a fool. Quick to strike, quick to anger."

"Are we enemies?" I asked. "I don't think we need to be."

The warg looked at me for a long moment. I put my dagger back into its sheath, and then he sat back on his haunches. "I suppose not."

"Okay then," I said, adopting a pose of ease while still being ready to move at a moment's notice. The warg could likewise leap the fifteen feet between us in the blink of an eye. So, while we'd agreed not to kill each other, there wasn't much trust there, yet.

"I did not see that this was your territory," stated the warg, cautiously.

"In the human fashion it is, but I have no need of it at the moment."

"Well then, I shall hunt here. Are there any buildings beyond the circle of fire?"

"A few, but they seem to be in poor condition," I said. "Would you like to live in a building?"

The warg paused for a moment before scratching behind his ears. "Yes. Once one has gotten used to a roof, it is hard to go without."

"Well, if you could be of use, then I could let you live in the town," I offered.

"The circle of fire will burn me," he noted, his ears going flat again.

"The fire burns whom I tell it to burn," I said gravely.

Kappa watched me for a long moment, before another fit of scratching got him. "If I can go through the ring of fire without being harmed, I may choose to help."

"Before you do, tell me something: Why didn't you go back to the other goblins?"

Kappa snorted. "Would you? The calling has never been strong for me."

"Calling?"

The warg sat on his haunches for a moment, thinking. He scratched his ear some more before responding. "One of the goblins was able to call to me, to all wargs. I alone learned how to ignore his screeching. My rider was using magics to make me more docile. Without his magics, I was able to decide not to return to them. They have fleas."

With that, the warg shook himself mightily, as if casting off something foul. He stood perfectly still for another moment and then nodded. "Shall we go?"

I agreed and the two of us walked through the tall grass together. Wolf speech wasn't like human speech. If I wasn't looking at him, I couldn't really understand him. The yaps and barks were somewhat useful, but they really didn't communicate any deeper meanings.

Of course, after this one short exchange, I spoke Wolf now. That would have seemed so odd just a few short days ago. Fortunately, there was a prompt that I promptly selected.

**You have learned about the Language of Wolves. You
are proficient due to your Lore skill. It was a Ruff day.**

The Lore skill allowed me to talk to animals. Fascinating. That
was another very useful sidebar to my abilities. Of course, Kappa was
quite intelligent. I'd have to interrogate another animal to see if they
were all this useful. The thought of interrogating a squirrel for his
nuts was flickering through the back of my mind as I walked through
the barrier.

Kappa stopped just outside of it, having been carefully watching
for it. I brought up the menu and found the controls of the barrier. I
was pretty sure I could let him in, but hadn't actually worked through
it yet. I saw that, right now, the barrier was set to automatically block
all creatures of darkness and any monsters. Looking at Kappa on the
interface, he showed the bright red of a targeted creature. I mentally
clicked on him and he changed to green.

Green meant neutral, not resident. If a resident attacked someone in the village, then the barrier wouldn't do anything. If a neutral
attacked, though, the interface would switch and the barrier would
target them. As they would already be in the town, this would not
end well for them.

"You are free to access the town," I said. Kappa simply stood
there for a moment before dropping to his haunches. After a moment
I asked, "Problem?"

"No, I am just reviewing my prompt," he answered. As he sat
there, I saw his facial expressions change. To one who could understand Wolf speech, he was basically sounding out the entire process
to himself. He didn't seem to have menu time; he had to do his menus
in real time.

I wondered if AvaSophia had menu time or if it was just me.

"I will not attack anyone while I am in the village," he said finally. "But if someone attacks me, then the barrier will not activate?"

"Not if they are a resident," I answered truthfully. "And the barrier will only attack you if you attack someone else. You should be able to get away from a farm wife and her children should they turn on you."

He flattened his ears, almost indignant. "I am not wicked. I will not attack a child."

"Good, then we understand each other." I grinned. "That said, be warned: they will probably want rides."

"Children do not always get what they want," he said coolly.

"They live under a roof with a warm hearth," I said in reply, as we started heading into the village.

Kappa walked a few paces before his head drooped. "One also gets used to a hearth. One can put up with much for a warm place to sleep."

If that warm place to sleep was actually being offered.

AvaSophia was less than pleased by the huge wolf. However, when I showed that he could be attached to an improvised harness, she relented enough for me to plow her fields for the next hour. Eventually, she became annoyed with my inept plowing and took over. She spent the remainder of the day at it while I tended to other things.

When I returned in the evening, the warg and the woman had reached an accord. He got access to the rug in front of the fireplace and a hot meal once per day. In return, Kappa had agreed to help her with the plowing and to do some hunting. Well, Kappa told me that's what they'd agreed to. AvaSophia was mainly of the opinion that the big dog was mostly harmless and seemed useful, seeing as how Kappa behaved himself the entire time. I was actually surprised it went that well, but Kappa was an intelligent creature making the best of his circumstances. He was willing to play ball for a price.

I was about to speak, when suddenly a massive prompt filled my vision:

> You have completed the Quest: Find a Draft Animal
> for <AvaSophia>. You earn 500 experience points
> and your village gains additional resources.

Blinking several times, I realized that I had left the quests set to notify me. I dialed that back down to an alert and noticed I had a skill prompt.

> - You have learned about Negotiation. You are Unskilled. You possess a silver tongue.
> - You have learned about Farming. You are Unskilled. All things in life come from the dirt.

Also, I saw that I'd leveled up in Rogue again.

> - Level UP, Rogue 3
> - You have gained one Perk. Please select it from the Rogue menu.
> - Your Hit Point total is increased by 10. Your Stamina is increased by 10.

I'd leveled up in Rogue due to the quest reward. Looking at my remaining classes, they were all moving closer to the next level, as well. I couldn't tell if any of the magical classes were advancing, but I suspected not. Rogue had taken longer to level because I wasn't doing as many Rogue-y things in the field. Checking my log, I'd gotten most of my Rogue experience from cleaning out the forge's secret room, and a lesser amount from looting the houses.

You got experience in combat for fighting like your class, which is why I was highest in Warrior. Virtually any action performed in combat earned experience for the Warrior class. Woodsman gained experience from Dual Wielding as well as fighting with daggers or a bow. Actually, Woodsman gained experience from a much larger variety of weapons than just daggers, but daggers is what got Rogue experience.

The Rogue class got me some experience from Dodging, but it

was slight. I hadn't been that effective with using my daggers in the last several battles. While my longbow could use my sneak attack, the longbow itself wasn't classified as a Rogue weapon. Using it actually got my Woodsman and Warrior to level faster, as they calculated experience primarily as damage dealt, with a bonus for kills or defeating an enemy.

When I'd defeated Shart (who was still currently unaccounted for), I'd done so by knocking him into a tree. The actual blow hadn't done much damage, but his horns had gotten stuck, rendering him unable to escape due to his stubby arms. That somehow counted as a win, and so he was defeated. I suspected that if I trapped a creature in a like manner, it would count in the same vein.

In any case, the challenge of earning experience for my Rogue class was making me reassess my perks. There were several attached to Dodging, making it more efficient or allowing me to wear heavier armor. I could Dodge while wearing light armor without any serious issues; that was just more ability to wear armor while Dodging. In so far as I could tell, Mobility didn't make Dodging better at avoiding attacks, but it did allow you to better position yourself afterwards.

I'd tested it; I could jump up to shoulder height easily in a conventional jump. This did seem to increase the number of SP I got for the Jumping skill slightly. Slam dunks would have been trivial. I could box jump well over six feet into the air, a world record back on Earth. The extra Mobility wasn't earning experience points, so I looked elsewhere.

There were no perks I had access to that allowed me to use more weapons, which would have been helpful. Even switching up to short swords would have vastly improved my experience point potential. There were Poison skills, but those required Herb Lore to acquire; I didn't have that skill yet. Furthermore, that meant a lead off time where I'd have to get the skill, learn Alchemy or the equivalent, and then start applying poisons to my blades. There was a chance that taking the perk would grant me those skills, but I was betting they just added something to your weapons base damage, which would be a slow path to advancement.

Then I noticed Shadow Walker.

It increased your Stealth ability by making you blend into the shadows better. As a passive effect, it also made your enemies have a more difficult time analyzing you through Lore. When I looked at a creature I had a Lore skill in, I gathered quite a bit of information: Hit Points, Mana, and Stamina, down to the exact number. If I didn't have the Lore skill for a particular creature, I could see bars; until I actually attacked them, I didn't know how deeply those bars went. That effect also occurred if they were a higher level than me.

I knew my amulet made it somewhat harder to detect my information with Lore, but possessing an even greater ability to hide seemed useful. I had gotten some Stealth experience, but I'd also been ambushed by those goblin sisters. Maybe being more difficult to find would prevent another such attack. I selected it.

In my vision, I always had an icon representing if I'd been seen or not. It was a little eye that watched me differently, depending on if I'd been seen and if the person looking at me was hostile or neutral. If it was glaring at me angrily, I'd been spotted. It also changed if I was stealthing, with the eye being completely closed or opened in stages, depending on who saw me or thought they saw me.

After taking Shadow Walker, the eye icon changed more. When I first attempted Stealth it appeared the same as normal. However, when I'd snuck into the shadows, the icon changed into a shadow of itself. I glanced at my arm and discovered, to my delight, that I was much harder to see even to my own eye. I blended into the background somewhat, almost like camouflage. While the icon showed someone could still see me, that had suddenly gotten much harder.

Armed with my new Perk, I waited until darkness fell and went to get more skins.

One of the first things I confirmed as I searched for some prey was that goblins did far more hunting during the night. I'd had to avoid several hunting parties in the North Woods before I'd finally gotten my first opportunity to even attempt hunting.

However, before I could even take aim, several goblins ran towards my hiding spot. They didn't notice me, but their running scared the deer I was stalking. The small buck turned around and ran the other direction, straight into another group of goblins, some distance away.

The deer didn't have a chance. Afterwards, while the hunters started to tend to the corpse, the beaters began searching quietly for new prey. Their process was mechanical. They'd find one, whistle, and then rush it towards the hunters, who would fill it full of arrows.

Ardently watching my Stealth icon, I was relieved to see that it never flickered once. They were not looking for me, so avoiding them was easy. As I watched through the night, something occurred to me. I didn't need to hunt; I just needed to get skins and maybe some meat. By the end of the night, and with much effort, the six goblins had collected three deer corpses and a string of rabbits. They were smaller deer, but still probably represented around 300 pounds of meat.

Their path took them exceedingly close to the village. All I had to do was set myself up and wait. Instead of hiding in a tree, I just picked a bush and waited in its shadow for them to take a forest path. They were walking down the narrow trail in a conga line of goblins, three pairs each carrying the carcass of a deer between them. They were talking and joking about how easy the night had been.

Time to change that.

I stepped out behind the six, driving a dagger into the last one's back. He didn't even make a noise; he just died. The goblin in front of him yelped, not out of any concern, but because his friend wasn't supporting his share of the weight anymore. I had the dead goblin's partner before he realized there was an issue.

At this point, the four remaining goblins realized something was wrong. Their conversation stopped and a couple turned around, not yet willing to drop their cargo. That's how I got the third one. He had just begun to turn to face me, but I was already in position. I fatally introduced my dagger into his kidney. The remaining three drew their weapons—a bow and two truncheons—and started to position themselves.

The closest goblin swung his weapon with all his might; I Parried his little club with one knife, while I gutted him with another. The second goblin rushed up behind me and I threw his dead companion at him, mostly because he'd become stuck on my knife.

The final goblin shot me in the chest with an arrow.

I'd sensed the arrow, but it didn't give me the same sensation as other attacks. It existed, but there was no danger to it and I hadn't recognized what it was. The arrow simply struck me in the chest before bouncing off. I glanced at my combat log; it had only done 4 points of base damage, which my defenses reduced first to zero. I tilted my head, staring at the final goblin as his friend madly scrambled to get free of the body I'd flung.

As the goblin continued to fire shot after shot at me, each bouncing off in turn, I began gathering up the deer carcasses. Throwing one over my shoulders like a bloody meat scarf, and dragging the other two behind me, I started back towards the village. The goblin eventually ran out of arrows and ran to his friend, freeing him. That one just ran as soon as he could and the other goblin screamed at me while I walked to the village.

Turning around with the town's glowing blue barrier as a backdrop, the wind blowing fantastically through my hair like a boss, I finally said something.

"Tell your friends Jim patrols this forest."

"What? I can't tell them that. That's stupid," the goblin said. "How can we face the others and tell them we got our asses kicked by something named 'Jim'?"

I brought the animals to AvaSophia, who stared in amazement. I was honestly concerned that this was too much meat and some would spoil before she came up with what to do with it. The village was short of many supplies that I theorized would be needed to . . . craft smoked meat. In the meantime, I got to skinning them and took the hides to the leatherworking shop.

I still suspected it would take longer to cure a hide, despite my previous experience and suspicions regarding time here; once again, I was done in minutes. My Skinning skill was at Amateur rank, so I didn't have a failure chance anymore. That made the process simple enough. Unfortunately, upon review, it was going to take forever to get the skill to the next rank. Still, I did have one Novice level success while Skinning, which gave me more leather to work with.

My next stop was the leatherworking shop. I began adjusting the basic tools there and trying to figure out what to do. Standing directly in the center of the workroom was a large bench, where I placed most of my tools. When I focused on it, a prompt flashed before my eyes.

You are in a Leatherworking shop. Quality: Poor.

Now that I had the menu, crafting was actually easy. I selected simple leather armor, because it required fewer materials than I had. First I had to make some twine and some leather strips.

I started with the leather strips. I selected them from my crafting menu, and my hands began moving, seemingly of their own accord. Taking a piece of leather, I quickly cut it into strips. My skill in any of the crafting professions was higher than normal, because I had the actual Crafting skill. Mechanically, it gave me a bonus and substituted for my actual Leatherworking skill. While I'd never actually done anything with Leatherworking, my strips came out as if I'd been doing this for years . . . well, months, at least. I'd had a 0% chance of failure, but lacking the Leatherworking skill I would have had no chance of getting an improved result.

That task finished, I went out and made twine. That was easy enough and could be made from a variety of sources. I used the bark of many nearby immature trees and ended up with a decent-sized spool after a short while.

Having gathered all my supplies, I checked to see how much I would need of each. Home Depot, eat your heart out; with my menus, I could tell exactly how much I had versus how much I needed. Given that I wouldn't be failing at all, I could afford to make myself an entire set of leather armor plus a helmet.

The process was similar to the way it worked before: I selected the option on the crafting menu, and my body more or less went through the motions automatically. I could stop mid-process with a small chance of damaging the item, but I could also restart the process.

I had never made armor on Earth, but I got the impression, once again, that it was a much faster process here. The chest piece took about fifteen minutes, with the rest taking substantially less time. It looked rugged enough when I examined it.

- You have acquired: Poorly crafted Simple Leather Armor (Chest). Defense 4. Durability 30/30. Draining.
- You have acquired: Poorly crafted Simple Leather Armor (Pants). Defense 3. Durability 20/20. Draining.
- You have acquired: Poorly crafted Leather Armor (Gauntlets). Defense 3. Durability 15/15. Reinforced.
- You have acquired: Poorly crafted Leather Armor (Boots). Defense 3. Durability 15/15. Stealthy.
- You have acquired: Poorly crafted Leather Armor (Helmet). Defense 4. Durability 20/20. Open-face.
- You have acquired: Poorly crafted Leather Armor (Bracers). Defense 3. Durability 25/25. Item can block; +4 Defense.
- You have acquired: Poorly crafted Leather Armor (Set). Bonus Defense +1 to all pieces.

So, with my new armor on my defenses improved:

Defense:

- Head: 14 (9 base + 4 helmet +1 set bonus)
- Torso: 14 (9 base + 4 armor +1 set bonus)
- Legs: 13 (9 base + 3 armor +1 set bonus)
- Arms: 13 (9 base + 3 armor +1 set bonus)

You are lightly armored due to Simple Leather Armor set, which provides a total of 18 Defense. Your total Defense is now 14. This increases the cost of your Dodging skill by 50% and increases your Damage Mitigation by 4 points. Several pieces of your armor are Draining, reducing your Stamina recovery over time. After more than eight hours in the armor, your Stamina will recover only 75% as quickly, with longer times further reducing recovery. Your armor has the Stealthy property, improving your Stealth skill by 5%. Your helmet is open-face; strikes to your face ignore armor. Your bracers can employ the Block skill. Successful Blocks grant them a +4 to their Defense skill and can be used to block strikes against another part of your body.

Your Light Armor skill reduces the penalty to your Dodge skill to 0. Further improve your Light Armor skill to discover other abilities.

Standing and moving around in my new armor felt like I was wearing regular clothes, for the most part. They didn't breath as well; I could tell that eventually I'd have to remove them, but that was for later. Now, I was actually geared up to kill me some goblins head-to-head. I selected my quest menu and found "Goblin Menace" and sensed several opportunities.

To the north of the village was the forest, and to the south was the ocean. Both were pretty majestic sites, however none of my quest targets were in those directions. There were many of them to the east, so I climbed the wall on that side of town to get a better look. It was the first time I'd gotten any elevation to see what was going on around my village. As I looked, I realized that I could see mountains in multiple directions. Looking around further, I could see them closest to the west, and somewhat more distantly to the east. The mountains to the north were quite a ways off, at least several days.

We're in some sort of valley, then.

With my Perception and Lore skills, I was able to pick out the signs of a camp to the west. This was also where one of my quest targets were located. The camp looked reasonably large, but I'd have to get closer to really do an in-depth investigation. I wasn't sure that was the best idea at the moment.

Taking my supplies, I went back over to the Creek House and spoke to AvaSophia.

She was sitting in the house, the plowing complete due to the assistance of Kappa. That left her with quite a bit of not-farming to do. She's spent the time working on the house and tending to her children and Kappa.

AvaSophia had also used her Food Preservation skill, which of course, was a thing. She had built a crude smoker out of a hollow log, standing it up and hanging bits of meat inside. By building a fire at its base, and placing steel at the top for a roof, the salted deer meat had been smoked for hours. By doing this, none of the meat would go bad and have to be thrown out.

The warg was sitting on a rug with EveSophia, who was using him as a pillow. She was telling him a story about some dumb talking dog that solved mysteries with his stoner friends. Every so often, the fire would pop or she would stop and the warg would sigh. While the fire cared not for the wolf's murmurings, EveSophia would simply continue reading. Meanwhile, JoeClarance was brushing tangles out of Kappa's fur.

In short, the warg was living the life. AvaSophia looked less dubious about the whole plan now that the planting was done. She was currently spending her time mending one of JoeClarance's shirts. He had only two, insofar as I could tell.

"I'm going west to deal with some goblins," I said nonchalantly.

AvaSophia's eyebrows raised. "To the Western Gate?"

"If that's where they are, certainly," I replied. JoeClarance suddenly stopped his brush work and looked up at me. This led to another sigh from Kappa.

"There are a lot of goblins there," he said, while staring at me with near-terror in his eyes.

"Well, I've killed quite a lot of goblins, so I'll be fine."

AvaSophia watched me for a moment. "We were captured near the Western Gate."

Put my foot into it, I thought. "Well, all the more reason to deal with it now."

Putting down the shirt, she glanced away before looking back to me. "My husband died there, along with many other people from my village. They were skilled hunters and fighters, but when the goblins came, it didn't matter. Those monsters killed some and captured the rest."

EveSophia had stopped speaking and Kappa turned to me. "It is very dangerous there," the wolf said.

"I need to kill whoever leads the goblins at that gate. Do you know who he is, Kappa?"

"He is a very bad goblin. He does things to humans that are best left unmentioned." Kappa then placed his head on the teary-eyed EveSophia and pushed her farther into his fur before saying, "Especially children."

I couldn't stand for that, I thought. "I'm going to do it. And to be clear, I'm not asking permission from anyone."

JoeClarance was trying to behave, but EveSophia was gently crying into the warg's fur. Not the sendoff I had wanted. I stood up and left the house, but AvaSophia chased me down.

"If you are hell-bent on doing this, I need to tell you something. After the goblins ambushed our caravan that was escaping Harcharles's army, the survivors were dragged through the old Western Gate Fort to the valley. I didn't get a chance to see much while they marched us through the courtyard. However, when the goblins marched us away from the gate, I saw a large crack in the inner wall, facing towards the valley. It didn't look very safe or durable, so it may not be as well defended as the rest of the wall." Then she knelt down and scratched out a rough picture in the dirt. Her map showed up clearly and she circled the southeastern tower when she was done. "Here. But be smart. If there are too many, you can come back without getting yourself killed."

I took the stick. "Where did you see the crack?"

AvaSophia gestured to a spot and I drew a large X there. "Thanks," I said, noticing a prompt.

You have learned about Cartography. You are Unskilled. Never Eat Soggy Waffles!

I blinked several times. All I had to do to get a world map was draw an X on the damn ground? It was so fucking simple that it had never even occurred to me. Inhaling sharply, I calmed myself. Of course, that's how it worked. I could hear Shart laughing in my head.

Quest: Please Come Back Alive. Your town needs you. The entire population of your town desires you to return alive from your next quest. Bonus 25% experience.

The entire population of my town was a statue, the residents of one house, and myself. But heck, I'll take bonus experience.

Thanking AvaSophia, I left.

CHAPTER 17

JOURNEY TO THE WALL

- Jim
- Hit Points: 115/115

- Stamina: 125/125
- Mana: 40/40

NEW SKILLS:
Combat Skills:

- Shadow Walker: Amateur

IMPROVED SKILLS:
Non-Combat Skills:

- Cartography: Unskilled

- Leatherworking: Amateur

"WELL, THAT IS A PARTICULARLY BOLD PLAN," SAID SHART as I was walking west. He had finally reappeared as I started my trip outside the village, landing unceremoniously on my shoulder with a wet plop.

"Given there is a non-trivial risk to my person, I thought you'd be opposed to it," I replied.

"Hardly. I need you to level up or I'm never going to get through my Demon Door," said the demon as he made himself comfortable on my shoulder.

"Which I won't be opening," I stated coldly.

"We'll see. I have faith in you, my boy," replied Shart.

The map was immensely helpful, especially after I figured out how to add a mini-map to the edge of my awareness. I do mean awareness, not vision. The map did not occupy any visual real estate; I could just sort of sense it at all times to know where I was and where I was going. It wasn't Google Maps by any account, but it was far better than nothing. Bluntly, it looked like an untalented kindergartner with a crayon had drawn it.

Earning Cartography experience was easy enough; you just had to expand your map. I checked the skill menu, but there were several sub-skills tied to the map that I couldn't make out. I had figured out one, Exploration, before I left town. Simply going to the square was enough to unlock this skill.

You have learned about Exploration. You are Unskilled.
This is a sub-skill of Cartography. You find it easier
to discover points of interest on your map.

On my map, icons represented all the buildings in the village. One was for my home, which showed up as a house. The town square itself appeared as a star. The ruins of the church were marked by a cross, and the town hall was represented with a velociraptor—I had no clue why. I figured out how to assign icons by the time the town came up. I gained some Cartography experience for that.

While I was walking, I started reviewing my maps from my previous adventures in the forest. These had been made before I possessed the Cartography skill, so they were vague, to the point of being useless. I had an approximate idea of where I first landed in this world, but nothing got detailed until I possessed the skill. I suspected I could find my way back to the Grove of Demon Smiting if I was required to, but even that was dicey. I was able to append the town map into my realm map. That got me to about the halfway point of the next level.

Now my map was less crude, but still not great. It was like a *talented* kindergartner with a *fancy* crayon had drawn it.

Overall, I guessed that unless I found a large, detailed map that I could copy, I was going to get most of my experience in this skill from walking around. Special locations, like the Western Gate Fortress, would gain me a bit in my Exploration skill and experience.

I was now several miles away from the village. While there had been a road cut through the forest at one time, it was presently overgrown; thus, I was avoiding it. This left me moving in a zigzag pattern through the forest as the mountains loomed larger to the west. I spent my time gathering berries, hunting small game, and otherwise doing Woodsman stuff. It was relaxing for the most part; I was getting used to my new equipment and the forest didn't seem as hostile as it had in the past.

The only point of interest had been a cave. Coming off a sharp rise, it almost looked like a skull. Rocks around the entrance appeared as teeth, with a downward spiral leading into the cavern. I could just imagine descending down into its depths, almost as if I was a bit of food sliding down an esophagus. *Looks creepy, but what the hell?* I thought, as I'd started to enter. I actually made it to the rock teeth before Shart chimed in:

"I wouldn't do that, but then again, I like not begging for death," he commented. I was getting a solid "evil monster lives here" vibe from the location. I decided it would be better to search that particular area *after* I'd dealt with the goblin menace.

I parkoured from rock tooth to rock tooth, leaping away from the gaping maw and returned to the forest.

Eventually, night fell. I found a good place to rest in the crook of a tree; it required me to make a truly epic vertical leap and then I used my Shadow Walker skill to all but vanish. I dozed off for several hours before hearing a noise in the forest below. I cracked an eye open to see several warg-riding goblins, carefully marching through the area.

"He vanished," declared a goblin below me after a long moment.

"Must have jumped into a tree," said another. "Make sure he doesn't drop down on us."

"We've been chasing him for hours. He must have known we

were following him. Why go down so many jagged paths otherwise?" said a third.

"This could be the cave all over again." The goblins and several of the wargs sucked in air at that comment. They all looked around carefully, staring deeply into the darkness.

With Shadow Walker, I'd mastered the ability of standing so incredibly still that I became invisible to the eye. One of the goblins unknowingly pointed his crossbow directly at me, while his warg stomped around and sniffed the air. I checked my quest log; none of them were my quest markers.

There were five goblins and five wargs, as far as I could tell by looking. Using my Lore skill, I examined one.

• Goblin: Warg Rider, Level 5	• Warg: Level 4 Beast
• Health: 40	• Health: 60
• Stamina: 50	• Stamina: 80
• Mana: 5	• Mana: 5
• Skills:	
• BOW: Amateur	
• SWORD: Amateur	

This warg is based on a common Mountain Wolf. They are known to be disloyal but are quite common.

"Maybe he covered his tracks."
"But then the wargs should find him."
"Oh, yeah. They did such a good job at the cave."
"He must be in the trees," one yelled again, and they continued searching the trees with their crossbows. One shot a bolt into the air, while the rest pivoted around to see what he shot at. A moment later, a raccoon fell from the tree and struck the ground. Within seconds, several of the wargs were snarling and tearing at the meat.

That was my chance. I drew my bow and readied the first arrow. I could jump from this tree to a slight rise in the earth. It wasn't far to some underbrush, where the goblins would have trouble staying on their wargs. I partially considered just leaving them be, but they might stay below me all night. More pragmatically, if I couldn't kill five goblins, I probably had no business attacking a fortress full of them.

I shot the first one as he was trying to control his mount. The arrow tore through him, knocking him from the saddle onto the ground. He landed precariously close to where the snarling wargs were tearing at their fresh meat. Their lack of discipline coupled with new goblin meat caused the barely controlled feeding to collapse into utter confusion. Two of the goblins, the ones whose mounts were farthest away and seemingly more controlled, started looking into the trees. They didn't quite know where I was or even if that had actually been an arrow; their companion, for all they knew, could have simply slipped. The other two goblins were having even more trouble now that there was extra meat for their hungry wargs. They also did not seem to be impressed by watching their companion being torn apart by their mounts.

As the other two cast about looking for their unseen attacker, I realized that my Shadow Walker perk had stopped. I was still up in a tree at night, hidden by leaves, but I was no longer invisible. I drew back for another shot, the strain in my muscles apparent as my Stamina bar began its slow drain. I needed to hit one of the other targets unaware, so I would get my sneak attack bonus. Ideally, I would do so in a way that didn't reveal my position to the other one. Also, I had to hurry because it sounded like the warg fight was letting up. Glancing down confirmed the wild wolves were down to goblin bones.

After a long moment, my next shot presented itself. One of the riders turned his back to me as he continued walking and his companion was clearly not looking in my direction. I loosed the arrow, which buried itself in his back. The goblin bucked forward and died. The other goblin with him twisted around in his saddle, looking up into the trees near me. Suddenly, my Stealth icon exploded into an eyeball, although that particular goblin appeared to continue searching.

One of the goblins in the Warg food fight had been knocked

from his saddle but, still being alive, he'd managed to roll away to avoid being eaten. It was he that had noticed me take the shot. He leveled his crossbow and fired at my chest.

I learned a few things in that instant. When an opportunity to Dodge occurred, there was a point where you could consciously recognize that a Dodge was necessary. You had the briefest of moments to choose if you were going to Dodge or take it. Furthermore, you got some basic sense as to how difficult the attack would be to Dodge, and some idea of how much damage the attack would inflict. So, when the crossbow fired at me, I became aware that the cost of the Dodge was very high and the damage was also going to be very bad.

Jerking to the side, I watched the bolt fly past me and impale a nearby tree with an audible crunch. The bolt buried itself down to the feathers in the tree and I was abruptly aware that my arrows barely pierced down past the arrowhead. I was also aware than I had just spent 32 Stamina to Dodge a bolt.

Two more goblins had loaded crossbows. The one that had just fired was running his warg to the tree while drawing his short sword. I fired at one, who took the arrow in its side and screamed, but did not die. His warg jerked forward, running him out of my line of sight, leaving me bereft of targets. I then heard the heavy footfalls of another warg bringing his rider towards me.

Drawing my short swords, I got ready for him. I caught sight of the warg as he leapt into the air, the goblin launching himself off the back of his mount. He had only a single blade; I instantly realized that my dual blades would give me an advantage. His smaller size let him maneuver in the trees more easily than I could, but my larger size gave me a real advantage in strength.

What I didn't anticipate was that all 420 pounds of the warg would slam into the tree at nearly the same moment. The tree I'd selected had been reasonably large, but it had not been some massive monstrosity. There was a limit to the amount of force it could take. The tree shook violently, and my branch suddenly shot nearly a foot over to the side. Mobility made it easier to Dodge and move, but it didn't do anything to keep you on top of a rapidly bucking tree branch.

Reaching out, I realized that I had swords in both hands and by the time I'd released one I was already spinning down to the ground. Fortunately, my Mobility let me land on my feet. Unfortunately, both remaining goblins with crossbows had them aimed at my chest.

They fired in unison and I watched the cost of the Dodge spike well over anything I could expend to use it. I opted to evade one, at the insane cost of 64 Stamina. The second caught me in the chest, driving through my breastplate and deep into the shoulder. The force of the impact was enough to propel me backwards several feet, leaving me momentarily stunned.

My health bar dropped sixteen points from the strike, which had a special ability to ignore Defense. It looked like the goblins' crossbows were classified as heavy weapons and that prevented the Damage Mitigation skill from activating while wearing light armor.

Learn something new every day.

Sixteen points of damage was actually quite a bit better than I thought it might be based on getting shot by a crossbow at short range. I didn't dwell on that, though, because it was then that I noticed the wargs charging towards me, snarling. Their riders just dropped their crossbows, which were attached to the saddles with a strap, and drew their short swords. I doubted they could reach me from the backs of their mounts. Then again, I doubted that they needed to reach me, considering what their mounts were.

Tearing the bolt from my chest—which caused a Bleeding condition—I rolled to my feet. Launching myself towards one of the wargs, I was able to cut off the other charging animal. The remaining wargs were scattered. One was recovering from his literal run in with the tree, another was nursing wounds received in the rush for food, and the final appeared to have fucked off into the forest.

Reaching into my opposite bracer, I grabbed a dagger I had stowed there. I quickly leapt with it and my short sword at the ready.

The warg lunged and we met in a snarling, snapping strike. It bit at my right arm, the one with the sword, which I blocked with the bracer. I drove my knife into its throat twice, before the other warg got close enough. The second warg started snapping at my heel. I took my knife from the first Warg's throat and drove it into its eye. It yipped, releasing me, just as the second warg grabbed my ankle and dragged me away.

I could feel blood flowing from my arm where the now deceased warg had done some damage, but that was nothing compared to what was happening to my foot. Blocking effectively doubled the armor of my bracer, but the defense on my foot wasn't anything like that. Just getting my leg chewed on allowed the damage to mount quickly. Even using Mitigate, I'd still suffered over 10 more points of damage already.

Driving my heel with my other foot into the warg's nose for the first two strikes didn't seem to do much, but I'm nothing if not persistent. The third strike caused it to loosen its grip, allowing me to wrench my ankle free. This, of course, caused even more damage. Not only that, it also left the warg in position to jump at me again; with my damaged ankle I couldn't make use of Mobility. I could barely even use Dodge. I noticed a status icon appear and realized that it meant some form of leg damage.

I quickly realized why the goblins didn't have spears. With as aggressive as the wargs were, they were far more likely to stab their own mounts with them than add any meaningful damage to enemies. They seemed to use their swords more to goad their wargs at targets than for attack, though the one that leapt at me demonstrated they could do that as well. With my attention focused on the one in front, the warg behind me lunged, just as the one in front did the same.

My Perception allowed me to see both these wargs, as well as the warg nursing his wounds. He was being slashed at repeatedly by his goblin rider, desperate to bring him into the battle. The unmounted one was slinking around, but not attacking. That's when I realized the futility of aiming at the wargs, who would simply slink away without their riders.

The warg behind me finally leapt and grabbed my bad leg, causing the status icon to refresh. The warg I was facing snapped at my neck. I allowed it to chomp down on my left arm's bracer this time. As it did so, I drove my short sword into the belly of its surprised rider. He tried weakly to defend himself, but he was too far forward on his mount. I was able to drive the blade into him repeatedly, before cracking the warg on its head with the pommel of my weapon.

The warg released his grip on my bracer and stepped back, dreading a rider's command that was never going to come. The second rider realized my strategy and, at a barked command, the warg tossed me away. I landed in a heap, my leg refusing to work as I tried to roll back onto my feet. Then, I heard a scream cut through the air like thunder.

From the tree, the airborne goblin jumped down at me. He held his short sword in a two-handed grip, blade pointing at my chest. I didn't fully understand the math behind the strike, but it seemed like that would do a whole bunch of damage. Waiting until the last moment, I rolled to the side, but not before bracing the pommel of my short sword into the dirt directly underneath the goblin.

His blade sunk deep into my bracer, splitting it and causing even more blood to pour down my arm. But he landed on my short sword and the blade impaled him. It entered through his groin and shot out the back of his neck, piercing every vital organ on the way out. It seemed a particularly miserable way to die. Unfortunately, that left the blade buried in such a way that it was going to be challenging to get it back.

I drew my second dagger from my other bracer and stood, ready for the ankle biter. That was when the bolt slammed into my side, driving me back to the ground. Glancing over, I saw the warg still licking its wounds, but the rider was spending his time far more productively; he was getting ready to reload.

Things got fuzzy, leading to the realization that I'd dropped below half health. I pushed myself back up as two goblins stared at me in disbelief. Wait a minute! Hold the phone. Five minus four is one. I was fuzzy, but not that fuzzy. Where the hell had that other one come from? Had there been six all along?

"How is he still alive?" cried the ankle biter's rider.

"He's not fast anymore. Just start shooting him until he dies. It has to happen eventually," said the new goblin, as he strode towards me.

I saw my bow on the ground and started crawling for it. Checking my status page, I had the Hobbled condition.

You are Hobbled: base 8 hours. −2 Spirit. −1 Endurance. You are hobbled for 5 hours. Demonic Boon reduces long wounds to a tenth of their normal value. Your total time hobbled will be 30 minutes. 29:37 remaining.

Well, that was terribly not useful.

"He's going for his bow," called the distant goblin. His cohort realized this and led his warg over to the direction of my bow. As he got closer, I hurled my dagger at him; it slammed into his chest with a meaty thud. The warg snarled but the goblin continued heading it towards the bow, so I threw my second dagger. It hit a few inches away from the first with another sickening thud. The goblin struggled in his seat for a moment. I could see his life bar; he was still alive, just horribly injured.

"You are out of weapons," he shouted and turned the warg towards me. The wolf was smart enough to recognize an unarmed target and, after a few apprehensive steps, began running towards me in earnest. I painfully pushed myself to a standing position, as if to bravely meet my death.

Of course, I wasn't unarmed.

As the warg lunged, I blocked with my left arm and reached down with my right, tearing the crossbow bolt from my side. I jerked the wargs head around and drove the bolt into the goblin's leg, causing blood to spill out of the wound. I tore the bolt free and began driving it into the warg's neck until he let go and ran, his rider tumbling away behind him.

I grabbed both of my daggers from the goblin's chest and waited a moment as the final, surprise-appearance goblin readied his crossbow again. As he loosed, I whipped the body of his newly dead comrade into the path of the attack. The bolt exploded through it, striking me in the face. My helmet provided no protection from the attack, but the goblin's body had stopped about half of the damage.

Tossing him aside, I tried to rally. The pulsing red in my vision had become much worse as my Health continued its downward spiral. I sat for a moment as the goblin examined me. I yanked the bolt out of my cheek and tossed it to the ground, reaching for my bow.

"No," said the goblin as he continued to wind his crossbow. "It is not possible . . ."

I had to stand again to shoot, which continued to become more painfully difficult every time. I got to my feet once more, just as he got his weapon ready. I felt the meaty crunch as his bolt slammed into my leg, but the limb was already dead weight. I miraculously kept my balance, even as he spun his warg around and began to run.

I fired arrows at the fleeing goblin. I will admit that it was more just wildly firing at this point than actual aiming. The first slammed into his side, causing his small body to tremble. The second tore through his arm, as I staggered from my injuries. The final arrow caught him in the neck, causing him to tumble from his mount. The surviving wargs trampled him as they fled into the forest.

- Jim
- Hit Points: 12/125
- Stamina: 18/135
- Mana: 40/40

- You have gained a level Warrior
- You have gained a level Woodsman

NEW SKILLS:
Combat Skills:

- Conditioning: Unskilled

IMPROVED SKILLS:
Combat Skills:

- Swords: Novice
- Shields: Novice

"Well, you got your ass kicked," commented the demon.

"If you could have helped me, you would have, right?" I asked.

"Most certainly. But as I'm a giant floating ball, I'm pretty much just here for moral support."

After a few minutes of checking to ensure I wasn't bleeding out, I began taking stock of myself. I had three wounds on my leg. The first was a 15-point wound that would reduce my movement 50% until it healed. My Endurance had reduced the duration slightly, but, even with my enhanced healing, that was around four-and-a-half hours for the wound to heal. On top of that was another four-and-a-half hours to recover the hit points. I also had two additional wounds at lesser levels that were essentially the same thing, at 12 and 9 hit points each.

As wounds healed in series, I was going to be at half-movement speed for a bit over ten hours. I was looking at another thirty hours of healing after that. Several of the wargs had escaped. If they returned to whatever place they came from, possibly the Western Gate Fortress, someone would figure out what had happened. My only hope was that the dead goblins had something on them that would be useful.

I quickly searched the three mostly intact goblins. Two of the others had been dragged off by their mounts after they died, and the other had been torn to shreds.

The goblins' short swords were worse than mine, but the crossbows were interesting.

You have found: Goblin Crossbow. Damage 16–20. Durability 10/15. Heavy weapon. Penetrating 12. High velocity. Mechanical (high velocity).

Focusing on the properties of the weapon, I was able to find out some additional details. Heavy weapons meant that it affected heavy armor normally. Penetrating reduced my Defense by a like amount—12 in this case—which explained why they did so much damage. High velocity meant that it was much harder to Dodge than normal, which I was very much aware. Mechanical was another property; having the Mechanical property allowed the device to have an additional augmented property. In this case, that property was high velocity. However, it also required that the device be maintained. So, a normal high velocity weapon would be hard to Dodge; this weapon made it extremely difficult.

I grabbed the best-looking crossbow and several bolts. The disadvantage of these weapons is that it took around twelve seconds to reload them. This long reloading time made them challenging to use in a regular fight. However, they were very effective, from what I'd experienced so far. Also, firing them in volleys made the total cost of the Dodge increase. If multiple goblins shot in unison at a target, that target would be in deep trouble.

Opening their pouches, I found an assortment of mostly junk. There were some small coins and useless goblin knick knacks. I kept the coins. I also discovered several large pieces of jerky and what I thought were seasonings, based on the smell of several smaller pieces of meat.

I sniffed one of the pieces and took a bite. It wasn't terrible, just jerky. It did have a strange, indescribable aftertaste. I decided to try it with a piece of the dried root herbs, which didn't improve the flavor much. It was very bitter. I was about to spit both out when I noticed a new prompt, a glowing heart.

> You have gained the status Slow Heal. You will
> recover 1 hit point per minute for the next 6 minutes.
> Due to your Spirit, your recovery period is 1 hit
> point every 50 seconds. Due to your Endurance, the
> duration increases from 6 minutes to 7 minutes.

> You have learned about Herbalism. You are
> Unskilled. You possess a green thumb.

Of course *there would be herbs.*

I pondered this. There were herbs and my attributes directly affected how well they worked. That also meant that my Herbalism would probably impact them. Instead of recovering 6 hit points, I would recover 7. As I had a total of five herbs, that would give me a total of 35 hit points recovered. Assuming that it affected my wounds the same as natural healing, I'd be able to walk at normal speed after the last of the herbs finished working.

After verifying that the other goblins didn't have anything else useful, I started hobbling towards the goblin shish-kabobbing my short sword. I removed the blade, which had its durability reduced by 5. I then took two herbs and spent several quality minutes trying not to puke up said herbs. The first thing I needed to do after this was find some water to cleanse myself. Also, clean my sword. Goblin guts stink.

I was in terrible pain and the herbs were not doing much to reduce that. I noticed that I had a Level UP prompt and figured that the extra hit points would probably reduce my pain somewhat. It was worth a try.

I dreaded going into menu time when injured. Whatever level of pain you were in is where you stayed during that time. There was no decrease or abatement whatsoever. The promise of sweet relief from extra hit points coming out of menu time still made it something I didn't want to put off any longer.

- Level UP, Warrior 4
- You have gained one Perk. Please select it from the Warrior menu.
- You have gained a stat buff. Please apply within 24 hours or it will be randomly assigned to your lowest stat.
- Your Hit Point total is increased by 10. Your Stamina is increased by 10.
- Level UP, Woodsman 4
- You have gained one Perk. Please select it from the Woodsman menu.
- You have gained a stat buff. Please apply within 24 hours or it will be randomly assigned to your lowest stat.
- Your Hit Point total is increased by 10. Your Stamina is increased by 10.

Stat buffs. *Finally.* I hadn't gotten any of those since I started here. Looking at my Warrior sheet, it appeared that I gained a stat bonus every four levels. That seemed pretty normal from my D&D experience, come to think of it. It looked like level 5 was the Class Specialization level, so I had that to look forward to.

I lacked any form of instant, magical healing, and even using the herbs still left me horribly injured for hours in the case of serious wounds. My Strength and Endurance both impacted hit point recovery equally. It seemed that the higher those got, the faster I would recover.

Strength improved my blocking skills. I decided to put one point into Strength and one point into Endurance. My hit points expanded. After leveling, I went up to 145 hit points but, adding in the stat bumps, I'd further increased Health significantly. I was now rocking 175 hit points. Reviewing the numbers, I'd discovered that each rank of a statistic was cumulative; while increasing my Strength to above average only increased my hit points by 5, going to good increased them a further 10 points. Endurance was even better, as its base was 10 points per rank. Good Endurance granted a total of 20 hit points and 20 Stamina, up from my previous rank.

What was even better was that my health regeneration had doubled. Before, I'd estimated forty hours to fully recover. Now I was looking at twenty. Better still, was that the three remaining herbs I had were going to give me an additional minute of healing each. That made them much more effective; I'd recover an additional 27 hit points. I'd already gone through two, which had netted me 14 hit points. That was 41 total, which would at least take care of my leg injuries and start healing me afterwards.

I also had two perks. I started with Warrior, looking for anything to do with reducing pain at all. Being stabbed sucked and getting shot with crossbows sucked, so anything that reduced that pain was great. What I found was Iron Will. It allowed you to use Stamina to reduce injuries and passively caused you to feel less pain. I took it. Breaking out of menu time, the throbbing ache that filled my body diminished into something a mere mortal could stand.

An outside observer might wonder why I "wasted" a perk on Pain Mitigation, when I could have taken Improved Damage or something else . . .

"Hey, Dipshit, why did you just waste a perk on Pain Mitigation?" Shart asked.

"Because I'm tired of being in agony all the time," I responded.

"You could have taken something useful, like Improved Damage or something," argued the bloody bowel stain. I chose to ignore him. He harrumphed but said no more.

The reality was that being in agony for days at a time was starting to really get old quickly. If something wasn't done soon, I'd probably start finding excuses to stay in the village just to avoid it.

I was still left with a Woodsman perk. That list was a bit more complicated. Lore was very useful in a non-combat sense but, now that I'd gotten my pain managed, I needed to do something that improved my combat ability again. My next level seemed to have more abilities to choose from, but right now I was still locked into the starter perks. Lore was the big Woodsman one, like Mitigate was for Warrior, and Shadow Walking was for Rogue. I flipped through my options.

At this level, there were no more Dual Weapon fighting perks I could take. There was a single sword perk called Blade Works Best Alone, which focused on one-handed weapons. There had been times, such as when perched precariously in trees, when having an open hand would have been nice. Presumably, there was a higher-level perk that fit into the other hand like Single Handed Casting or maybe a Hand Crossbow and Sword. However, I didn't really have a good one-handed blade.

I eyeballed Marksman. It had an improved chance to hit and damage, but I still wasn't really missing my targets very often. Now that I was really paying attention, though, I noticed that it opened up the Marksman Tree. That sounded like it had potential, but did I really need another talent tree?

Looking through the rest of the perks, I saw one for Woodsman's Herbalism, which I briefly considered taking. I wasn't sure it would be worth having though, since I could probably figure out how to harvest herbs on my own. I was assuming it would function like Woodsman's Lore. Woodsman's Lore was considerably better than normal Lore. However, if all the perk did was make me harvest faster, what good was it? I had plenty of time to do that on my own.

Selecting Marksman, I saw another tab open up on my character sheet called, unsurprisingly, Marksman. It also removed Bows from my skill sheet and transferred all that experience into Marksman. Apparently, the perk superseded the skill.

The Marksman page showed the Marksman talent in its center, which looked like a glowing gold disk, with a group of other disks around it. As the disks were adjacent to something I knew, I could read all of them. Each disk listed a type of shot. There was: Power Shot, Piercing Shot, Stunning Shot, Pinning Shot, Frost Shot, Fire Shot, Lightning Shot, and Magic Arrow. I had one choice to select which shot I'd like to start with.

Making choices on a talent tree was different than just selecting perks. I could tell instinctually that the only way to improve this talent tree was to do damage with my ranged weapons. If I earned enough of this Marksman's Experience, I could earn more choices on the Marksman shot tree. With each choice, I could either learn a new shot or improve one I already knew. Unlike my main perk trees, I could see every option in Marksman and there were not that many selections. Most of the shots took Stamina to use. However, some took Stamina and Mana, and Magic Shot took only Mana.

For example, Magic Shot created an arrow made of magic that could be fired towards a target for the cost of 2 Mana, instead of costing Stamina. Its base damage looked like that of my normal arrows, but the fact that it only took Mana was useful. I tended to end a battle with all of my Mana intact, but not much Stamina. Anything that used just Mana would be helpful. I also reviewed Fire Shot, which cost 2 Mana and 5 Stamina to shoot and added 3 points of fire damage to my arrows. Adding elemental damage would also be useful, but that meant that if either my Mana or my Stamina was depleted, the shot was useless.

Normally, shooting my bow took 3 Stamina. With my recover rates, I could fire one shot per five seconds and completely recover my Stamina. I could fire slightly faster, at once every three seconds, and still have some degree of accurate fire. Unless I somehow learned to aim more quickly, three seconds was going to be my limit.

I was also trying to get to Mage level one. I had attempted several different ways to earn "magic" experience that would level me up in the magical classes, yet nothing so far had worked. Shart was useless—big reveal there—as he didn't even know why I was able to level in *any* of my existing classes. This left me guessing at possible ways to level into the magical classes. Currently, my idea was using Mana in offensive attacks, since just dumping magic into Shart hadn't done anything. If this didn't work, I'd have to go find a Wizard somewhere to teach me to cast spells, if that was even possible.

The demon was sitting on my shoulder again. "What are you doing when you are quiet like this?" I asked.

"I've used my Mana to construct a false reality where I'm surrounded by demon babes," Shart replied.

"You can't be serious." His hips moved a bit. *Oh crap.* I tried to prod him off my shoulder, but he appeared stuck. *Why?!*

Finally, I selected Magic Shot, all while still attempting to vigorously remove the demon, unsuccessfully.

I ate another herb and drew back my bow without an arrow nocked. Nothing happened. Focusing on the skill Magic Shot, the bowstring suddenly began glowing blue. However, when I pulled back on the bowstring, the effect stopped. Focusing caused the bowstring to glow blue again; this time, I felt it carefully. It gave my fingers a prickly sensation as they ran over it, but there was definitely something there.

Slightly tightening my fingers onto the blue string, I pulled it back while leaving the real bowstring in place. This time, the string went back and a glowing blue arrow appeared on it. If it had been golden colored, it would have looked much like Hank from the old D&D cartoon. I focused on aiming, and the targeting dot appeared. My Mana depleted by 2. I released the arrow and it flew across the clearing, leaving a bluish trail in its wake. It exploded in a flash of energy against the tree I had targeted. One thing I noticed was that it flew straight, unimpacted by gravity or wind, unlike a regular arrow.

I walked over to examine it. The damage was remarkably similar to my normal attack. I fired at a different tree three times in rapid succession. Each shot reduced my Mana by 2, but not my Stamina. I noted that even without aiming, I was very accurate with the bow. I only really needed the reticle for longer shots. I tried to do the shot without drawing the bow and was unsuccessful; part of the magic was tied up in the act of properly using the weapon. I could cheat a bit though: I didn't actually have to release my fingers to loose the arrow, as I could just will it to fire.

Improved Simple Bow. Damage 12–16. Durability 27/30. (Durability –10 due to Improvised Tools).

Experimentally, I picked up the goblin crossbow and looked at its mechanism. There was a crank on the end that one had to wind up for firing. I tried to will the shot to activate, and the string actually started glowing. I drew the weapon up to the firing position and activated focus mode, which caused a dot to appear where I would strike. That was far superior to the single wooden pole that served as the crossbow's actual sight. Targeting a nearby tree, I released the magical bolt, which had two effects. First, it struck the tree in a slightly larger and different magical blast. Second, my mind recoiled and I saw a status effect pop up.

Glancing at the status effect, it read:

Science and Magic. You have tried to combine a mechanical object with magic and have suffered

the Mana Lock condition for 30 seconds. You cannot
spend Mana for 30 seconds. All Mana costs on
mechanical devices are increased by a factor of 5.

Sure enough, my Mana now had an odd locked shape and all 23 points of it were unavailable to me. Mana regeneration was also blocked during that time, so the 30 seconds ended up costing me another 3 points of Mana that didn't regenerate when it should have. At least the Mana Lock wasn't painful, just unpleasant. When the effect ceased, I fired another magical crossbow shot with the same effect.

That sounded silly, but I realized I could shoot the crossbow at a target and then follow it up with a Magic Shot a few seconds later. That gave me the ability to use the Magic Shot as sort of a double tap from the crossbow. Of course, switching between the crossbow and my regular bow was going to get clumsy.

Content with my choices, I focused on my quest prompts again. I'd need to go back to the village to heal, considering how badly wounded I was. One would have to be a strong kind of moron to go into battle with wounds from another battle so fresh. Knowing the location of the goblin bosses was useful in that regard. However, when I looked through the prompts, I no longer saw the one to the west.

Mentally cursing, I brought up my map and realized that if those wargs were running, they could get back to the fortress in ten minutes. While all the riders had died, it probably wouldn't be hard to track where they came from. Alternatively, the goblins might just have someone who could speak Warg. It had only taken me about three minutes to learn that language, after all. If they did have a fluent Warg-speaker, it would take mere seconds for the goblins to know exactly what happened and where.

It had been at least fifteen minutes since the attack, probably longer. If the goblins were moving on wargs, they could be as few as five minutes away. I doubted I could make it back to the village, as that was nearly three hours east of here on foot. To the south, there was the ocean, but who knew what was in there. Turning north, I decided to trust my sneaking and . . . I paused.

If the boss had left his fortress, then his fortress was not well guarded. While I didn't have any healing potions, that didn't mean that no one did. If anybody did, it would be the goblin boss of a fortress. Sighing inwardly, this strong kind of moron started calculating the best route to get to the fortress. I snuck out of the clearing as carefully as I could while covering my tracks. I activated my Sprint skill and continued on with my zig zagging trail, heading west.

CHAPTER 18

TO THE WESTERN GATE FORTRESS

- Jim
- Hit Points: 69/175
- Stamina: 160/175
- Mana: 40

I SPENT THE NEXT TWENTY-ONE MINUTES "SPRINTING" TO-wards the fortress. If one wonders how someone sprints with a 50% movement penalty, the answer is poorly. That twenty-one minutes represented the amount of herbs I had eaten. On top of their recovery, I'd gotten back 2 additional hit points from my improved regeneration. Thus marked the end of the herb enhanced healing. Fortunately, when I leveled, I just gained the additional hit points; the fifty I'd earned were added to the mix, making me healthier than a horse.

I meant that literally. I could see a horse through the gate and it only had 60 hit points. Her name was Patches.

I'd found a spot on the eastern side of the Western Gate Fortress that appeared unguarded, as if the goblins were unconcerned with the area. I was just outside easy bow shot range and still protected by a cover of trees. The fortress itself was only marginally maintained and was basically surviving on the fact that it was large and made of well-crafted stone. It stood nearly eighty feet tall on the western side, which was a wall with the makings of a portcullis in it. That side looked like it would be a real challenge to assault.

The eastern side, where I was, looked far easier. Whereas the large western wall was both massive and imposing, the far smaller eastern wall was both shorter by about fifty feet, and only half as thick. Both walls were anchored by mountains on each of their sides. The mountains themselves were sheer enough that climbing would have been next to impossible. The area between the walls and mountains was boxed in, making a nice camping area for the goblins. I could see the tower that AvaSophia had described. There was a crack in the wall that I could easily climb. It looked like whatever had damaged the wall had also taken out the walkway to the tower. Presumably, the goblins avoided it. That said, there were still several goblins walking the eastern wall. They seemed attentive enough. However, their patrol pattern had gaps. My Lore skill and Tracking abilities told me there would be an opening soon enough.

While I was waiting in my protected patch on the eastern side of the Western Fortress, I'd actually found an herb. I could tell because in my vision it was highlighted with a greenish hue. While I didn't recognize it, I had gardened before. I carefully went about removing it.

You have found a Blue Moss herb. It has unknown properties. It is raw.

If it grows in nature, it must be good for you, I thought and started chewing on it. I instantly felt my Stamina recover slightly more quickly. Of course, it was nearly full anyway, so that wasn't all that useful at the moment. I found some more Blue Moss, now highlighted in my vision more clearly, and took another piece.

"What'cha doing?" asked Shoulder Shart.

"Getting ready to charge into a heavily defended enemy fortress," I answered. "Isn't that pretty obvious?"

"I was just checking. You seem like the strong kind of moron that would do something like that. Still, I had to check."

"Any advice?"

"Beyond 'Don't go in there, Dum Dum'?" He made a show of looking around. "No, you'll be fine. Just get in there and do hero things and try not to die. I'm surprised. I thought this place would be more heavily defended."

"Well, I mean—" I started, but then remembered that he was spending most of his time in that demonic spank bank he'd made himself. Who knew how much of the last goblin slaughter Shart was even aware of? "I'm sure it will go fine."

Finally, I spotted the opening. After checking that the goblin boss was not showing up in my quest menu, I sprinted towards the wall. With my Mobility, climbing the wall was easy. Each handhold was more secure than any climbing wall I'd ever been on. I could easily lift myself one-handed whenever the need arose. I climbed all thirty feet of the wall and ended up on top without any real effort.

I quickly encountered my first problem. As soon as I landed, I saw two goblins sitting within some broken rubble on the wall, playing dice. I could tell from their vantage point that if either had bothered to look, they would have seen me, too. However, due to the speed of my climb and their involvement with their game, they had failed to notice me.

Throwing both daggers as I landed, I scored two sneak attacks, as both goblins slumped to the ground soundlessly. Checking their pouches, I found two more herbs and assorted trash. Taking the herbs, I threw both bodies over the side, letting them splat to the ground outside the wall.

The interior of the eastern side of the Western Gate Fortress was uncomplicated. There were a number of structures built against the weaker eastern wall, but the barracks and armory were built into the western wall. The western wall had a giant portcullis that looked big enough to easily drive a semi through, much like the semi that killed me.

Talk about a sneak attack. NO. I can't think about that now. I have hero-ing to do.

The eastern wall had a similarly sized opening, but it was partially covered by a tattered wooden gate. Between them was a football field–sized courtyard strewn in misery.

There were several human bodies tied up to poles, some alive and some dead. There were also several cages full of people against the rough mountain walls in the north and south of the courtyard. The caged people were totally exposed and many looked emaciated. There were several carts, some damaged and some not, in the middle of the courtyard. Goblins were tearing into them, spilling out grains and other foodstuffs while searching for treasures.

I was surprised to only count about twenty goblins and no wargs. Six of the goblins were in the middle of the camp, searching through the carts. Eight more were on the high western wall; many of those had crossbows. The remaining six I could see were on the eastern wall walkway with me, walking in pairs and looking out into the darkness.

Not really considering whether it was a good idea or not, I got to work. The top of the wall was dark with the moon being mostly obscured. My Shadow Walking perk tied into my Stealth, allowing me to move quickly and quietly behind the nearby wall guards. I went through them like a hot knife through butter and had them all slain before my first newly found herb ran out.

Moving closer to the cages, I realized that they were all locked with some good, quality locks. I doubted my bow would be able to do much to them. Then again, I did have that goblin crossbow with its magical properties.

Before I saved the people, I needed to try to thin out the goblins some more. I started with my bow, looking to the western wall. I observed the goblins for a few long seconds. They were divided into three groups. The first group was largest; they were talking and looking to the west. The second was farther away, but both goblins were bent over dicing, seemingly totally distracted. The final group had one goblin watching the cages and one looking over the wall.

I shot the goblin looking over the wall first. The shot was challenging, as my Aiming ability showed true. Things like the wind blowing through a mountain pass caused it to dance everywhere. I was just about to try something else when I noticed that there were several flags whipping around and I could base my timing on that. I launched my first arrow and then had the second one away towards the cage guard before the wind picked back up. Both struck true and the goblins collapsed, which was both good and bad. It was good that they were dead. It was very bad that the one watching the cages fell off the wall and landed with an audible crack that everyone in the fortress could hear.

I loosed another arrow quickly, before anyone could act on the loud bang of the body. Just as I was firing my arrow, the dicing goblins looked up. The arrow pierced the left foe's eyeball and impaled his skull, causing his head to spin around 180 degrees. It looked horribly gross and unnatural but was presumably fatal. The wind picked up before I got another arrow away. His game partner started screaming. Everything broke into confusion. The majority of goblins in the courtyard had run over to see who fell by the cages, with two still too engaged in digging through the carts to care. The group of four goblins still on the wall had begun to look into the courtyard. However, upon noticing another goblin gone from the wall, they immediately moved under cover. They were pressing against the western wall searching for an attack from outside, while actually presenting their backs to me.

The only goblin who knew for certain they were being attacked from inside the fortress, the still alive dicing goblin, was actively looking around. He was trying to get everyone else's attention, but everyone was yelling too loudly for him to be heard. I took aim at him. However, the wind picked back up, making my aiming mark impossibly erratic. Remembering that the Magic Shot was immune to gravity, I guessed it was immune to the wind as well. I readied a Magic Shot, watched my aiming point neatly solidify, and fired.

As I watched it explode into a magical flare, the goblin picked himself up and dove behind cover. I instantly recognized that I had screwed up badly. The other goblins on the wall all saw me glowing blue and they all ran to the battlements.

Wow, I really am *a strong kind of moron*, I thought, as I stared at the neat blue trail running the length of the courtyard, giving the goblins an exact aiming location.

Grumbling, I dug up my combat log. All of my other arrow strikes had been sneak attacks, while the glowing blue arrow had not been. Without the bonus sneak attack damage, I couldn't quite do enough to kill a goblin in one shot, unless I got a very good shot. Because every center of mass shot I'd done had killed a goblin, I hadn't bothered to aim better. Now, I was going to have to aim much more carefully without that damage bonus.

Flipping back to real time, I figured, at the very least, the goblins would have a difficult time hitting me at this range. Their crude weapon sights, in addition to the wind, should provide me with a degree of safety from their arrows. As their volley of unerring death raced towards me, I was able to use the Dodge skill to dive behind the battlements on my side of the fortress. That Dodge had cost me over 40 Stamina, though.

How the hell did they shoot that accurately with those crude sights? I wondered. The strong moron in me then realized, *Hey, Dum Dum, they probably have the same aiming skill I do.* Their crossbows were also going to be much less affected by wind due to the heavier, faster bolts. You didn't need a good sight if you could just rely on a magic dot to see where your shot was going to land.

I stood back up. The goblins who were firing at me had all hidden to reload their crossbows. I knew from experimenting with mine that I'd have at least twelve seconds before they managed to get them wound. The single goblin I'd hit before spotted me the moment I spotted him. We both fired simultaneously.

This time, I aimed for his face. The Magic Shot wasn't a laser; the arrow still took a moment to cross the distance between us and, in the meantime, he'd released his own bolt. My arrow, unimpeded by wind, exploded into his face. This explosion caused his brain to boil and liquify, oozing out of his nose and mouth. His bolt flew at me, but it was a single shot at range. My Dodge skill allowed me to easily avoid it. It only took 4 Stamina, too. The battlements were giving me a bonus for Dodging into their cover, it seemed.

Meanwhile, all six goblins on the ground had merged back

together. They were screaming to the—unbeknownst to them—dead goblins on the eastern wall. All of them began pulling out shields as they ran towards me. I took a moment to fire several arrows, both magical and normal. Their Block skill allowed them to swing their shields around. Despite me finding "openings" that should have allowed hits, my arrows amounted to nothing.

I chewed on some Blue Moss while allowing my Mana to recover. I readied another shot as the goblins on the west wall all stood as one and took aim. I was faster than them; my Magic Shot released, striking one in the head. His crossbow fired erratically, flying off into the woods. The other three fired as one.

I again Dodged, ducking under the battlements as the bolts struck all around me. Shards of rock pelted my face, but it had only cost me 18 Stamina to Dodge this time, due to fewer shots being fired. With my herbs, that was almost manageable. I felt the quest marker change in my vision; that meant that the goblin boss had come within the radius of the quest. The goblin boss had realized, all too soon for my liking, that while he was searching for me, I had avoided him in my trek to the fortress. That put a timer on this. I had only a few more minutes to finish this battle before he came back.

With my Perception, I'd been keeping tabs on the cages. The two medium-sized cages on the south wall were filled with women and children. There also appeared to be some older and possibly sick people in with them. The third cage stood by itself on the north wall. As soon as the first arrow flew, at least three of the men and one very burly lady in it had instantly moved to the door, trying to break it open.

The shielded goblins were running up the stairs towards me. They'd still have to deal with the stairs in the dark, so I had a few more seconds. While the crossbow goblins were reloading, I dropped my simple bow and grabbed the goblin crossbow. The goblins charging at me slowed. The crossbow could penetrate their shields, meaning they had to be more careful. However, they were not my target.

Lining up on the lock for the northern cage, I fired the crossbow.

The bolt slammed into the lock, ruining it. Unfortunately, it still held. One of the men was kicking the cage with everything he had, trying to break the door open. Focusing, I charged up a Magic Shot and fired a second time, feeling my mana seize up as I did so. This time the bolt hit with enough force that the durability of the lock was reduced to 0 and it broke apart. The man's next kick caused the door to fly open.

Being unable to use magic, I did the next best thing: I charged towards the six goblins running up the stairs. Drawing my short swords, I launched myself at the lead one feet-first in an impressive drop kick. The goblin responded by activating his Shield Block skill. It was an odd sensation as my feet slid off of the shield, diverting almost all the force of my strike elsewhere. I landed on my feet, but was dramatically spun around, causing me to slam my elbow into the shield.

Of course, the shield struck my funny bone. There was no way that wasn't going to happen, given my luck. However, I still applied most of my large body's mass against that shield at a good rate of speed. The goblin was knocked backwards. Several things happened in quick succession. My left hand lost the grip on my sword, which clattered down the stairs. The goblins on the stairs were all bowled over by the lead goblin being knocked back into them. However, my feet were well outside of what would conventionally be described as "solid ground." With my left arm temporarily useless, I had to drop my other sword to free my right hand. I heard the sword land somewhere on the walkway as I grabbed the edge of the wall to avoid falling thirty feet into the courtyard.

This terrible position gave quite the target for the goblins on the western wall. They all fired their crossbows at my exposed, nearly-impossible-to-miss self. I sensed that the cost of Dodging would be extreme. Swinging my nearly useless left arm around, I somehow managed to knock one bolt out of the air which caused a glancing wound. Another just missed burying itself into my crotch. The third slammed into my right leg . . . again. In total, I'd lost 15 points of health from the attacks.

"I could use some help right now!" I called out to my dipshit demon.

"You got this," replied a voice that sounded like it was coming out of a barrel nearby. "I believe in you!"

Growling, I pulled myself up with my right arm, flipping onto the top of the stairs. The goblins on the staircase were still trying to right their balance and reorganize. A dagger would be a poor choice to deal with their shields, so I cast around for a larger weapon. I spotted a barrel and one of my swords. Grabbing the barrel, I lobbed it at the third goblin in the line. The barrel was half empty and half full of worthless garbage, but it hit with enough force that the goblin was knocked off the stairs and down to the courtyard below.

As the barrel continued to fly into the courtyard, I heard a little demon voice, growing fainter as the barrel flew farther away. "You son of a bitch."

"You got this!" I called after him. "I believe in you!"

The humans breaking out of the cage had run everywhere. There were at least a dozen of them. Several were digging through the wagons and a few more had grabbed anything they could use as clubs. One was already at the fallen goblin, grabbing at his sword and shield. Unfortunately for the escapees, the western wall goblins had momentarily decided that they were easier targets and had begun firing at them. I saw at least one go down as a bolt slammed into her side.

I moved to block the top of the stairs. The five remaining goblins were back on their feet and trying to force their way onto the battlement. While the stairway was big enough for one man to ascend safely, goblins were smaller. Two could fight almost shoulder to shoulder. However, between battlements, there was a walkway that was wide enough for two men to stand. That would allow just about every remaining goblin to rush me at once.

I'd realized that kicking was out of the question, as the shields would be able to knock me seriously off balance. That left me with my sword and hope. I held the top of the stairs as both goblins surged forwards, slashing low and to the middle with their short swords.

I couldn't give any ground, so I relied on my Parry skill and foot-work to keep the goblins from advancing. They scored several strikes against my legs, but those didn't cost me anything more than a few hit points. I scored on one as he slashed at me, cutting a bloody wound down his sword arm.

The other lunged at me, but I blocked it with my bracer. That left him fully exposed to a powerful thrust of my own. Twisting the blade as I pulled it loose, the goblin collapsed to his knees, gurgling in front of me. As another goblin rushed to take his place, I grabbed the shield of the newly fallen goblin and pulled his body forward. The shield came off easily enough, but I didn't have time to put it on. The next goblin moved forward, finding a gap in my defenses. He used his momentum to drive a power strike into my chest, piercing my armor and wounding me.

However, now I had a shield. This was useful, as I could already sense that the crossbow goblins were ready for another shot. As they fired, I ducked down, covering as much of myself with the shield as possible. The goblins who were rushing forward didn't quite under-stand, as the one on the end was skewered by a bolt. The other bolts both struck the shield, piercing it. Whatever the rank was to redirect the force, I did not have.

Goblin Shield. Defense 10. Deflection 6.
Durability 2/20. Deflection contacts penetration
attacks on a point-by-point basis.

Suddenly the goblin in the rear screamed as a heavily bearded man charged up behind him with an axe. Before the goblin had real-ized what was going on, the lumberjack had chopped down into his shoulder deeply enough that it must have cut through his clavicle. It really didn't look like a survivable wound, especially considering all the blood and meaty bits flying through the air as Mr. Lumberjack fought to get his axe unstuck.

The goblin agreed with me, promptly dying.

The scream of their comrade distracted the other two goblins attacking me. This was not good for them, as I managed to drive the short sword into the side of one's neck. He survived the initial strike somehow, but fell several seconds later, bleeding everywhere. The final goblin found himself outnumbered and I managed to strike at his head. It's pretty easy to deal head wound damage when you are three feet taller and on a higher step than your opponent.

"Don't try it. I have the high ground," I warned.

He stumbled towards me, leaving his back exposed for the lumberjack to hack apart.

Huh, I guess high ground doesn't matter all the time.

Suddenly, I was in the clear. Grabbing another shield, I looked up to the ramparts where several other humans, including the rather burly lady, were throwing the screaming goblins off the western wall.

"Well, that was easy," I said, tearing the crossbow bolt out of my leg.

"You damn fool!" shouted the angry lumberjack.

CHAPTER 19

RESCUE

TWO MINUTES LATER, AND AT THE URGENT INSISTENCE OF a very angry lumberjack named OttoSherman, I had been brought down to the central part of the courtyard. The locks were being hacked off of the two cages at the southern wall. A dour-looking bearded man was standing there with the burly woman. She also looked dour, but you can't just describe everyone as dour.

The dour-looking bearded man glared at me for a long moment, so I used Lore on him.

- Fenris: Warden, Level 6
- Hit Points: 76/80
- Stamina: 70
- Mana: 25

Warden is a sub-class of Woodsman, who stand to defend the forest and nature. They are skilled at defending an area. They prefer to use traps, swords, and shields over more common Woodsman weapons.

"Who are you?" he barked.

"You can call me Jim."

He inhaled sharply. "I'm in no mood for games."

The woman elbowed him. "He's telling the truth. Poor guy."

I frowned at her and she just shrugged.

"I am Fenris and this is SueLeeta," he said, gesturing at the woman. "What were you thinking?"

Fenris was a tall, dark rock of a man, with broad shoulders that seemed unbowed from his captivity. He was glaring at me with piercing brown eyes. SueLeeta, on the other hand, was looking at me far less angrily and far more curiously with her own green eyes. Her auburn hair was in a tight braid that went just past her enormously well-muscled shoulders. She was almost pretty, but her shoulders were so ripped that I wasn't sure it was appropriate to think of her that way.

"Well, I was thinking that you had been captured and thrown in cages, so I should probably rescue you," I replied. He seemed madder than I would have figured. I pondered why. Breathing in deeply, I suddenly recognized the smell. It was the odor of wargs. Looking around, I could see many warg tracks. One of the buildings nearby had the smell of a kennel, meaning it smelled like shit. Literally.

"Do you realize what you've done?" asked the burly woman.

- SueLeeta: Hunter, Level 5
- Hit Points: 73/75
- Stamina: 60
- Mana: 25

Hunters are a sub-class of Woodsman, who travel the forest searching for animals to hunt. They are skilled at picking out targets and eliminating them. They prefer archery but are skilled with a spear. They frequently have animal companions that assist them in their adventures.

I frowned. "Saving . . . you? I attacked when the wargs left. They posed minimal danger to you."

She paused for a moment before examining me more critically. "But they will come back. They tangled with something in the woods tonight. Ten Wargs went out this morning with riders, but only five came back. All five were wounded and returned without their riders."

"Yes, it was a bad fight," I said.

Fenris's eyes narrowed. "You know who fought them?"

"*I* fought them," I replied coldly. "I came here to kill the leader of this place."

Fenris's nostrils flared. "You came to kill Grou'tuk, the Warg

Master? Well, why didn't you say so? That's just easy-peasy. It's a wonder no one has ever thought to kill him before." Rolling his eyes, Fenris continued, far more seriously. "You do realize how many men have died trying to kill that bastard, right? Only the Weird Sisters are worse."

"They are pretty tough." I nodded, spitting out my healing herb and chewing on another. Fenris glared at me, while SueLeeta continued examining me with her own Lore skill. "Are we going to get this place defendable or do I need to do it myself?"

"Well, I suppose we'll have to," snapped Fenris, "given that we don't have any other options. A bunch of unarmored humans with goblin weapons against Grou'tuk's best wargs. Should be real fun."

"I said I'm here to *deal* with Grou'tuk," I reminded him. "When I'm done with him, I'll help with the wargs."

Fenris was about to launch into a hot retort when SueLeeta elbowed him. Her hands flashed into two quick movements and Fenris examined me. I recognized that they were both using Lore on me but wondered what they were getting. With my amulet and Shadow Walking, they should have had a pretty hard time figuring out that I was lower level than either of them. However, my own Lore ability allowed me to recognize several of the hand gestures that SueLeeta was making. They were Ranger Speech used by Woodsmen. She said "Jim, Negative Health, Herb," or in longer form, "Jim's health isn't affected by that herb."

I signaled back, "Herb good, Health good."

Fenris deflated slightly as he watched my Health slowly inch up as the herb did indeed work. But unlike his Health, which was fully recovered after two minutes, the 2 points of Health I recovered were only 2 more of my 175 hit points. It was only a drop in the bucket, so to speak. My hit point total was literally greater than both of theirs together; to Fenris, that could only be from me being absurdly higher level than them. "I didn't realize. If you think you can defeat Grou'tuk, it would be greatly helpful."

I nodded. "Get that gate blocked."

As he walked over to the gate to cover the eastern approach with a cart, I deliberated for a moment. I could reasonably bail on these people, either going out the western gate or skirting the mountain and running back to my village. Part of me questioned why I was doing this in the first place.

Because, honestly, what else do I have?

Other than the village, I didn't even have a safe place to sleep. There were goblins everywhere and each group of people I found described everywhere else as being war-torn and terrible. So, either I could make my village bigger and safer, or I could wander off into the unknown alone and probably be much worse off.

"Shart?" I questioned internally. He didn't respond. *Damn demon.* Looking down to where the barrel had landed, I could see some demonic tracks. They vanished rapidly, though, as the demon must have flown off to pout.

CHAPTER 20

PLANNING THE BATTLE OF THE WESTERN GATE FORTRESS

WE ONLY HAD A HANDFUL OF MINUTES BEFORE THE HOST of wargs plodded up to the eastern gate of the Western Gate Fortress. The gate to the west could be shut properly, having an oak door a foot thick. It covered a heavy steel portcullis that was unblemished, despite the long years it had stood unused. Given the unblemished walls, an attack from the west would have been impossible. Unfortunately for me, they would have to attack from the east and that was not in nearly as good condition. I'd certainly not had much trouble getting past the eastern wall, especially with the huge crack in it.

Now I had only four men guarding the wall with crossbows and spears to keep others from penetrating it. There was a certain poetic irony to it, if you were into things like that. The eastern gate led to a tunnel through the ten-foot wall that still had an impressive door on only one side. The other side of the door had been shattered years back and was wide open. We had jammed two carts into the tunnel and cut off their wheels. It would take a serious effort to break through. That would, at best, limit the number of wargs that could pass through at one time to a hopefully manageable number.

We had thirty men and women who claimed they could fight, and my Lore skill mostly agreed with them. However, several of them were just listed as townsfolk and that was troubling. Every warg and every rider was listed as a combatant. There were forty of them, including Grou'tuk. I finally laid eyes on my approaching target, from my perch on the eastern wall. I used Lore.

Grou'tuk: Warg Rider, Level 10

I didn't get any other information. Just a name and a level. I was feeling confident right about now.

Not.

Grou'tuk was a nearly-five-foot-tall specimen of goblinhood. He had short tufts of black hair on his green skin and his legs looked oddly splayed, as if he were very used to being in the saddle. His warg—and one must consider *his* warg—was also huge for the species. That translated into quite a bit more than huge for a goblin. Both were covered in scars and were wearing leather harnesses.

Mentally, I pegged Grou'tuk at between 120 and 150 hit points, and similar in Stamina. I also guessed he had skills in Crossbow, Sword, and Shield, given that he had all of those things obviously displayed on him. His warg, cleverly named "Grou'tuk's Warg," had 100 hit points, far more than your average warg.

Easy-peasy, I considered, as I brought up my crossbow and sighted on the powerful looking goblin. The little green dot lined up with his mouth. I was contemplating what special shot to use when he called out.

"Which one of you strong kind of morons talked the rest of the weak kind of morons into doing this?" he shouted, in a surprisingly deep voice for a goblin.

"That would be me," I shouted back. "Get off my lawn." With that as my only warning, I brought the weapon back up and took aim . . . and the targeting dot promptly started flowing everywhere but on Grou'tuk.

"Are you the one that killed my scouts?" he yelled back.

"Well, they were annoying me and I figured you wouldn't mind," I said, again trying to aim at him and failing utterly. I could see Grou'tuk with my zoom feature; up close he was uglier than I'd initially given him credit for.

"It will be a joy to kill you," he declared, before turning to his troops. The goblin boss was giving orders. I tried in vain to line up a shot on him, but I could tell in my heart that if I fired, the arrow would miss.

"Sir, what are you doing?" asked Fenris.

"Trying to get a better look at him," I said, attempting to get any sort of aim point on him. I was just playing around with my crossbow at this point, and it was not helping.

"See," hissed SueLeeta. "He's just trying to see the enemy commander's face. He knows you can't fire at range at an enemy leader during battle."

GODDAMNIT, why can't anything be easy? I thought, as I stopped aiming and glanced back at Fenris. "He's ugly, but don't worry, I've dealt with worse." Fenris bought it. Turning back, I commanded my twenty archers to get ready for battle, as well as the six who were to use spears if the goblins broke through the makeshift gate. I checked the crack; four men were also there, just in case the goblins got frisky.

"What is the plan, J— Sir?" he asked. For the first time, I noticed that Fenris was looking a bit worried. I was out of my depth and was just about to tell him so, when I remembered something. I possessed a source that was chock-full of useful information and was always happy to tell you how smart he was and how stupid you were.

Bringing up my menu, I noticed there were a few prompts. I ignored them. I needed to talk to my pouting demon, and I was going to do just that. I quickly tried dumping a few more points of Mana into him via the bond but, of course, nothing happened. Desperate, I tried something I'd specifically been told not to do.

I tried to draw Mana *out* of the bond. The cosmic link between the demon and me was a bit like a networking cable. Inside the bond, there were many strands, including the one to transmit and receive Mana. Before, I'd grabbed the whole string and, since Shart had wanted to get power from me, he'd let me do just that. On the other hand, Shart was really fond of his Mana, so the mystical connection for taking it from him was a bit harder to grasp.

That said, I was annoyed and desperate. After a few moments in menu time, I got it. However, getting it was only the first problem. I next needed to find a point to draw from, which took quite a few more moments. I searched and searched across the strand until I finally found a point that was a bit weaker than other spots. Scratching it with my metaphysical thumb, I exposed the tiniest bit of the surface and tried to draw mana out of it.

"YOU KNEW I WAS IN THAT BARREL!" came a screech from the back of my mind, as the demon materialized into my menu vision. He was no longer an amorphous blob, but an imp-like avatar of himself, all black and wicked looking. The fact that he was monstrously pissed off was just a bonus.

"I thought you could handle it."

"Every time I assume you aren't a total idiot, I am left disappointed." Shart glowered. "I got my Mana and I did what you asked, so I've been off dancing in my own tiny Mana pool, trying to forget this horrible event ever occurred."

It's hard to point your finger at someone in menu space, but I successfully poked him in the chest with my mental cursor. "I've needed your help, repeatedly."

Brushing my cursor away, which felt like someone grabbing your hand and throwing it to the side, he said, "No, you really haven't needed it. You figured it all out on your own."

"I nearly died several times," I reminded him.

"But you *didn't*, and I wasn't worried. You could take any five creatures in the valley at this point; it'd take an army to kill you."

"Turn around."

"Mother Fucker!" screeched the demon, as he first turned towards the goblins and then back towards me. "You always seemed like the kind of guy who just pisses people off, but seriously, why do you have a death wish?"

"I got a quest."

"You got no brains!" screamed the demon. "Is this mass combat? Oh shit, it *is* mass combat. Which one of you idiots is the captain? *You* are? Shit! What the hell were you thinking? You've never even been in a mass combat before."

"That's why I need your help. Why can't I target the boss?"

"You can't because that's against the rules. Didn't they have war on Earth?"

"We could target commanders on Earth!"

"Seriously? Wow, your wars must have been weird. Okay, I have a plan. Go to the Mass Combat tab and find out where it says leader."

Glancing through my menus, I found that I now had a Mass Combat tab. Also, I discovered some points to spend in Marksman, but that was beside the point. Clicking on the Mass Combat tab, I found where the leader was listed. No surprise, it was me. I also found the commander of the other side, Grou'tuk unsurprisingly, and the relative force comparisons for easy reference. There was a girthy red bar for his side and a tiny little green bar for mine.

That can't be good.

"Okay, I found it!"

"Good," said Shart. "Now, click on yourself. Then, when you receive the prompt, you can try to hand it off to someone else. Alternatively, and I highly recommend this, just select abandon field and then we can run the other way."

"I'm not leaving these people to die."

"But *you* will die," cried the demon. "And if you die, I'll have to find another person to escape with. I'm so low level, it's going to be really hard to find someone worthwhile."

"So, if we all die, it would be inconvenient for you," I said, just to clear the air.

"I would be moderately inconvenienced if *you* die," clarified the demon. "I'd be stuck here for decades while trying to replace you. Why can't you think about *me* for once?"

"Because, when you leave this place, you are going to kill me," I said, remembering the root of our problem.

"But that's *then*. They are going to kill you *now*."

"Can you *help* me now?"

"Yes, but I don't want to. You are a stupid asshole," replied the demon, sniffling. "But I'm great, so I'm the only one who can."

"Cool. Also, the demonic regeneration works great."

"Of course it does. All my powers are awesome," said Shart, as I felt him start knocking around in my character sheet. In case you are wondering, it felt like a demon playing around with my soul, and not in a good way. "You have unspent Marksman experience, because you are stupid. No free class Perks, though."

All at once, it felt like my soul was being torn apart as Shart rooted further into it. "Wait, you *are* an actual idiot. A big heaping mound of buffoonery, covered in stupid, with a side dipping sauce of moronic fool. You didn't spend your Founder perk!"

"I have a Founder perk?"

"Yes! From when you claimed your village. So, I'll just toss some demonic energies into the perk and change it to a Warlord perk. Boom."

It felt like someone had just taken a sledgehammer to my skull. I would have collapsed, had it been possible in menu time. The entire interaction with Shart had taken less than a second in real time. Glancing back at my sheet, I saw that I now had a Warlord perk. At first level, all I could choose was War Leader talent, so I did. It was similar to Marksman, in that talents were perks with their own experience tracker and skill tree after it.

Several things happened all at once. The green bar for our humble army got bigger. Much bigger. It wasn't as long as Grou'tuk's, but it wasn't a heel of bread to his great loaf of power, either. A local map appeared, showing the battlefield where several of the defensive points were listed. The map also detailed where to station people on the wall so they could earn bonuses from my War Leader talent. Then, to my shock, I noticed my new Warlord perk was oozing purple, instead of being the usual gold color.

"Why is that perk oozing purple?" I asked. It was a bit troubling.

"I told you: I infused it with demonic magic. It's 50% more powerful than it would be otherwise."

Glancing down at the War Leader talent, it was at Rank 1. A brief description offered itself, informing me that War Leader allowed me to have a second in command, assign station commanders, and create auxiliaries. Furthermore, it allowed me an overhead view of the battle and the ability to grant some of my weaker perks to my men. They also got a flat bonus for me being their leader, which was amplified by +50% from my demonically-infused talent.

Now that I was aware of the battle outline, I slotted everyone into place. Another nice thing about the War Leader talent was that I could instantly know who was best suited for each position. Dropping their names into the spots, I noticed that Fenris was almost always listed as the best man for the job. When I checked on second-in-command, only he and SueLeeta were visible. Reviewing the list confirmed what I had already guessed: they were the two highest level people here.

I opted for Fenris as my second-in-command and placed SueLeeta as the captain of the archers. This was the only position she outperformed Fenris, and I was confident in my placement of them both. Filling up these two important roles increased my green bar further. To round out my forces, I selected the lumberjack, OttoSherman, to command the cracked south tower. I also placed one of the townsfolk in charge of the auxiliary healers, as she seemed to have some talent for both healing and leadership. I finished my battle plan and a prompt appeared:

**You have completed your battle plan. Would
you like to issue orders? (Yes/No)**

Pausing for a moment, I switched to Marksman. It was now up to Rank 2, which gave me additional damage on all ranged weapons. I also had one more talent point. I tried to push that into Magic Shot, but the next rank of that talent took 2 points. I also noticed that Magic Shot was earning experience points. It looked about halfway to reducing the cost of Magic Shot 2 by 1 point. However, I didn't have 2 talent points now. Instead, I went over and chose Powerful Shot, which used Stamina to increase damage.

You have learned Powerful Shot. You can make a powerful shot costing 5 additional Stamina to do 5 additional Damage.

Assuming it was anything like Powerful Blow, from my Simple Weapon skill, Powerful Shot shouldn't be complicated to execute. I figured it was better to have an ability that I knew how to use now, than to have to figure out a new one during battle.

I had no more talents, or perks, or buffs, or alerts, so I went back to my prompts.

I selected "Yes" to issue orders and returned to real time.

For me, several minutes had passed; to Fenris, I'd been standing still for about two whole seconds. Suddenly, I felt something overtake me. It was like the spirit of Patton entered me and began issuing orders for a successful battle. I gestured with my hand at OttoSherman. "Get to the South Tower and defend it at all costs."

The man looked surprised, but nodded. "I'll not fail you, Sir!"

"SueLeeta," I said, "you will be in charge of the wall archers. I'll need you to kill every damn one of those wargs before they get close."

"Sir," she replied, looking pleased, and then ran off up the stairs to where the archers were waiting.

"Fenris," I started, looking at the man. "You will be my second. If I should fall, you will ensure that the battle continues."

He nodded, his expression changing as he did something. I

recognized it as him looking at his menus. He could access the war map as my second-in-command. I could see Fenris's level on my map. However, a quick glance showed my own image as having a star instead of a level. Hopefully, that's what Fenris saw, too. Otherwise, he would realize I was lower level than him pretty quickly.

I flipped out of menu mode just in time to see Fenris's eyes shoot open. I wasn't sure exactly what he had seen in his menu mode, but he looked far less dour now. He had a determined glint in his eye as he proclaimed, "We can win this."

"Of course."

"That's the elite warg cavalry," he warned. "They should have a much higher Battle Strength than us."

"We are in a well-defended fortress. That is going to offset their advantages tremendously," I replied. I was trying to look commanding despite not understanding what the hell he was getting at.

"When I fought them with more men, we were in a well-defended spot, too, although we didn't have near this Battle Strength," explained Fenris, his expression suddenly shadowed. I deeply hoped that Fenris wasn't harboring any doubts about his leadership skills, given the terrible conclusion of the last battle he fought.

"Well, we'll still lose if we don't fight our best, so let's kill some goblins."

Fenris nodded slowly at first, then with more conviction, before moving down the stairs to the east gate. The five men, plus Fenris, would keep the gate from burning, while we all filled the goblins with enough arrows to keep them away. As I confidently looked around, surveying the goblins with disdain, I came to where SueLeeta stood, also surveying the battlefield.

Actually, looking at the goblins with anything other than an expression of utter confidence in their defeat was challenging, now that I'd activated War Leader. I wasn't sure I actually liked losing control over my body like that. When I'd given orders in a crisp clear voice, it had not been my own, but rather my body acting out the motions of the plan I'd drawn up. In an indirect way, I'd been in control back then. Now, my facial muscles were locked up into an expression I had very little control over.

"Excellent plan, Sir," whispered SueLeeta, as I stood next to her.

"Thank you."

She grinned, tearing her gaze off the battlefield to flick to me for a moment. She, too, was compelled to quickly look back at our common enemy. "You held off on showing your plan until the last minute. You let Grou'tuk start moving his troops into position and preparing to order an attack before you committed us."

I had indeed seen the goblin forces moving right before I activated the plan. Now, they seemed to be hesitating.

"Interesting strategy," she said. "Grou'tuk was ready to attack us poor, unorganized defenders but, suddenly, we have a strong defensive plan. Now, he doesn't know what to think. To top it off, there is you, and you are going to kill Grou'tuk yourself. Goblins never count the commanders in their battle calculations. All you need to do is kill the goblin leader, and we are going to win this easy."

I wasn't sure how putting people places constituted a strong defensive plan, but the logic of this world was well outside my understanding. It seemed more like a last ditch Alamo-type situation. However, if SueLeeta wanted to believe I had a "strong plan" . . . well, whatever it took for her to willingly go into battle.

"Remember, the eastern gate of the Western Gate Fortress!" I shouted.

CHAPTER 21

PRE-BATTLE JITTERS

WE STOOD EYEING EACH OTHER FOR SEVERAL MORE MINUTES. The goblin leader was adjusting his strategy and I wouldn't respond. He'd shift it around more; I wouldn't respond again. I was defending, ultimately, and I had some very strong defenses. Adjusting them would have exposed some holes that his fast-moving wargs might have been able to exploit. Instead, I just kept my troops in position, archers at the ready, and melee fighters where they were most likely to do some good.

Hopefully, we'd kill enough of them on their way in that they would break. If the goblins had siege equipment, they could have peeled through the crumbling wall easily. Thankfully, they didn't, which left me wondering what was going to happen. I could climb the crack, so, presumably, some of them could as well. Who, though? Also, in my previous battles, when the goblins had died, their wargs usually bolted. It seemed they bolted back to Grou'tuk, who was now on the field with them. Would the wargs stay and fight just because he was here?

I could see the durability of the still standing partial gate at the eastern tunnel. What was left of it was not impressive. Even with the carts jammed into the hole and against the gate, it was still one of our two main weak points. Our second weak point, the crack in the wall, would be much easier to defend via the archers. As I contemplated these fragile areas, I continued to watch the goblins. They were busy shifting resources between the two unsound targets. They kept at least five attackers for the crack, but sometimes they had up to fifteen.

Had Grou'tuk just placed troops and let it go, I probably wouldn't have noticed anything suspicious. However, closely watching his constantly shifting troops led me to discover that there were always the same five brown wargs assigned to attack the crack. I finally managed to activate Lore on one of them.

- Chode: Warg, Level 4
- Health: 60
- Stamina: 80
- Mana: 10
- Climbing: Novice

These Wargs are based on mountain dogs, renowned for their surefootedness and climbing abilities.

I hadn't seen any wargs with Climbing skill before. I guessed that it was a difference in breeding and that this particular breed could actually climb the badly cracked portion of the wall. I wondered how quickly. That also left thirty-five other wargs for the gate. Fortunately the gate and its blocked opening were not large enough for all of them to attack at once. Still, at least four or five at a time could probably get in on the action. That left me wondering how they were planning on breaking through the bottleneck.

The intact gate door had just enough durability that the goblins couldn't break through before we shot them to death. Hopefully. I considered that they might burn their way in, but it would take several minutes. Anything that kept them in the killing field outside the wall was to our advantage. Even a few minutes would buy our archers time to break them.

Everything was going to be decided in the opening minutes of this battle. If the goblins got pushed back, they would lack the numbers to make a second attempt. Furthermore, it was getting light out; I could see the beginning of orange and yellow that heralded dawn in front of me. It was so far my experience with the goblins that they fought less well in bright light. If they stalled and waited until tomorrow night, we could fortify the wall much better. Any time they gave us strengthened our position substantially.

CHAPTER 22

BATTLE OF THE WESTERN GATE FORTRESS

MORE TIME WAS SIMPLY NOT TO BE. GROU'TUK FINALLY DEcided that I wasn't going to bite and shifted his formation one last time. It was a configuration that was almost identical to his first formation. I knew this because I went back into menu time and carefully reviewed it, before deciding I didn't really need to change anything in response. Had it been a more open battle, and had I been more confident with my troops, I might have changed something. Perhaps I could have come up with a more detailed plan. However, the harsh reality here was that I was going with a very basic idea of holding the wall, because the goblins didn't have many options.

I was suddenly aware of SueLeeta's eyes on me, but I just nodded back at her. She was in charge of the archers, so she got to issue the order to fire. I was content to shoot with the group, though I did notso-subtly indicate to her that she might want to hurry it up. As she prepared, a glowing green area suddenly appeared around the wargs, indicating where she wanted us to fire.

The goblins started marching for a moment, tightening their ranks while still outside of bow range.

"They're quick. Fire low," I said, calmly.

SueLeeta glanced over at me for a moment. I saw her shift the targeting area down to where the warg's would be as soon as they started running. "When will they charge?"

"Soon. It will take several seconds for our arrows to hit them. They will start when we shoot," I said confidently.

SueLeeta thought about it for a moment and then nodded before screaming, "LOOSE!"

There were twenty archers on the wall and we did a good impression of a volley. As soon as we fired our bows, the wargs dashed towards the wall. The ground outside was mostly barren and somewhat uneven, though not nearly enough to bother the wargs. They moved with a speed even more impressive than I'd thought, but SueLeeta was not deterred. She had a Hunter's eye. The volley hit them just north of center.

If we'd had twice as many archers, it would possibly have stopped them. As it sat, only about ten arrows actually hit, which I thought was very good. Two of the wargs collapsed as they suddenly became riddled with arrows, falling mid-run and crushing their riders beneath them. Another goblin bucked back as well, an arrow sticking out from his eye socket. However, his warg kept charging. I guess that answered my query regarding the wargs' behavior in the presence of Grou'tuk.

"Loose!" called SueLeeta again. She was actually singing a song about archers as she released. I was close enough to some of the other townspeople that I caught them lightly humming along. It kept everyone firing on tempo, I supposed.

Our second volley was about as effective as the first. By this time, the wargs had covered nearly a third of the distance required to get to the wall. We might get one more volley in before they were too close. Then, we would shift to single targets. Another warg fell and three more goblins, including one of the riders of a brown warg. I spotted all five of those wargs heading towards the south tower, as expected.

I pivoted, intending to fire at one of the massive brown wolves. Yet, when SueLeeta cried "Loose!" again, something compelled me to pivot back and fire with everyone else. This third volley was the last, as the wargs were now much closer to the wall. We were firing every six seconds, but they could cover an absurd amount of distance in that time. They were covering 120 yards or so between volleys, moving with speeds I'd more commonly associated with a car.

Right before we released the third and final volley, the five Wargs broke from the main group. As the final volley was targeted at the main group, none of them took any hits. Two regular wargs and another rider fell, as the goblin's main line finally got close enough that they needed to slow down.

The brown wargs, however, did not. They started leaping towards the cracked wall, scrambling up it with a speed even I hadn't been able to manage. Considering their massive size, it really was quite incredible to see the huge wolves charging up the side of the tower. The first one got to the top before any of the defenders had a chance to fully appreciate what was happening. The warg, without slowing at all, prepared to leap onto OttoSherman.

That's when I fired my first Power Shot at the wolf's head. I hadn't just picked Power Shot frivolously. In this world, crossbows were easier to aim than conventional bows, because their shot traveled faster and was heavier. It ignored more of the atmospheric conditions than a regular arrow. Power Shot basically made my arrows function the same way as crossbows, but with the added benefit that Power Shot knocked the target silly when it hit them.

My arrow slammed into the neck of the warg, spinning it around like some sort of bad ragdoll effect. When the warg stopped spinning, its front paws were in the air away from the wall. It vanished over the side as gravity snatched at it.

Unfortunately, the second warg was just behind it. That beast didn't snap at anyone until all four of its paws were firmly pressed onto the hard stone of the wall walkway. One of the defenders jammed a spear into its side, causing the creature to howl, even as its goblin rider fired a crossbow into the man's chest.

The warg survived, the townsman did not.

I was already rushing towards the vertical line of wolves and several of the archers had suddenly changed their aim towards the wall climbers. By the time I'd gotten there, six more arrows had found their mark, with another climbing warg falling to its death. The defenders had managed to spear another warg dead, though its goblin then leapt onto his stead's attacker, stabbing him repeatedly with a short sword. The ensuing scuffle sent both tumbling over the wall's edge.

OttoSherman was attempting to use his axe to split the skull of another warg, however, he missed. He did, however, succeed in headbutting its rider, as the monster tried to protect his mount. The lumberjack's thick skull and high strength caused his headbutt to send the goblin flying backwards off the wall and into the rocky earth below.

When I got there, only two wargs were still standing, with only a single rider between them. I leapt with both my short swords, sailing over the cracked portion of the wall and straight into the side of one of the wargs. The creature had already taken too much damage and the impact of my strike drove it back several paces, where it collapsed.

The final goblin brought up his crossbow and fired at me. The Dodge was expensive at that range but, as I had little desire to get hit and plenty of Stamina, I jerked out of the way. Two of the remaining spear men managed to pin the last warg against the parapet. The goblin laughed and jumped at me, but I side-stepped his attack and drove a short sword into him. At the same moment, OttoSherman brought his axe down on the head of the last brown warg. This time, he did not miss.

Almost too easy, I thought, and instantly regretted it. I heard ten clanks, as grappling hooks were flung up the wall.

As the archers began either firing down at the climbing goblins, or attempting to remove the hooks, I noticed that they were not having much luck with either. The stout ropes were quite thick, and almost none of the archers even had daggers. What I didn't understand was that goblins didn't have a Climbing ability, as far as I remembered. Without warning, my War Leader ability activated.

Enemy Commander Grou'tuk has used a
battle action, Grapple Attack, granting his
goblin soldiers the rapid climbing ability!

Well ... that isn't good.

I quickly checked and found that I didn't have any battle actions, which was unfair. Seeing as I couldn't do anything about that though, I looked back to the goblins. They were climbing towards the lightly equipped archers. One-on-one, a man usually had an advantage on a goblin, but these were well-equipped goblins versus poorly equipped humans.

I grabbed a nearby grappling hook in one hand and attempted to pull it off the wall, failing miserably. The line was taunt, and the goblin on it was bobbing up and down rhythmically as he climbed. Now that I was looking, I realized that the rope's end was in a warg's mouth; they were playing tug a war with the freaking wall. And since they were 400 pound dogs, they were winning.

The brown wargs had just been a distraction.

Using the short sword in my left hand, I hacked at the rope twice before it severed with a snap. SueLeeta, likewise, took a broad headed arrow and, after carefully aiming for a moment, fired it at the rope, which also snapped. That was it, though, because then the goblins were among the archers.

The eight goblins went to work attacking the archers. SueLeeta managed to shoot one before a second one attacked her from behind. Another was knocked bodily from the parapet by an archer, who used a nearby unlit torch as a poor club. Then, the screaming of the townsfolk started. One archer got stabbed in the back by a goblin, while another goblin slit the throat of an archer who had been lining up a shot to save her friend.

I started wading through the goblins, striking at them with my short swords as the archers fought for their lives. I managed to kill two before I saw SueLeeta stand up with a bloody broken arrow in her fist. Another goblin was flung inside the wall, landing with a sickening crash on the cobblestone courtyard.

We'd responded quickly, in spite of the shock of climbing goblins. With the spearmen assisting, the archers managed to kill the two remaining goblins. We'd succeeded in killing all ten goblins at the cost of three humans dead, another six wounded, and a minor delay in shooting at the wargs below.

I got back to the top of the wall and got ready to shoot almost straight down into the mass of goblins and wargs below. I'd only loosed my first arrow when I saw two wargs running away from the fight, purposefully. Which is when I noticed the ropes trailing from the wolves.

Taking aim, I lined up on the first rope. It was attached to the harness of one of the fleeing wargs. This type of harness appeared to be one a sledding dog might wear, similar to the one Kappa now used to plow. It was designed to let a dog pull with all its strength. I released and watched the Power Shot blast into the dog's back, grazing the rope. The warg yipped but kept on running. When the rope went taut, it snapped, unable to support the tension.

The other rope was fine, however, and an audible crunching came from below. To my horror, I watched what remained of the eastern gate flying outward. We'd blockaded the half of the door that was missing, with the expectation that they would force their way in on that side. The hinge wasn't even set up to let the door swing out. I saw why that didn't matter: the hinge was still attached to the door. The powerful wolves had ripped the entire door *and* all of its hardware free of the wall.

I had not for a moment considered that as a possibility. The civilians had moved inside the western gatehouse, which would briefly offer some protection. There were even a few possible fighters among them, but not enough to really matter. For a moment, I was overwhelmed. I needed to think.

Remembering menu time, I retreated into my mind. I spent about thirty seconds just trying to calm down. Yes, this was bad, but, according to my Battle Strength menu, we were actually winning the fight . . . slightly. Half of the goblins and ten of the wargs were dead already; we'd only lost five people, though several more were badly wounded.

Fenris had actually found time to rig the wagons to burn. According to the close up on the battle map though, there was a red X through the cart. The trap had probably been destroyed upon the violent removal of the remaining door. The cart's contents were spilled liberally on the ground.

Breaking out of menu time, I glanced down at the remains of the wagon. There was a barrel of oil lazily pouring itself out into a mass of straw and cloth. I already knew my Magic Shot couldn't start fires, so I glanced over at SueLeeta. Her horrified expression was similar to the one I had worn only seconds ago. "Burn that," I ordered. "I'm going to go kill Grou'tuk."

With that, I jumped off of the wall into the inner courtyard.

CHAPTER 23

HERO WORK AT THE WESTERN GATE FORTRESS

THIS WAS, IN FACT, A TERRIBLE IDEA.

The walls were not ninety-degree, modern-construction, perfect edifices. So, technically, I was just moving down a very steep eighty-eight-degree ramp. At least, that's what I told myself, because it sure felt like I was falling pretty much straight down. I jammed my two magic swords into the wall, causing a shower of sparks. This, combined with my Mobility, Mitigation, and Damage Resistance, only had the fall costing me 12 hit points of Damage. I did certainly get down much faster than I would have otherwise. My precious swords, however, were both down to 0 and 2 points of Durability, respectively. I discarded them and drew my daggers.

Grou'tuk was there. He had stepped just inside the short tunnel through the eastern wall that was now totally exposed. From here, he was immune to the archers above. At his shouted command, warg after warg were rushing in to kill us. He grinned when he saw me land in the middle of this mess.

Asshole.

I had left six defenders down here, as well as the young woman who was serving as lead healer. Even now, she was attempting to drag away one of the wounded men. Three separate wargs, each with a rider, were already inside the courtyard, attempting to kill my remaining men. Fenris was fighting one by himself. Another man, bearing a sword and shield, was also engaged in one-on-one combat. The last goblin/warg duo was being engaged by two men with spears, until a crossbow bolt exploded out one man's back and he collapsed, soundlessly.

Suddenly, the man with the sword vanished as the warg grabbed his leg. With a practiced motion, the wolf flung his victim to the pack. The man landed next to several other wargs and his screams were pitifully—but mercifully—short. The goblin glanced around and took aim at the young woman who was still desperately trying to drag away the first wounded man. He fired.

I took all this in at a glance with Perception, so my next move could only be described as particularly stupid. Swinging with my bracer, I smacked the bolt away from the healer before rushing towards the warg. He turned to face me as I closed in, but he wasn't fast enough. I got near enough to drive a dagger into the side of its neck, as well as another blade into the goblin riding him. Only then did I notice that I hadn't deflected the bolt, so much as caught it in the forearm. It caused me 9 points of damage.

Stupid.

The warg was already wounded from his fight and died at the same moment his master did. The death of the swordsman had caused a slight delay in the warg reinforcements. Their unplanned fresh meal gave me a moment to run to the aid of the spearman. He was still locked in mortal combat with one of the wargs in the tunnel. He was trying to step back and give himself room to use his spear effectively, with the warg focused on trying to strike around the sharp weapon. I struck from the side, driving both daggers into the warg's unprotected flank.

With all my bonuses and the sneak attack, the warg died instantly. The goblin rider snarled, but before he could leap at me, a spear took him in the chest. The spearman grinned. All at once, I heard the click of Grou'tuk's crossbow. I dodged instinctively, the bolt flying past me. The Dodge cost less Stamina than I would have expected, but then I remembered where I was standing. The shot meant for me had instead struck the spearman straight in the heart. The bolt didn't stop there. It exploded out the unsuspecting man's back, leaving a gaping hole the size of a walnut. A very bloody walnut.

He died still grinning. Looking around, only Fenris and I were still standing. The other spearman's throat had been torn out while I'd been fighting elsewhere.

Two more huge wargs and their riders were next to Grou'tuk, preparing to enter the fray. Several things occurred simultaneously. Fenris managed to shield-bash the goblin rider off the warg he was fighting. It had almost managed to break out of the tunnel into the courtyard, causing the goblin to lose the grip on his crossbow. The still-loaded weapon clattered to the ground next to me at the same moment that SueLeeta finally figured out how to light up the oil.

I was secretly hoping for a fireball. What I got was something more akin to a respectable bonfire. Grou'tuk and his warg were in the tunnel, and not even so much as a cinder came his way, despite the fire being right behind him. The same could not be said for the other two wargs. As they were covered in hair, the oil seemed to coat their tails and hindquarters. Both ran forward, yowling at the top of their lungs and bucking their riders into the flames. The wolves charged past me into the courtyard, where no relief awaited them.

"I seem to have gotten you alone," I said, holding out my daggers.

Grou'tuk chuckled. "I was hoping it would come down to this. I'm going to let my warg eat your balls." The warg growled hungrily. With the fire behind him, and the sounds of battle all around, it was quite the sight. Especially considering he was at full health and I had . . . 42 hit points.

It happened so very quickly. Grou'tuk's warg began to hunch down, preparing to lunge. I started rolling forward, towards him. Grou'tuk threw his crossbow to the side and drew his short blade. The warg recalculated his lunge, now that I was so low to the ground. I grabbed the crossbow. Grou'tuk's sword was pointing towards me in a guard position. The warg lunged. I fired a Power Shot into its chest from the still loaded crossbow.

My Power Shot didn't just travel fast and do a bit of extra damage. It also had knockback, and that was important here. When the bolt struck the warg in the chest, it caused him to go flying backward nearly a yard, despite the fact that he was in mid-process of launching himself at me. Flying backwards from his position meant flying into the fire, with a shocked Grou'tuk still on his back.

It was not without cost, unfortunately. My Stamina replenished quickly, and I had a lot of it. It didn't instantly replenish, though, and I'd been making extensive use of it. Furthermore, using any Marksman ability with a Mechanical Weapon increased the Stamina costs, as well as the bonus effect, by a factor of five. I'd depleted a big hunk of my Stamina for that one shot.

The warg bounced and kept on rolling. He had some oil on him, he was on fire, and he had suffered a 42 point wound from just the crossbow. But he was still alive. SueLeeta and the other archers fired several more arrows into him a moment later. However, Grou'tuk was not with his warg. He had been knocked clear on the initial impact and, due to his Ride skill, had managed to get to his feet immediately while in the burning oil.

While the burning oil wasn't doing anything for his complexion, he didn't plan on staying there very long. He only managed to suffer about 20% health loss before exploding out of the fire and straight towards me. He had a short sword that I suspected was magical. Meanwhile, I was armed with a discharged crossbow that was a bit undersized to use as a melee weapon.

So I Magic Shot his ass.

His eyes widened as I dumped Mana into the weapon and fired off a second bolt. It was an immediate second shot from a crossbow that I had just shot moments before. He saw a Magical Bolt that required an absurd amount of Mana for a non-casting class. In fact, it had cost me nearly all of my Mana; I hit a Mana crash status, even after my thirty-second lockout was over. It was a talent that he couldn't have reasonably expected me to have and something that cost a fortune in Stamina to Dodge.

He couldn't afford to. It would have cost 80 Stamina to Dodge at this range; that was half *my* Stamina pool. He'd been riding hard to get here and had been fighting and Dodging strikes from my archers. His Stamina pool wasn't full by any means. The Magic Shot exploded against his chest in a fountain of light, blinding him momentarily. This bought me a few precious moments to roll backward and grab my daggers. He was down to about half his hit points. I was far worse off but couldn't back down now.

Goblin fighting relied on stabs in vital locations to reduce mobility, followed by attacks from blind spots. A quick glance at his fighting stance showed Grou'tuk would not be deviating from tradition. If I'd had a long sword, I might have been able to keep him away; with my paired daggers, I had to have a different strategy.

He slashed at my leg; I cut his shoulder. He cut my thigh; I stabbed his arm. He kept attacking me and I kept attacking him. I made strike after strike, so that Dodging all of my blows would eat up too much of his Stamina. My strategy was pure counteroffensive strikes. Anytime he struck me, I struck him back.

He had better armor than I did, but my Defense was higher due to my Resistance perk. I spent Stamina on Mitigate, when appropriate, and Dodge, when it was cheap enough. Still, I kept on the attack. It was a knife fight where both sides managed to nearly gut the other for nearly thirty agonizing seconds.

Finally, we broke apart. I was having to commit Stamina to avoid a Bleed effect I'd gotten, and my Stamina was dangerously low. I was down to a little over 13 hit points, having lost a total of 30 in the battle. Due to my Iron Will, I could feel the injuries; they were terrible. I was still able to function, though. Grou'tuk's hit points finally dropped to 25% in the last moments of the previous clash. They were continuing to tick down as his own Bleeding status took its toll.

Outside the gate, arrows rained down on the remaining wargs who were unable to break past the bonfire. Fenris managed to drive his sword into his opponent's chest. The healer finally managed to drag her patient outside the tunnel.

Grou'tuk's expression was bleak. I wanted to collapse, but my perks were keeping me on my feet, even despite a status effect I had involving a dagger strike to my groin. Whatever perks the goblin riders had, Iron Will was not one of them. He staggered, until the weight of all of his injuries overcame his determination.

"You will pay for this!" he screamed, turning and running out of the tunnel. I made no effort to pursue.

"What are you doing?" screamed Fenris, as he stood over the bodies of the other warg and its rider. "He's getting away!"

I just stood there. I could do nothing else.

Grou'tuk ran towards the other goblins. Finding a nearby warg, he leapt onto its back and twisted it around to run. At that point, an arrow whizzed through the sky and into Grou'tuk's skull. Instantly, the remaining battle collapsed. The wargs were entirely done with this mess, as whatever hold Grou'tuk had over them ended as soon as he did.

My Stamina ran out and I dropped to my knees. Fenris's look of elation at the battle being won turned to horror as my health bar continued to drop. I had quite a few Bleed effects on me *and* that groin wound. I brought up my character sheet just to check; I had 11 hit points and 22 points of bleed effects over the next 30 seconds. I was going to die.

I considered calling for Shart, but I had Mana Crashed. I didn't have any Mana to do anything with. The Iron Will saved me from the headache and pain, so I just felt distant. I called for the demon once, all the same, but he wasn't listening.

Breaking out of menu time, Fenris suddenly rushed over towards me. He grabbed me and started pulling a bandage out of his pack. The pretty blond healer angel pushed him aside and opened my mouth . . . and spit into it. She was really going to town, all but regurgitating a mouthful of something—something that tasted bitter, like Healing Root and something else. I didn't hesitate; I started chewing the already moist, pulpy mass. I learned the second flavor was something called Staunch Berry. I loved Staunch Berry, because Staunch Berry halved the effects of bleed damage for a very short time. They also tasted like raspberries.

I slid into unconsciousness.

CHAPTER 24

AFTER THE BATTLE OF THE WESTERN GATE FORTRESS

- Jim
- Hit Points: 7/175

- Stamina: 87/175 (Stamina wound)
- Mana: 4/40 (Mana Crash)

I AWOKE SHORTLY THEREAFTER, MUCH TO THE SURPRISE of everyone.

"Well that sucked." I coughed, as Fenris and SueLeeta both stared at me in shock.

"How are you awake?" gasped SueLeeta, who then obviously stared at me for a long moment, finding my health. "You have less than 5% health!"

"I have a perk for that," I wheezed, looking around. The fire was out, and there were dead wargs and goblins everywhere. Most of the people nearby were either being ordered about by the pretty blond girl or standing there trying to figure out how they were still alive. The healer had been in charge of the auxiliaries, or healers, and I didn't even check her name when I assigned her that role. The Battle Leader menu had just more or less placed her there, though she probably would have done it anyway, I guessed.

- Jarra the Healer: Alchemist Initiate
- Hit Points: 25
- Stamina: 35
- Mana: 40

- Alchemy: Initiate
- Herbalist: Novice
- Glassmaker: Novice
- Healer: Novice

An Alchemist Initiate is someone who has devoted their life to the pursuit of Alchemy. They frequently pair this skill with Herbalism to find herbs from which to make their potions. Some also practice the skill Glassmaking in order to build the other items of their craft.

I could also delve deeper into her character sheet with my Lore skill than others I had seen. She had Novice Cooking, for example, but that didn't show up unless I was really looking for it. It seemed that Lore auto-sorted to the class's relevant skills, so Combat skills were listed more broadly than someone's Bread Making ability.

She had Novice Bread Making.

Fenris watched me as well, again activating his Lore ability. He was trying to puzzle me out, I suspected. I'm not sure if he found what he was looking for, but he said, anyway, "We are alive and free, thanks to you."

"Yes," I groaned. "What are your plans now?"

SueLeeta leaned up against a well and looked over the destruction. "Honestly, I don't know. We were trying to head to one of the River Cities, but we skirted too close to the old mountains." She gestured towards the stark peaks on either side of the fortress.

"But," she continued, "there is a war going on out there. And worse. I don't know if we can make it anywhere."

As she spoke, she eyed Fenris. "We lost people getting even this far. We think we might be able to get some of them back, but we aren't sure. Fenris isn't going to leave the valley until we at least check."

Suddenly Jarra the Healer was among us, eyeing the three layabouts with near outright hostility. She was tall for a woman, around five foot ten inches, and had long blond hair. She was wearing a simple green dress that had seen better days. Despite everything, she marched, not walked, towards us. Her posture was perfect and her shoulders squared. From what I could tell, she still had a bit of curve on her, despite her recent mistreatment. She had somehow found the means of cleaning her face off, too. As I'd noted a few times, she was pretty, even possibly beautiful, but her expression was very serious. She struck me as the kind of girl who wanted to succeed on her own merits and not on her looks, a real no-nonsense kind of girl.

Fenris retreated wisely, moving towards the wargs with his skinning knife already out. SueLeeta held up her bandaged arm as if that was her excuse. Without my Healing ability, and with a very limited number of healing roots, it was not wise for her to be doing much of anything. Compared to me, though, her wounds were still trivial.

As Jarra turned to look at me, her expression softened somewhat. In that distracted moment, SueLeeta abandoned me as well. There was a critical appraisal of my injuries from Jarra that one only really sees from a healer, stern but compassionate.

"Thank you for helping us," she said after a moment, brushing several strands of her long blond hair behind her ear as she spoke.

"It was not a problem," I responded. I was too tired to posture or flirt. Iron Will stopped the pain but, deep down, I knew I was still very badly injured. That does wonders to shut down one's libido. Also, I was married. Well, I was sort of married. I had vowed till death do us part and I'm pretty sure I died.

A philosophical debate for another time.

"I am Jarra the Healer," she said to me, almost cutely. It was almost like a girl trying to save a wounded puppy, but I'd take it. I'd never really looked at my own face since the truck event, but I was aware that I was younger now than I had been in some time. She was likewise young.

"Hello, Jarra the Healer. I am Jim."

She processed this a moment, her eyes getting slightly wider, before turning away. Coughing, she replied, "That is an . . . ahem . . . unusual name."

"I've heard that."

"Are you from around here?" she asked, after a moment. She was watching the people milling about, some gathering supplies, some talking amongst themselves quite loudly.

"Yes," I replied. "I am fairly well-acquainted with the local area."

She stood motionless for a moment while two of the men started yelling at each other. They didn't quite come to blows, but it was a near thing. After they were separated, she finally spoke again. "We don't have a place to go. Fenris was taking us to the City of Narwhal, but I don't know that they would even have taken us in. They certainly won't now that we have no supplies for a bribe. I don't know if we could make that distance now, anyway."

She got quiet for a moment, her shoulders slouching ever so slightly. "We need to get to someplace where we can hole up and plan out our next move. Do you know anywhere defensible in the valley?"

"Well, I know a place that you could set up that's very defensible."

CHAPTER 25

TO THE VICTOR

SIMPLY TELLING JARRA THAT I KNEW A PLACE WAS ENOUGH for her. She set upon the idea with vigor, ordering nearly every person around to prepare for the journey. Fenris didn't even put up a token protest, as she commanded him about like a general commanding a lowly soldier. As the minutes passed, everything of any value, including pelts from the slain wargs, was loaded back onto the three still-functional wagons.

The meat was left to rot. Apparently, whatever caused the transformation from wolves to wargs made the animals inedible to humans. I just stayed where I was and chewed Healing Root like it was my job. After all, I was grievously injured. Besides that, I had already freed them and given them a place to go. What more could they reasonably expect from me?

Jarra finally got herself and all eighty-six refugees ready to go. I wasn't actually counting them, but my Battle Map had many uses that I was now able to flip through. You know, *after* the battle. The majority of the people had hidden during the battle; most were not battle-ready and many were elderly or children. The healthier people fashioned a cart for the invalids, which Jarra prepared to have me loaded onto. I chose to walk, like the badass savior I was. I was doing much better by now. I had 14 hit points and my Stamina had just dropped out of its crashed state, so it was slowly refilling.

Now that I was fairly sure I wasn't going to die, I looked at the various types of prompts. I saw levels as well as skill boosts; there was also a third icon that I guessed was for talents.

- Level UP, Rogue 4
- You have gained one Perk. Please select it from the Rogue menu.
- You have gained one Buff. Please apply it to the stats on your character sheet.
- Your Hit Point total is increased by 10. Your Stamina is increased by 10.

- Level UP, Warrior 5
- You have gained one Perk. Please select it from the Warrior menu.
- You have gained a Specialization. Please choose your Specialization.

Glancing over to Woodsman, I saw that I was almost, but not quite, at the next level. The formula for experience was slightly different for each class. I'd earned more Warrior experience than Woodsman experience, because I had done more Warrior actions. Rogue had leveled, but I'd been pretty close to leveling in it, anyway.

The Specialization was new, so I flipped to Warrior first. The Warrior menu still had the normal skill tree that I was used to. The difference came with the tree's trunk. It now broke into three very large branches, each topped with a specialist node. There were Duelist, Knight, and Man-at-Arms. The Duelist was best at fighting one-on-one battles against single opponents. The Knight was a heavily armored warrior who was best at fighting from a mount, though it didn't specify a horse. The Man-at-Arms was a general warrior who was broadly skilled in many abilities.

The Man-at-Arms made up the middle section of the trunk. It carried on straight up the tree, whereas the Duelist and Knight sections branched off. Based on what I could tell, a Man-at-Arms would be good at everything but great at nothing. Moreover, both Duelists and Knights had some unique perks that the Man-at-Arms lacked. Reviewing all of my recent battles, each had come down to a one-on-one duel with someone. That made Duelist a clear favorite.

On the other hand, Knights were not just skilled in riding, but they also had perks that improved their Mass Combat abilities that the Duelist totally lacked. Man-at-Arms had perks for fighting duels *and* commanding men, but neither went very deeply. So, the question came back to "Did I want to be decent at everything, or good at a few things?" Also, did my Unbound talent allow me to learn those perks elsewhere?

I considered that briefly. Unbound let me choose perks that were outside my level to be certain; I still had to meet all of the other prerequisites, first. So, by taking Man-at-Arms, I would be sacrificing the higher power perks from Duelist or Knight.

I was finally able to eliminate one when I found an issue with Knight. While it was effective in certain situations, such as with a mount or in Mass Combat, its primary focus was on the heavier weapons side. It sacrificed abilities while wearing lighter armor to concentrate on medium and heavy armor. I didn't even *have* any medium or heavy armor.

I would undoubtedly find some, but, until then, would taking Knight be worth it? The Duelist specialization utilized all kinds of armor and weapons, which seemed to synergize with my other classes better.

Finally, I chose Duelist.

- Specialization selected: Duelist.
- You gain one rank in Strength and Dexterity.
- Your Hit Point total is increased by 10. Your Stamina is increased by 20.
- You gain the Talent Duelist Strikes.
- Your skill in: Swords, Axes, Maces, and Spears increases to Initiate.
- Your skill in Heavy Armor, Medium Armor, Parry, and Block increases to Novice.
- Several of your skills were already to the correct level. Bonus skill experience has been moved into your Duelist Strikes talent. You are at Rank 3 in Duelist Strikes.

Well, that was handy. I glanced at the Duelist Strikes. It was a talent tree similar to Marksman, but for one-handed swords. I verified that meant short swords, long swords, and the ever-popular rapier. Glancing over at the nubs of my old short swords, I decided to allocate those points later.

With Rogue, I took my buff and placed it into Charisma, as I had a note to do just that. I trusted the old me that left the note. He must have had a plan. I was just winging it.

Glancing down at Rogue, I was disappointed to see that I didn't have as many perk choices as I would have liked. My first problem with Rogue was that it was harder to level because of the limited weapon selection. There was nothing available to counteract that. The second issue I was having was the whole getting-horribly-injured-all-the-damn-time thing. I didn't see anything that worked on that, either.

Well . . . I brought up Poisoner. That looked suitably Rogue-like, but I wondered what poisons were made of. I was betting herbs, and I was right. After I selected Poisoner, I noticed several herbs suddenly appear in my vision; they were highlighted in purple. Also, the warg droppings became a shade of violet. I was suddenly sitting in a field covered in violet shit. The Poisoner perk gave me the ability to make poisons from commonly found herbs . . . and warg feces. Whether it would only work with warg feces or simply feces in general was an experiment I was not interested in conducting. According to the perk, normal Alchemists could make poisons, but they had a penalty. In addition, a critical failure during application of the poison caused the alchemist to poison themselves. What was more important to me was that Poisoner granted me Novice rank in Herbalism and Alchemy, so I didn't have to just make poisons. I could make potions with the Alchemy I would be granted.

Next, I flipped over to my newly improved skills. The Weapon skills worked about like you'd expect, with my Dagger skill improving because of my goblin throat-slitting extravaganza. My other Weapon skills improved due to my specialization. That meant improved Speed and Damage. I'd also improved my Two-Weapon Fighting skill and

Twin-Weapon Strikes skill, but not enough to move up a rank. I'd inexplicably picked up an Unskilled rank in Martial Arts, which I resolved to explore later.

My Block skill went from Amateur to Novice, which granted me the ability to transfer force away from myself. A knock down attack would suddenly be much less serious. There was a Stamina cost in line with Powerful Blow, so it was probably very useful.

Parry had also increased. Amateur Parry had let me block blows with some reliability. Novice Parry gave me a chance to riposte; that chance was augmented by my Weapon skill and the actual weapon. That might prove to be interesting in the next battle.

I had gotten both Medium and Heavy Armor skills. Medium Armor at Novice rank allowed me to move as if it was light armor. Heavy Armor at Novice rank further upped the armor's defenses. As I had no medium or heavy armor to test against, I moved on.

Herbalism went from Unskilled—where I could notice some kinds of herbs—to Novice, where I could notice most of the local herbs. Most were green in my vision; some were purple. The purple ones were poisonous. Novice Herbalists were able to chew two herbs at once and gain both effects. Furthermore, herbs I ingested were more effective in general. I additionally gained some Poison Resistance from the Rogue-specific perk.

> You have the status Slow Heal. You will recover 1 hit
> point per minute for the next 6 minutes. Due to your
> Spirit, your recovery period is 1 hit point for 50 seconds.
> Due to your Endurance, the duration increases from
> 6 minutes to 8 minutes. Due to your Herbalism, the base
> effect of the herb is increased by 50% to 1.5 hit points
> per minute. You have 4 minutes 23 seconds remaining.

That was a much better effect. It would give me just over 14 hit points per root and, even from the tunnel looking out into the valley, I could see a few likely contenders for more Heal Root.

If I can find enough Heal Root, I could take over the world.

The next skill I reviewed was Alchemy. It let me craft potions, unsurprisingly, and poisons as well. It functioned similarly to other crafting skills, meaning that my basic Crafting applied to it. Hopefully, this would allow me to make better potions than my skill level would otherwise dictate. I would need some time to experiment to really see what it could do.

I had figured out how to tune out the constant interactions of my Improvised Tools skill, because the world was starting to look like that one scene in *The Lego Movie*. Now, I relaxed a bit and glanced around at my options. I immediately turned it off again, as apparently goblins were great building blocks; parts of them were at any rate. I shuddered.

Walking to the body of Grou'tuk, because everyone had looted everything else while I was unconscious, I flipped through his stuff. He had a ring that I obviously took. His sword looked to be of decent quality for a short sword, but not very special aside from that. I still took it. The only other significant item in his possession was a key.

The key didn't have anything magical about it; it certainly didn't feel mystical or mysterious. I was guessing it was human made. There was only one place a key could have gone in the fortress and that was the tower. I didn't allow myself to believe I would be that lucky, though. With my luck, this key probably went to some private outhouse in another long-forgotten town. Still, I headed to the tower.

"Finally," said Shart, as he latched onto my shoulder.

"You seem to vanish when other people are around," I said, cautiously.

"Yup," replied the demon, before he whispered in my ear, "I can never be too careful. One of them might have a Demon Finding perk."

"Why would anyone want to find you?"

"My boy, I'm hurt. I'm a demon and every bit of me is soaked in magical power. They might want to get a little bit of Shart, if they can manage."

We were both quiet for a moment, as I finally made it to the door of the tower. "We won."

"I had every confidence that my powers would let you win. You can thank me by opening up the Demon Door for me."

"What do I have to do so you won't destroy me when I open the door?" I asked.

Shart got quiet. "Sorry, my boy. I like you. I really do. You are like a stupid, ugly, dumb pet. Yet, when I get back, I need to overwrite you. I need to use your soul to kill the Dark Overlord."

"So, I need to kill the Dark Overlord?"

Shart looked at me for a moment. Finally, he sighed. "Yes. If you kill the Dark Overlord, I'd leave you alone. It's impossible, though. He's a Godling. His soul is incorruptible. You don't even want to know how many hit points he has."

"If I did, though . . . you'd let me continue to exist?"

"Yes. But you'll die."

"I'd rather die fighting than be erased by you."

Pushing the unlocked outer door open, I entered into the darkness of the Western Gate Fortress Tower. I almost regretted it, as the place stank. Maybe this really was an outhouse. The tower wasn't just putrid; the air felt heavy, like you were breathing in some form of disease. Goblins and wargs had been using everything as their own private bathroom and the stench was overwhelming. I mucked through it, climbing stairs until I came to a door that had obviously been left intact. Using the key, I stood mesmerized as it actually entered the keyhole and turned. The lock clicked open easily, and I carefully stepped inside.

It must have been the captain's quarters. There was a main room that would also have served as an office, as well as a side room that appeared to be his chambers. Stepping through the pile where at least one warg previously slept, I stepped into the bedroom. It was not much better, but one spot stood out; nothing had been piled on top of it. Brushing away a coating of dirt and muck, I found the outline of a safe in the floor. It had a clever-looking lock attached to it. However, the goblin had left it undone. After a moment of looking for traps and finding none, I opened it.

Inside, there was a small, folded piece of paper, as well as four bright red potions that glowed faintly purple in my vision. Pulling the stopper from one, I inhaled sharply.

> **You have found Potion of Healing. It will restore 20 hit points over 10 seconds. The potion contains Deathroot poison, which will cause 60 hit points of Damage over 30 seconds. Deathroot nullifies Active Healing for 10 seconds. Your Poison Resistance will lower the damage by 18 points. Your Endurance will lower the damage by 9 points. Your Endurance will increase the healing by 3 points.**

Well, that was just evil. If you didn't have the Poisoner perk, you would think you had a good old healing potion. Unless I could either mitigate the poison or improve the effects of the healing, these potions were basically useless. Still, into my pouch they went. There was also a small amount of gold, silver, and copper coins, which I took.

The folded piece of paper appeared to be a note, but it was chicken scratch over parchment. The goblin had written it down for some reason, but, despite my ability to understand the goblin language, I couldn't read it. I wondered if perhaps one of the people downstairs could. Folding it for later, I carefully placed it in my pouch as well.

Unsatisfied, I looked over the room once more and prepared to leave. Just before stepping out of the room, a tear in a tapestry caught my attention. The tapestry itself hung above the main door to the chambers. It contained a roughly sewn picture of a hot BDSM scene. Not like *50 Shades of Grey*, either. Like, real hardcore shit. The stuff you can only do on a Saturday night because you got to take your ass to church right after . . .

Just kidding. It was the field with the town behind it.

The tear happened to be in just the right location for a glint of metal to be seen, if the light caught it in a certain way. The door was short enough that, with a bit of stretching, I could reach under the tapestry. As I pulled it back, I could see the upper edge of a shield.

I carefully took down the dusty metal shield from its place on a hidden shelf. On the bulwark was a strange crest. It was orange and black in color. At first, I thought it was a cross. Further examination led to the realization that all four sides were the same length. This made it more of a plus sign than anything else. A fancy plus sign, but definitely a plus sign. Farther back on the shelf lay a sword. The weapon was in much better shape than it had any right to be, though it needed a good cleaning to wipe away the fine layer of gunk that coated it. Underneath the grime, the sword was still sharp and seemed to be of good quality. I carefully examined it, but the blade was not magical.

You have found: Soldier's Longsword. Damage 14–20 (2–8 Base + 6 Strength + 6 Skill). Durability 75/80. Durable. Enduring.

I focused on the qualities. Durable weapons had double the normal Durability and Enduring weapons took Durability damage at half the usual rate. They also didn't rust or tarnish under anything less than the most trying conditions. Rubbing the filth off the blade demonstrated its sharpness, as I felt my Mitigation skill activate.

I turned my attention to the shield.

You have found: Soldier's Shield. Defense 24. Durability 18/40. Rotted.

The straps that hold this shield to armor have rotted. Take it to a leatherworker to get the rotted condition removed.

There wasn't a scabbard for the blade, but I slipped it into my belt anyway. I figured my armored leg was tough enough that it couldn't really cut me unless I got stupid. The blade actually had a ricasso, or unsharpened part, just past the hilt for gripping. I, of course, knew the term ricasso because . . . reasons.

Knowledge being rammed into my brain hardly bothered me anymore.

After I scanned the room one last time, I decided that I'd had enough of the smell and headed out. The air outside smelled of crisp mountain breezes and the sea. I inhaled deep lungfuls, trying to clear them of the scent of shit.

"Jim," called out Jarra. There was a hint of longing, or maybe hope, in her voice. She had followed me to this semi-isolated, though filthy, spot. Things were looking up.

I smiled, walking towards the sound and spotted Jarra, picking up a small dog. "Yes?"

She blushed prettily. "Um . . . Jim, this is my dog. Jim."

CHAPTER 26

THE TOWNSFOLKS AND THE VILLAGE

AFTER WE LEFT, I MADE SOME INQUIRIES OF THE TOWNS-people and found that Jim was a name they gave to little dogs. It wasn't like naming your dog Carl or Mark. It was like naming your dog Spot. My name was this place's equivalent to Spot. If that wasn't going to make it hard to be taken seriously, I didn't know what was.

No one said anything, though, as I kept walking off the path and coming back with handfuls of herbs. Jarra the Healer had been impressed with the goblins' herb supply, but she quickly realized that the valley was full of them. The ones that were freshly picked tasted much better than the ones stored in goblin pouches, especially if you considered that the goblins typically stored their pouches under their loin cloths.

I'd found twelve by the time we got to the edge of the forest and I hadn't seen a single goblin. Fenris had been following me, and not very discreetly. I had initially believed that he was trying to protect his people, but then I realized it was something else. He wanted a favor but didn't know how to ask for it.

"Spit it out," I said finally, as he tried to steel himself up for the third time.

"That obvious?" He sighed. "You may have heard that we were ambushed. Well, the goblins captured some of our people and took them into this valley. Not very many of them. Three, to be exact."

"Okay," I said, reaching down. I gathered another strip of blue moss and placed it into my pouch. "What do you need me to do?"

"Your tracking skills are undoubtedly better than mine, and I need to find them quickly."

"Who got taken that is so important?" I asked.

"My family. I know you are much higher level than me. You have no reason to help, but I don't know if I can do it myself." The last words came out like a crossbow bolt being ripped from his leg.

You have been offered a Quest: Help <Fenris> find his family. Reward: Increased loyalty from Fenris.

"Of course, I can," I smiled. "We will go together to find them."

Fenris thanked me profusely and we walked back to the main group.

We finally crossed out of the forest and everyone got a good look at the village. To me, it had started out as a broken-down ruin. To them, the reaction was slightly different.

"It has a town wall!" gasped OttoSherman, as he actually wiped his eyes at seeing the place.

"Well, it's damaged, but I'm sure we can fix it," I said, scanning for goblins. For once, they thankfully appeared to be absent. Actually, looking at the wall, there were a few large rents in it, but those would not be impossible for this many people to seal off.

"What's that blue tint?" asked Jarra, as she stood mesmerized by the town. With the clouds behind it, the blue tint of the magical barrier was quite visible against the backdrop.

"It has a barrier to keep the goblins out. You said to take you to a safe place."

"It still has a *barrier*?" questioned SueLeeta reverently. Several of the people collapsed to their knees. A few wept openly.

"Just how rare are barriers?" I asked, gauging the mood of the group.

"Extremely," replied Fenris. "It is said that the Dark Overlord of

Legend destroyed most of them in his great war with Grebthar the Destroyer. A few remain, but they are all in the Royal Cities. It was thought that only the kings still had them."

"That's interesting," I said. "Shall we continue? It's almost lunch time and I'd like to get something to eat."

"Wait, that's a town," stated Jarra. "We need to ask the mayor for permission to enter. Who is the mayor?"

"I am, of course."

"The mayor is named Jim," said nearly everyone in unison.

CHAPTER 27

THE MAYOR OF NOOBTOWN

DESPITE MY TEMPTATION TO LEAVE EVERYONE OUTSIDE, I relented, mainly due to the near constant string of apologies. Jarra even vowed to rename her dog. Eventually, we got to the barrier and everyone took a turn pressing their hand into it. Each and every one claimed they could feel it as they stepped through.

I brought up the town menu and changed them all to residents, beginning with the children. No need to start an accidental fire.

I showed my eighty-seven new neighbors the road to the market square in the center of town, which had the giant velociraptor symbol on the map. They could set up camp there and figure out what to do next. I took Fenris and started off towards the Creek House, hoping food would be available for the noon meal.

"I would prefer to go out looking immediately," he said as we walked.

"I would prefer to get one warm meal in us before we go," I countered.

"We must hurry, though," said Fenris, after a moment.

I agreed and we walked at a brisker pace. The village wasn't tiny, but it wasn't large either. We had only been walking a few minutes when I saw the outline of the Creek House. It was still in much the same shape as when I left, complete with a small amount of smoke from the chimney's near-constant fire.

Then I saw JoeClarance and realized that I wouldn't be getting a hot lunch. Fenris made a choked cry and started running before his mind caught up with him. JoeClarance heard the noise and looked over at me. His attention was then drawn to my companion. The boy shrieked, before he, too, began to run. Fenris was on him in seconds, grabbing the boy to his chest and sobbing.

AvaSophia heard the commotion from inside the house and came out brandishing a cudgel, only to drop it. She also ran towards Fenris. EveSophia, seeing her mother depart the residence, followed her out. The little girl also ran towards her father.

That was an easy quest, I thought, as I noticed Kappa's head pop up in the window with a look of utter confusion. Now was probably not the best time for Fenris to discover his family's new pet. I shook my head at Kappa and gestured for him to go out the back. He frowned but disappeared. A few moments later, the warg stepped out the side door, holding his carpet in his mouth. He flipped it over the banister in a practiced motion and then trudged off the porch towards the southern fields. Off to do some hunting, I supposed.

I turned around to leave, but was stopped by Fenris calling out, "Did you know?"

"I wasn't sure," I replied honestly. "And I didn't want to be wrong."

"You saved my family and brought everyone else here to safety," he said. Then, "*Why?*"

Because I am the mayor around here?

Because I'm a goddamn legend?

"Because you are a heartless asshole who won't even open one little Demon Door," whispered Shart through our bond.

"Because no one fucks with the Mayor of Noobtown."

The End . . . for now.

FROM THE AUTHOR

THANK YOU FOR READING. Get ready for Jim's continuing adventures in the next book: *The Village of Noobtown*. If you liked *The Mayor of Noobtown*, please take the time to review it. If you didn't, then stay away from that ratings section! Haha, I kid, I kid. Seriously, you have no idea how much a rating can help an author like me.

Keep on the lookout for the next Noobtown book! You can follow its progress on Noobtown's Facebook page. I'm very responsive and love to hear from my fans. Thanks again for reading my writing! Hope to hear from you soon.

ACKNOWLEDGMENTS

THANK YOU to everyone who helped make Noobtown possible over the years. It truly does take a village. My deepest thanks to Sarah, Lenny, David and Isabella, and Victoria.

ABOUT THE AUTHOR

RYAN RIMMEL is the author of the Noobtown series. When he's not writing, he is playing *Dungeons & Dragons*, upgrading his computer, or doing other dorky tasks.